Other novels by Chuck Walsh

A Month of Tomorrows
Shadows on Iron Mountain
Backwoods Justice
A Splintered Dream

Chuck Walsh

A Passage Back
Chuck Walsh

Vinspire Publishing
Ladson, South Carolina
www.vinspirepublishing.com

A Passage Back

To Mom

Chapter One

I often seek comfort in the recollections of my youth.

And in those remembrances, I run the streets of time, into a familiarity as warm as sunbeams on a young boy's shoulders. It's not into the physical world I run but, rather, the deep corners of my mind, where memories exist in a separate world altogether.

Not too long ago, those roads were actual streets. I simply had to open my eyes and ears and experience what would one day become the memories I now seek. In that era, submerged in a world of endless summer days and warm autumn nights, I was surely going to live forever. Well, maybe not forever, but at least a couple centuries. For, in those days, the baseball field was the land of eternal youth, the backyard held endless possibilities of childhood fantasy, and the smell of chicken frying, along with the buttery aroma of yeast rolls baking, ensured Mom would always take care of me. It was these things that made childhood more a state of being, frozen by time. Or it sure seemed that way.

But the endless summer days have long faded, slipping quietly by like a fallen leaf in a swift stream. Because of my inability to concede that youth was gone, I found myself waist deep in the metaphysical river of life, trying to slow time with my bare hands. Sadly, it slipped through my fingers like a raging river, and there was nothing I could do to stop it. I couldn't turn around, couldn't go back. Ever.

And so I began to hold childhood memories close in my mind, and even closer in my heart. Nostalgia became an endearing friend, and all things past held a tender spot in my life. Simply watching Mom and Dad in their den watching television brought comfort. The morning alarm stirred my thoughts to days when I lay in the warmth and comfort under my blankets in those quiet, predawn hours before school. The aroma of eggs and bacon bubbling in the skillet reminded me of breakfast in the kitchen with my brothers, jockeying for position by the space heater. My shaving razor sparked the recollection of Dad standing at the sink in our small bathroom, getting ready for work, in pajama pants and a white tank-top undershirt. The crisp smell of linen reminded me of Mom washing and folding clothes on our back porch.

I guess I was supposed to just sit back and take it like a man. I thought of Dylan Thomas' plea, 'do not go qentle into that goodnight,' and it became my mantra. I'd decided I was going down kicking and screaming. I didn't want to be thought of as old. I didn't want to turn gray. I wanted to ride my bike down the streets of childhood again, surrounded by familiar faces, the sun on my shoulders, yelling to the world that time had lost its grip on me.

I didn't want to be the guy sitting in the bleachers watching baseball players half my age playing the game I was born to play. I wanted to put on my uniform, walk to the pitcher's mound, stare down the batter, and strike him out. Instead, I threw batting practice to kids thirty years younger than me, trying to transfer the knowledge of my baseball days to someone who surely didn't appreciate the sport the way I did.

Middle age stood at my door, ready to administer a dose of reality without giving me the option to refuse the medicine.

I began to notice the passage of time in subtle ways, in many places. I saw it in the mirror and in the fine lines forming along the corner of my eyes. I heard it in the airwaves, when songs from my high school days played on the 'oldies' station. I felt it in the irreverence shown to landmarks and places that were once part of my childhood. All around me were signs that youth had slipped away, where every strand that linked me to my childhood was fraying, ready to snap at any moment.

The two constants that remained in my life, those strands that linked me to my past, were my parents and my boyhood home. Whenever I wanted to return to the comfort of younger days, I'd recline on Mom and Dad's couch and sip on a glass of sweet tea. It was no different than when I was a child.

But the final threads began to give way, and my grip on the past loosened. Mom and Dad began dealing with aches and pains, small ones at first. They began missing family events — grandchildren's baseball games, picnics, and birthday parties. I realized, watching them walk to the car after church one day, holding hands, they were doing so as much to keep their balance as to show their love for each other. I saw age creeping up on them like shadows stretching across our lawn when dusk drew near.

As the aches and pains grew, they found they could no longer take care of the house, nor the large yard that had been home to half the neighborhood kids years ago. When they told us they were thinking of moving into a smaller home, with a smaller yard, I offered to do the mowing, the raking, the cleaning, just to get them to stay. But, as time went on, I couldn't avoid the fact that they needed to move.

When I watched the realtor stick the 'For Sale' sign in the yard, she may as well have driven it through my heart. I began spending as much time as I could at the old house, knowing that the days of tranquility and contentment, it offered were coming to an end. I tried to fake excitement when Mom and Dad found a patio home in a great part of town. Maybe the old house wouldn't sell, I told myself, and they'd have no choice but stay. But, in less than a month, the offer came and it was too good to pass up.

I reluctantly helped with the packing and wrapping up remnants — forty years of family life stuffed into boxes, destined for the attic or garage sales. I fought tears as I boxed up my childhood. When the house — *my* house — was finally empty, I volunteered to lock up the place and give the keys to the realtor. After my family headed to the new home, I walked through my empty house, and I had never seen anything so lifeless. When I locked the door behind me, I closed the door to my childhood forever.

I've been told that a house is nothing more than bricks and mortar. That home is a state of being, not a place bound by walls and a roof. But I believe it's the walls, the rooms, and the design of the house that hold the memories: the kitchen table, Dad's recliner, Mom's vanity, the bedroom wall lined with pennants.

And so, for weeks after the house was sold, I struggled through the fact that strangers would soon inhabit that place where I grew up, shaping the walls and rooms into some new design common only to them.

I began to have dreams of the old house, dreams that I was young again. I would awaken and find myself trying to fall back to sleep to recapture that incredible feeling. But the night I dreamed a most hideous dream, I awoke in a cold sweat. It was a nightmare in the truest sense. In that dream, she lay in a casket. Strange organ music played, and people surrounded her, weeping. Her face was pale blue, and when I reached down to kiss her on the forehead, she opened her eyes. The jolt shook me from my sleep, and my heart pounded so hard I could feel every vein beating within me. Perhaps the dream should have prepared me.

For there she lay, her casket cloaked in flowers, people weeping for her. Other than her inability to open her eyes, I realized how similar the dream was to the real thing.

I sat in the front row of the church, sunlight slipping through the stained-glass window and turning the carpet into a kaleidoscope of purple and violet. Roby Gentry, his bony fingers wrinkled and worn by time, began to play the fiddle, and I fought tears as the first notes let me know what was coming.

"I was standing by my window on a cold and cloudy day," he sang in a country twang, "when I saw the hearse come rollin' for to carry to my mother away." That hauntingly beautiful song now ripped at my gut. When he sang, "there's a better home a waitin' in the sky, Lord, in the sky," I was certain that applied to Mom. "Will the circle be unbroken, by and by?" he asked in song. In my heart, it was as broken as broken could be.

As I looked behind the piano out a hopper window, I spotted a child zip down a metal slide into a woman's arms. She squeezed him to her chest, and he cackled. The scene repeated itself for several minutes, and I was jealous of the boy who surely had no clue that the sanctity found in his mother's arms was finite in time. Oh, to have the chance again to be so blind.

I glanced down at the program sitting on my lap. The front of the program contained a magnolia flower in full bloom, underneath the words, 'I am the way, the truth, and the life.' On the back of the program was her picture, taken by Dad as she stood by a 'Welcome to Florida' sign on their honeymoon. I touched her face with my thumb. Her smile jumped off the page. I couldn't decide whether to fold the program and place it in my coat pocket, or set it on the pew beside me. I settled for the pew. Again, I looked out the window. I couldn't bring myself to look at the casket.

Flowers of red, pink, and white adorned the metal stands in front of the mahogany box, almost masking the presence of the casket entirely. Dr. Long began to speak, surely words intended to soothe, and though maybe they did for the congregation, it had no effect on me. I didn't want words. I wanted to be anywhere but there. Alone.

When the service came to an end, and we were escorted out the side door to a long, black limo that would take us to the gravesite, everyone in the family stepped inside the car. Everyone but me.

"Where are you going?" my wife, Blake, asked when she saw me heading toward the road. She touched my sleeve. I turned, the tears filling my eyes. I tried to speak, but looked skyward for a moment.

"I can't do this," I said. I rubbed my tired eyes. She took my hand, but I pulled away. Human touch was the last thing I wanted, unless it was from my mother. I saw my high school friend, Ed, walking to his car. "Eddie, can you give me a ride home?"

"Chase, you can't leave," Blake said. "We still have the gravesite service and the burial."

"You'll have to do it without me." I looked at Eddie. "Can you give me a ride?"

Eddie looked at Blake, and she told him with her eyes that it was okay.

"Sure thing," Ed replied.

We didn't speak at all on that fifteen-minute ride. Ed pulled up in front of my driveway and, when I started to get out, he placed his hand on my shoulder. I looked at him briefly and nodded my appreciation. I'm certain he saw the sadness in my eyes. I walked to my car and fumbled through my pocket for the keys.

Soon, I was turning onto my old street, Brennan Avenue. Back home. Back in time is what I wanted. I heard a voice hawking multivitamins on the radio. The voice proclaimed, 'Life begins at forty.'

"What a crock," I said, turning off the radio in disgust. If life began at forty, somebody stick me back in the womb.

I drove on, expecting my old neighborhood to welcome me with open arms. It had to. It was my only hope. But, when my black, two-door sports coupe turned on to the road that led to my boyhood home, what I received was nothing more than indifference. Not in the physical sense, obviously, but one of a spiritual nature, like God closing the doors to Heaven. For the first time in my life, I was a stranger come to visit.

The distant sound of a push mower interrupted the silence of that Carolina afternoon. The sweltering heat rose from the street in a liquid haze, blurring the road that split the one-story houses like an asphalt stream dividing two rows of freight cars. I passed on the urge to ride by my old home, although I'm not sure why. Instead, I turned left onto Confederate Avenue. I stopped in front of Ben Ross' house, looking at the corner lot where we played football games on Saturdays in the fall. Mr. Ross had removed every tree on the lot so we would have a place to play. Somehow, he had been able to keep the grass thick and green, an amazing feat for turf that took the pounding it did. The once-manicured lot was now covered with waist-high weeds and housed an abandoned car. I continued down the block and spotted Mrs. Lavigne walking to her mailbox. It seemed only a short time ago that she used to outrun her son, Kenny, and me, in her front yard. Now, she looked too feeble to carry her mail back to the house. It sickened me.

On I drove to the parking lot of Belmont Elementary. It was the school where I grew from being a child who didn't want to let go of Dad's hand the first day of Kindergarten, to a pre-teen getting my first kiss outside the sixth grade classroom. At the time, the kiss had been as traumatic as that first day of Kindergarten — more so, if I was pressed to tell the truth. The 'kiss' took place on a spring day. A sixth-grader, I can still remember that pale blue sky stretched across the boundary of the earth, as though there were no limits to the heavens. Robins skirted along the pale green playground that bordered the baseball field where I played a pick-up baseball game with my buddies. The air was brisk, the northerly breeze erasing any thoughts of the muggy air that would hammer us come June.

It had been Valerie Jacobs' fault. She'd walked on the field and asked me to break the leather bracelet on her slender wrist. I'd done the gentlemanly thing and obliged. When she'd told me I had to kiss her for snapping the bracelet, I had returned to the game without giving it a second thought. Stupid girl. But later, when the final bell had sounded and I walked out Mrs. Barrett's classroom, I was the one who had looked stupid. Valerie, and every girl living in a six-mile radius, waited outside the door. It had truly been a wall of females, hands on their hips, waiting for me to fulfill my promise. After what had seemed like hours of unrelenting pressure, I'd seen no choice but to peck Valerie on the lips and dash through the parting gate of bodies.

I exited the car without bothering to close the door. The rusty, barren flagpole in front of the principal's office stood silent. The school was tucked away at the back of the small neighborhood, bordered by towering pines and heavy maples. When we were kids, we had been told that hobos lived in the woods behind the school, and they were said to kidnap and kill young boys. Of course, we'd believed those fabrications because we didn't have the sense not to. Those intimidating woods had stood in stark contrast to our school.

I looked around the courtyard, and I could almost hear the voices of my classmates playing in the grass and scrambling for their books when the morning bell sounded. Man, how we scampered when that bell sounded. But those echoes had gone silent a long time ago, and now the school sat desolate, its windows boarded shut. With the school still and lifeless, I knew it was time to go to the place that made life worth living, and I walked around the side of the school.

There it was — the baseball field. My shadow appeared to melt into a hazy curtain of orange and blue in front of me as the afternoon sun dipped behind a scattering of pewter-bottomed clouds. When I walked on the unkempt field, my black wool suit soaked up the heavy air like a parched sponge. Sweat seeped from above my brow, and I lifted the handle on the rusty gate beside the third base dugout.

Thirty-five years.

Thirty-five years since I first walked through the gate. I was seven-years-old, and my baggy gray cotton uniform had swallowed me. In a blue wool ball cap, black cleats, and a hand-me-down Spalding baseball glove, I'd felt happier than any kid had the right to be. I was joining an elite fraternity. I was, at that moment, a ball player.

And here I was on that dirt infield again, though no longer in uniform.

The ballpark may have been just a field of dirt and grass enclosed by a chain-link fence, but it was not called a diamond for nothing. It shined like the brightest stone on those summer evenings as our parents gathered in the bleachers. It was a game that connected father to son, joining past and present through a little rawhide ball. It was a fairytale world contained inside the confines of one Little League ball field.

I looked to the bleachers and nodded slightly to a vision of Mom. I removed my coat and tugged at the knot in my tie, lifting it from around my neck. I wondered what my family and friends thought about me leaving the funeral home where they'd gathered to pay respects to Mom. I wondered, but I didn't care. All I knew was that Mom was gone, and the ball field was a chance to bring her back, to bring my days of youth back, at least for a moment.

I walked into the dugout and rubbed my fingers across the aged, chain-link fence that enclosed it. The wooden bench was dry and splintery. When I sat, I dropped my head and sobbed quietly. Where had the days gone? How had they passed so quickly?

The day Dad had called to tell me Mom was ill had caught me like a left hook.

Though she was already in the advanced stages of breast cancer, Mom hadn't wanted us to know she was sick. Dad had felt otherwise, and called my brothers and me one morning while Mom lay down to rest.

It had been torture to watch Mom fade away, to see the presence of her being disappear. The hospital room where she'd spent her final days was cold and uncaring. She'd deserved so much more. She had always been the one who'd taken care of us all, and now she lay in a room devoid of color, as if some heartless decorator had done it that way to prepare her for her morbid date with destiny. I'd thought it ironic that Mom was in the same hospital where I had been born. We'd gone full circle, from the day of new life, to the day where life would be taken away.

During her last days, I'd tried to find an opportunity to be alone with her. I'd needed to tell her how much she meant to me, needed her to know she was the person I wanted to emulate. To be compared to her was the ultimate compliment. But I never got the chance. Family and friends were had always been there.

Then the final day had come.

We took turns sitting by her bed, watching her frail body strain to breathe. Tubes were attached to her arms, chest, and stomach to make her exit from the world as comfortable as possible--a comfort that was just not there. Her eyes fought to open when she heard the voices of our family. Dad sat to her left, holding her lifeless hand in his, watching his soul mate of fifty-two years slip away.

I ran downstairs to the gift shop in search of a yellow rose. Mom always thought it was the most beautiful flower of all, and I wanted to place it on her pillow in hopes its aroma might ease her pain. A stupid idea, I know, but I had to do something. But the shop didn't carry them. I remembered a tiny florist two blocks away and jumped into my car. I found one in full bloom, and I dashed back to the hospital. Surely this would help. As I walked down the hall I saw my family leaving Mom's room. Blake looked at me as she tried to console our daughter, Lauren.

No way.

A nurse was closing the curtain around Mom's bed when I walked in.

"Wait," I said. "She needs her flower." She needs her flower? What difference could that make now, you might wonder? Well, it made a difference to me. I stood at Mom's side. Her pain was gone. Her battle was over. She looked at peace, and I knew her soul was on its way to Heaven. I rubbed her hair and kissed her forehead. When I laid the flower on her pillow, I couldn't help but cry. For the only time in my life I felt deserted and alone.

The screech of a mockingbird on the green, tin dugout roof snapped my attention back to the tattered dugout at the ball field. There was only one thing to do now. I took off running for the car and drove the beltway across town. Once home, I swapped coat and tie for t-shirt, shorts, and tennis shoes. I grabbed the same for Brett and Lauren.

A black, dusty bat bag hung in the garage, and I strapped it on my shoulder and ran to the car. I drove to my brother, Bob's, house, where I knew my family and friends had congregated after the funeral. I figured they were all hovered around the casseroles and pies on the kitchen counter. I spotted Lauren removing something from the trunk of Bob's car, and I pulled up beside her at the street.

"Lauren, go get Brett," I said through the window.

"Dad, where have you been?" she asked. "Everyone's worried about you."

"There's no need. Go tell Mom I have to do something. Something with you and Brett."

Within minutes, she returned with her brother.

"What are we doing?" Lauren asked while looking in the open window of the passenger door and gently sliding her shoulder-length blonde hair behind her left ear. Her hazel eyes, bursting with bits of green and yellow, told of her worries.

"We're going to the ball field."

"What ball field?" quizzed Brett as he slipped into the back seat.

"The Little League field in Belmont."

I drove while they changed, and I could tell by their silence they didn't know what to say. I didn't know what to say either.

After driving up to the school, we soon climbed the curb of the parking lot and onto the bumpy school ground. We rumbled through knee-high, brown weeds that steadily rapped against the side of my car.

Lauren turned and looked at Brett with a puzzled look. She glanced over at me. "Dad, are you sure you're okay?"

"I will be in just a minute."

I led the way through the gate and removed two gloves from my bat bag, and tossed them to Lauren and

Brett. I reached in and found my well-worn Rawlings, a black Easton aluminum bat, and a scuffed baseball.

"Hit me some grounders," I shouted to Brett. "Lauren, you play first. I'll take third."

The ragged dirt infield was dotted with small patches of centipede and ragweed. No footsteps were visible, indicating that the field had been dormant for quite some time. The outfield was wrought with grass-choking weeds, whose only purpose seemed to be collecting empty beer cans and Styrofoam containers. I wondered if the neighborhood had become devoid of children. Having an unused baseball field was like having a grandfather with a waiting lap and no children to sit upon it.

I jogged to third base, kicked the sand off the bag, and rubbed my sneakers across the dirt, moving my leg back and forth like a windshield wiper chasing rain drops. "Gotta smooth it out so the ball'll take true hops," I said with my head facing downward. I paused and bit my lip, stunned how the passage of time had carried me into middle age. There I stood, beside the base I had defended like a loyal servant many years ago. Only now, I returned as a man searching to recapture youth with his children. It made no sense, and the thought of it sucked.

The texture of my glove was smooth as I placed the fingers of my left hand inside, and I closely inspected the tightness of the laces. Brett stepped beside home plate and began hitting me grounders. His biceps bulged through the faded green t-shirt he'd intended to trash when he had left for college the previous August. I scooped each ball and rifled it to Lauren. As I watched her throw the ball to Brett, I noticed the stark contrast of their appearances. Brett, strikingly handsome, wiped small beads of sweat from underneath the wavy locks of his dark-brown hair. The salty moisture produced a shimmer on his olive-toned face, causing his deep-green eyes to stand out like a Cheshire cat. Lauren had an athletic build combined with blonde hair and a peaches-and-cream complexion that gave her the look of a California surfer girl.

The dormant field had again come alive, and I felt as if I'd never left the diamond. I caught a sharp grounder to my left, and then backhanded a shot to my right. I still had the ability, and it made my body rock. It was as if the crack of the bat, in some sort of Pavlovian way, induced me to bounce as I anticipated the feel of the ball pounding into the web of my glove.

"Hit 'em harder," I shouted. "See if you can get one past me."

The balls came harder and faster and I fielded each one like a vacuum sucking up marbles. I had decided I was never leaving the ball field again. We could set up tents in the outfield and run electricity to the dugouts for the refrigerator and television.

Brett kept trying to get a grounder past me, and he ripped a shot down the third base line. I extended my glove to make the catch, and the ball hit the third base bag. After striking the corner of the base, the ball caromed upward and crashed against my head, striking me in the temple. I fell hard to the dirt.

"Dad!" I heard Lauren cry out.

I could hear them by my side, and I could feel their hands touching me. I could barely make out their shapes as they helplessly watched me slip out of consciousness.

And this is where the craziness began. You might believe it was a dream, and maybe it was. But to me, it was as real as anything I've ever experienced, and I'll cling to the belief that it happened for the rest of my life.

Darkness settled over me. I heard them plead for me to awaken. I barely felt Lauren's fingers rub gently across my face. Though I was lifeless, my spirit rose. The next thing I remember, I saw the field below me and my children kneeling beside my body. It was like a scene from a Ron Howard film. I rose above the school and the entire neighborhood. I drifted higher and higher, and I had never felt so at peace. I wondered if I was Heaven-bound.

The skies turned dark. My eyes closed and I couldn't open them. My body became still again. No movement. Soon I heard faint voices, muffled, like noise from the bleachers of a ball field. As the voices slowly became clearer, one voice in particular sounded eerily familiar to me. Slowly, I opened my eyes, and I tried to focus on the jade-green eyes peering deeply into mine. Those eyes and the soft smile looked so warm, so reassuring. I think you know where I'm going with this.

"Chase, are you okay? You took a nasty blow to the head." The vision brushed my blond bangs away from my face with long, smooth fingers. "Let's go to the dugout and make sure you're all right."

My legs were wobbly, and it took me a moment to stand. It was then I knew my eyes were privy to a sight I never thought possible. "Mom?" My eyes struggled to focus. Could it be?

"Yes, baby?" She seemed to notice the look of frustration in my eyes.

"What is going on?" I rubbed my temples and closed my eyes. I opened them again. "How can this be?"

"How can what be?"

"How can you be?" I stared into her eyes in absolute disbelief. I was unable to think coherently, and I reached out and touched her face. Her beautiful, incredible face. I shook my head and glanced downward while I rubbed my aching temple. I was wearing my Little League uniform.

"You'll do anything for attention, won't you?" a voice yelled.

To my left, standing in front of second base, a ball player nervously rubbed his right hand inside the web of his glove. "Joe?"

"That ball knocked the crud out of you, didn't it?" he asked.

I looked around as Mom led me to the dugout. All around me were teammates from my Little League team. No way could this be happening. No dream had ever been so clear in my head. I sat on the smooth bench in the dugout, feeling the chill of an ice pack surrounded by familiar hands. I looked up and into my mother's eyes. "Mom, is that really you?"

Her face was radiant. "Certainly it's me. Were you expecting someone else?"

I glanced down at my uniform. "Unbelievable." How would you have felt?

"Chase, can you play?" a deep voice asked. I craned my neck upward as Coach Cooper placed his hand on my shoulder. "How about it? You ready?"

I smiled. *You're absolutely right I'm ready.* I'd have mortgaged the farm to have the chance. "Yes, sir!" I sprinted to third base and my teammates cheered their approval. I looked around the field with a smile surely as big as Texas. I touched third base with my foot, the same base I had stood next to just minutes ago while Brett had hit me ground balls. The *Twilight Zone* could never top this.

The hitter stepped into the batter's box and I tried to keep my composure. Slowly, I shook my head and pounded my glove with my fist and stared at the batter. Jimmy Stocker. Jimmy was a lanky, left-handed hitter with an inside-out swing that pushed every ball he hit down the third base line. It was time for me to set aside the time travel and focus on the game. The pitcher, Rusty Richardson, fired the pitch toward home plate. Jimmy swung and the ball bounced my way. It was a high hopper, and I fielded it chest high before throwing it to first for the out. The bleachers came alive. But most of all, I came alive. I pointed my glove at Rusty on the mound, acknowledging his nod to me for getting the out. I smiled at Cary Gilliam at short and said, "Can you believe this?" He surely had no idea what I was talking about. And I didn't care.

Alvin Bailey, a strong, right-handed hitter, stepped to the plate and crushed the first pitch between Cary and me. I moved three steps to my left, extending my body horizontally in mid-air. The ball shot into my glove as my knees and elbows slid across the soft dirt. The feel of the ball landing firmly in my glove stirred my soul. Hopping off the ground, I dusted my pant legs and jogged to the dugout with my teammates. Life was grand again.

"Nice grab," Joe said, patting me on my backside. "Now let's see what you can do with a bat."

When I reached the dugout, I turned to see the faces of the outfielders as they ran off the field. It was easy to recognize all three of them, especially Perry Williamson, who would later become one of my closest friends ever. Perry had been a good ball player, but his interests would expand in so many ways besides sports when he'd became a teenager. The funniest kid I'd ever met, he was a Jim Carrey kind of guy whose antics at school would lead me to not only uncontrollable laughter, but to the principle's office for disrupting the class. When he came up to me, I shook his hand. It had been twenty years since I'd seen him.

"Hey, man," I said with a big grin, "how have you been?"

"No different than I was an hour ago when we walked to the field together."

I wasn't sure how to respond, as no one in the crazy dream had clued me in to what I'd been doing earlier that day in the past. "Yep, that makes sense." Looks like I needed someone to bring me up to speed on what I'd missed. I patted Perry on his cap with my glove and followed him into the dugout.

Coach Long called out the batting order. "Okay, boys, time to crank it up a notch. Gilliam, you're leading off. Richardson, you're on deck. Chase, you're in the hole."

I loved the phrase 'in the hole.' Though it meant I was the third batter due up in the inning, it sounded like I was a soldier leaving the safety of my foxhole to slay the enemy. I glided my hands across the knobs of the bats leaning against the fence and selected a thirty-one-inch wooden beauty. Wood bats had been replaced with aluminum ones when I'd begun high school, and every level except the Major League used them. The sound, feel, and even the smell of a wood bat, was baseball in its purest form. Aluminum bats were the silver, artificial trees of Christmas. I slid a blue batting helmet on my head, my fingers gripping the air holes on the sides. I kept my hat on because it was always a magnet for good pitches. I glanced at the scoreboard.

We're down two runs to these guys?

Cary stepped to the plate and singled up the middle. I moved up to the on-deck circle and looked towards the bleachers, and Mom motioned with a slight wave and a smile. She surely looked angelic sitting there and, though she probably was an angel in Heaven, to me, she was right there watching from the bleachers. A light breeze briefly eased the heat of the summer afternoon, and I slowly inhaled the soft fragrance of honeysuckle. The crack of the bat turned my attention to the field. Rusty doubled to the fence, leaving runners on second and third.

I stepped into the batter's box and stroked my fingers on the handle of the bat like a musician playing a flute. The handle felt smooth inside my hands. I eyed the pitcher, Pat McCarthy, a stocky boy who had served me quite a few homerun pitches in Little League. I took three practice swings, a batting ritual. Baseball players are well-known for having superstitions. Some guys might wear a lucky t-shirt under their jersey, others a particular batting helmet. I had played with a couple guys in college who had refused to wash their jock if they were on a hot streak at the plate. As I recalled, those guys hadn't had much luck on the dating scene during those streaks.

Finishing my swings, I crouched slightly, the bat resting just off my right shoulder. I watched the pitch roll off the pitcher's fingers towards home.

I lightly tapped my rubber cleats with the end of my bat and settled into the box. *Come on Pat, you know you've got no chance, so you may as well bring it to me.* Pat slowly wound and stepped towards home plate, releasing the ball. I cocked my body slightly towards the catcher and then began to stride toward the oncoming pitch. Pulling my hands quickly towards the plate, I rotated my hips as the sweet spot on the bat drove into the oncoming ball with all the power I could muster. The moment of impact, when the ball met the bat, felt as if the bat was part of my body.

I took off down the base line to first, but I kept my eyes on the ball. I knew it was gone, and now was not the time to look at the first base coach for instruction on whether to run to second base. The left and center fielders sprinted to the crescent-shaped fence behind them, watching helplessly as the ball left the yard. I wanted to raise both arms, but I tried to keep my composure. After all, it had been almost twenty years since I'd hit my last home run, so I had the right to celebrate. As I ran the bases, a path I'd run many times before, at that moment it was the greatest trip around the bases ever. Coach Cooper patted me on my backside as I stepped on third, turning towards home. My teammates waited anxiously behind home plate, and I couldn't wait to reach them.

Chills ripped through my body when my right foot touched the center of home plate. My teammates surrounded me, tapping me on my shoulders and my helmet. Joe put his arm across my shoulders as we made our way to the dugout. When I looked to the bleachers, Mom flashed a smile. Dad, slipping up from behind the back of the dugout, poked me on the shoulder through the fence.

"Way to go, son. You did good." All was right with the world.

Our team couldn't push across any more runs, and so we took to the field. Joe tossed me my glove as we ran to our positions, flipping it over his shoulder. I caught the glove in stride, as this had been our good luck routine for years. "This is it," Joe said. "One more inning. What do you say we go to A & W after the game and eat?"

"Man, it's been years since I've been to A & W."

Joe looked at me peculiarly. "We just went there last Friday, you moron."

I smoothed out the dirt in front of third base, disregarding what Joe had said. I looked around the field, watching my teammates settle in to their positions. The sun had sunk below the skyline of the trees behind centerfield, and shadows covered the field. A lazy breeze brushed against my skin, cooling the beads of sweat under the bill of my cap. I glanced at the bleachers that bordered either side of the backstop. Both were filled. J.T. Moore stood beside the third base gate, holding his grandson, Chip, on his shoulders. He held Chip's hands as he talked with Herb Benson, the vice-president of the league. J.T. had passed away when I was a senior in high school.

"Waddaya say now, Chase?" he said, his silver hair covered by most of his ball cap.

Coach me up, Mr. Moore. I'll make you proud.

J.T. had coached for over fifteen years, and though he had hung up his coach's shorts years ago, we all knew he still desired to coach.

Rusty Richardson struck out the first two batters before watching the final out land in Joe's glove in shallow right field. Coach Cooper shook hands with Coach Long, and they walked toward home plate. As I ran by, Coach Cooper removed his hat, lightly popping me on mine.

"Great game, son."

"Thanks, Coach."

Both teams formed a line, and we shook hands as we crossed home plate. Players from a generation ago together again—not just on a baseball field, but a field of perpetual youth. I smiled and looked in the eyes of each opponent as I shook their hands.

Guys, it's great to be back among you.

Coach Long unfolded a green duffel bag tucked behind the dugout bench and began stuffing the bats and helmets inside. I picked up the catcher's equipment off the dusty sand of the dugout floor and waited for Coach Long to finish packing the helmets. Standard post-game protocol consisted of players taking their glove, hat, and hopefully a smile, out of the dugout as quickly as possible. We kept the bats in the duffel bag because they were provided by the League. Bats were considered a luxury, and if a boy was fortunate enough to own one, he didn't dare bring it to the game. When league bats broke they were discarded. If a bat broke near the handle, I would take it home, repair the break with carpet nails, wrap the handle with electrical tape, and use it for pickup games.

"Let me help you, Coach," I said, clutching the mouth of the denim bag.

Coach Long looked a bit perplexed that a player was helping with the equipment.

"I appreciate the effort, Chase."

I placed the bats and the catcher's gear into the bag. I smiled as I looked into my coach's chocolate-brown eyes. I was so happy I would have dragged the infield and mowed the grass for the next game if they needed me to.

"You better go catch up with the team," the coach said. "You know how Coach Cooper loves to recap the game."

Coach Cooper walked with the team along the outfield fence. Like a sergeant leading his troops, he walked to a patch of ground beside a plump maple. The breeze kicked up the soft aroma of clover from the woods behind the scoreboard in left field. I found a soft spot of grass next to Joe. I couldn't hide my smile, still not quite convinced of what was happening.

"Now, boys," the coach said, "I'm proud of you. You played hard. You played with enthusiasm." Coach Cooper looked at the huge grin on my face. "Son, you look like you just found out Howard Hughes is your uncle."

"I'm just happy to be here," I responded, patting Joe on the shoulder. "I just want you guys to know how I enjoyed, uh, enjoy playing ball with you. It's been a privilege."

"Well," the coach replied, "I say we end it on that note. Drinks are on me." The team, except the coaches and me, sprinted to the concession stand for their free sodas. "Aren't you thirsty, son?"

"Thirsty doesn't even begin to describe it." I laughed, shook my head, and lifted my glove from the hunter-green centipede.

Mom chatted with Joe's mother behind the concession stand. Joe was lobbying for a trip to his favorite eating establishment, the nearby A & W.

"Please, Mom?" he said. "C'mon, it's Friday, and we won. What more reasons do you need?"

Mom interjected, "Maybe next week, Joe."

She glanced over Joe's shoulder and I followed her eyes across the school ground to Dad, who sat in his beige sedan at the edge of the parking lot. He tilted his head and took a long sip from a bag wrapped loosely around a bottle. That brown bag. Thousands of tears because of the brown bag. I looked into her eyes, sensing the uneasiness.

"Joe," I said, "let's get together tomorrow. Bring some of the guys and we'll pick up a game." Tomorrow? Would I be there tomorrow? Would my dream be over tomorrow?

I clutched Mom's hand tightly and we walked across the neatly trimmed, grassy path that connected the ball field to the yard of the elementary school. I smiled at the two silhouettes our bodies cast on the flat schoolyard, and thought it a most incredible sight. Letting go of her hand, I reached my left arm around her waist and her light blue cotton dress danced gently in the summer breeze. I felt like holding on forever.

Chapter Two

The long, black wing-tipped Plymouth pulled into the driveway. It looked like the Batmobile, but I wouldn't have traded it for a Lamborghini. Though Thomas Wolfe once said, 'You can never go home again,' he'd have been singing a different tune if he were hitching a ride with me that day.

Mom killed the engine and I stepped out of the car. I was temporarily paralyzed as, standing in front of me in all its modest glory, was my boyhood home. And, though every nook and cranny of it was tattooed into my brain, seeing it again in its infant stages, so to speak, sent chills through my body. The red maple beside the front steps, cut down the week after Lauren was born, was only an eight-foot sapling. I remember Dad wanting it removed not long ago because the limbs were smothering the roof, and the squirrels had made it their personal jungle gym. He'd cursed them daily and threatened to blow them apart with his Remington 12-gauge, which he was known to do. The azaleas, which Mom had kept shaped and manicured, stood barely knee high. Even the plump evergreens, which had stood like giant book ends at both corners of the house, were but puny shrubs that resembled a Charlie Brown Christmas trees.

Our home, a three-bedroom ranch-style home, sat on a slow-rising slope at the north corner of the neighborhood. The front yard was considered normal by neighborhood standards. It wouldn't have won Yard-of-the-Month honors, but it had always been neat and trimmed. That hadn't been our choice, necessarily. It had more to do with being allowed to eat and have a bed to lay our bodies on at night. At least that's the way Dad had presented it to us. The backyard, however, almost an acre in size, had been our Graceland. It would have won the Best-Yard-to-Play-Ball-In award if one had existed.

Mom walked in the side door at the edge of the driveway while I finished reintroducing myself to the front lawn. When I looked over my shoulder, Ricky, my younger brother, walked into the yard from the road. Rick's face was beet-red and showed the signs of a boy smack-dab in an active summer day. Tabasco and vinegar again filled his veins, stick-thin and cocky. Rick had been one of the few boys in the neighborhood who figured out life was more than playing baseball. My heart smiled at seeing Ricky energetic and wild, like an untamed colt, years before seventy-hour workweeks would tear down his unbridled enthusiasm.

"Beat you to the house," Rick yelled while he raced up the driveway. His lanky limbs pumped hard, his eight-year-old body moving chaotically as he tried to coax me into joining the race. He made it to the door and looked back at me while rubbing his muddy hands on his once white t-shirt. His sweaty, brown bangs stood at attention, and the tiny freckles on his pug nose were illuminated by the fading sun. He placed one hand on his hip, and waved me off with the other. "Wuss." How nice it was to again be the subject of questionable gender origin.

Familiarities of childhood exploded when I entered the den. Goose bumps rose up on my arms the size of marbles. Never had wood grain paneling looked so good. The glass trophy case Dad had constructed when I was ten sparkled under the slightly dusty swag lamp. A high-back, brown-and-gray sofa separated the trophy case from the eight-point buck Dad had killed on Thanksgiving morning when I was I was seven. It had been my first deer hunt, and Dad had bagged the buck in one shot while, two hundred yards away, I'd had my cap gun pointed at a mossy stump that I figured was some swamp creature. Beside Dad's deer mount was a brown gun rack with three shotguns and a .22 rifle. Our clunky Magnavox television had a wall to itself, and it stood out like a sentinel. I detected the faint aroma of apple cinnamon drifting from the kitchen as I scooted past Dad's tan recliner into the dining room.

"Check this out," Ricky said as he waited beside the dining room table, a table where we Watson boys were only allowed to eat when company came for dinner.

"Unbelievable," I said as I looked at his creation.

On display was a miniature scale of Fulton County Stadium—home of the Atlanta Braves—Rick had built with his vast collection of Lego blocks. The attention to detail was amazing: multi-row seating, portals for the exits, raised dugouts, and an upper deck, complete with plastic lights. Ricky could turn a can of Lego's into structures that would have made Michelangelo proud. He'd developed the knack by the age of five. I, on the other hand, could construct little more than a square tower. Maybe that's why I stuck to baseball.

"This is really good, Rick."

Ricky shrugged his shoulders a bit and walked to the kitchen. It was as if he wanted the focus on the creation, not him. It allowed him to hide behind his plastic wall of blocks, a defense mechanism that would serve him well through his childhood years.

"Put your uniform on the washer, Chase," Mom said from the kitchen. "I'll wash it after dinner."

I walked into my bedroom and rubbed my hand across the auburn school desk that sat in front of the window. My blue-and-red Cleveland Indians pencil holder sat at the back of the desk, overflowing with a collection of multi-colored pencils. It was at that desk that I had agonized over math problems, composed essays on summer vacations, written love letters that had never made it past the trash can, and devised lineup cards for imaginary baseball teams.

Walking across the ugly, oval throw rug that resembled a rainbow racetrack, I sat on the bottom of the pine bunk beds. I had always slept on the lower bunk because of my tendency to sleepwalk. For years, I had fallen asleep staring at the underside of the box spring above my head, convinced that bunk beds were required by state law to families who had more than one child. I looked about the room and confusion overwhelmed me. *How could this be happening*? It was a bit more than spooky, I admit. But, haven't we all said, 'Wouldn't it be great to go back in time and do it again, knowing then what we know now?' Well, I had said it many times and I was getting the chance. Be careful what you ask for.

As I tried to get a handle on the situation, the familiar aroma coming from the kitchen snapped my attention to something more important than solving the mystery of my journey back in time: Mom's cooking. I tried to peel off my uniform so quickly I fell against the bed as my feet got caught in my baseball leggings. I snatched a frayed pair of cutoff jeans and a white t-shirt with 'Dodgers' written in cursive blue across the chest. Cutoff jeans? Could my legs look any skinnier?

Waiting on the green Formica kitchen table were two plates of calorie-laden dumplings and a pair of opal Tupperware glasses filled with sweet tea. Well, actually they were imitation Tupperware. I grabbed a fork and knife with my yellow, dirt-stained hands, and began inhaling my food. Ricky matched me bite for bite, rarely coming up for air, and speaking to no one.

I watched Mom move about the kitchen, a woman content in her own world. A world where love flourished in the canisters of flour and sugar that grew in the mixer and baking dish. It wasn't that she was the world's finest chef—it was the care and gentleness that she put into it for her family. It was something I had learned early, and was something I've spent years trying to recreate in some similar form that I don't think I ever quite captured. Whether it was because my heart lacked the pureness of my amazing mother, I don't think I'll ever know.

I smiled in disbelief to see her so young, vibrant, and, most importantly, alive. Imagine seeing your mother, hours after attending her funeral.

I had forgotten how her dark, shoulder-length hair curled gently at the base of her neck. Her high cheek bones were softened by a hint of rouge, and her lips of cherry-red enhanced the sparkle of her smile. While I watched her, I heard Dad slip into his recliner in the den.

Ricky surfaced for air. "What's for dessert?"

"Chocolate pie," Mom said. Always a step ahead, she placed the pie in front of her hungry boys. *Jackpot.* Ricky inspected the pie laid before us, as if to make sure he wasn't getting hosed by receiving a smaller piece. After close inspection, Rick gave a 'thumbs-up' sign and we dug in. After wiping a small bit of chocolate crumb from the left corner of my mouth with my index finger, I said, "Mom, I sure have missed your cooking."

She walked to where I sat and placed her hand on my forehead. "Maybe that blow to your head today has you confused. Maybe I should take you to the doctor."

"I'm fine." Oh, man, was I fine.

Mom stepped back to the stove. "Nobody touch this," she said as she filled a platter. "Bobby's going to be home soon, and I know he'll be starving." Bobby was three years older than me. He was athletic, a huge prankster, and the only teenage workaholic I ever knew.

The front door opened and shut quickly. "Slow down," Dad yelled from his well-worn recliner. "You're gonna knock the door off the hinges one of these days," he shouted. "And I'll guarantee you, you'll be the one who has to pay for it."

Entering the kitchen, the prince of the family said, "Okay, feed me." He stared at me when he noticed me laughing. He had become muscular in his adult years, and it was funny seeing his licorice-shaped body of youth.

Bobby might deny it, but Ricky and I knew Mom pampered him as if he were Moses' brother. Until Bobby married years later, one could count on the hand of a thumbless man the amount of times he had prepared his own dinner plate.

"How'd your game go?" Bobby asked, the bangs of his brown hair flopping low, curving from left to right just above his eyebrows. Being the oldest, he had more freedom in the style and length of his hair.

"Great," Mom responded. "Chase hit a home run in the last inning to win the game."

"How a spaz like you can hit it out the park blows my mind," Bobby said. "You look better suited for badminton or croquet." Typical talk from my brother. Compliments-R-Us. He pulled a chair from underneath the table and removed the folded newspaper resting on it, plopping down his gangly six-foot-two frame in its place. He unfolded the paper and immediately turned to the sports section, totally uninterested in discussing his day with his siblings. Mom placed Wonder Boy's food and a tall glass of sweet tea on the table. Squinting as he read, Bob's liquid-blue eyes were barely visible, and he sported a look of someone reading VCR instructions instead of baseball box scores. Ricky took a sip of tea and squirted it between his two front teeth, barely hurdling the newspaper. The expelled liquid nailed Bob on the chin.

"Hey!" Bob shouted. "What's your problem?"

"Pipe down," Ricky said, disregarding the fact that he was half the size of his oldest brother, "or I'll take you out back and whip your ass."

"Ricky," Mom said. "Unless you want to spend the rest of the evening in your room, you watch your language." She pointed a rubber spatula at him.

"Easy, big fella," I whispered into Rick's ear.

The excitement at the table was interrupted by the sound of the refrigerator door opening. Dad's broad shoulders hunched over slightly as he grabbed a beer from the top shelf. Pains of disappointment, dormant for years, returned to the pit of my stomach. Mom breathed a sigh of frustration as she wiped the counter top.

"Chase, why don't you jump in the shower?" Mom said. "Ricky, go play with your Legos."

She had always been good at diverting attention from Dad when he'd been drinking. Beer in hand, he returned to his recliner. Rick wandered to the living room, where a mansion was being constructed on the cherry coffee table. Sitting on his knees, his hands moved slowly and deliberately. Each block had a purpose and

Rick was diligent in placing them, one by one, in the perfect spot. I watched him silently from the hallway as he again built a wall around himself.

Even though Mom was keeping us from harm's way, I really did need to take a bath. I was filthy. When I was a kid, dirt hadn't bothered me. At that moment, however, I reeked and couldn't stand it. As the tub filled, I sat at the side, rubbing my hands through my short, sandy-blond hair. The water approached boiling point, and the only things missing were potatoes, carrots, and a cannibal with a giant fork.

"Aaaaaah!" I screamed when I stepped in.

"What in the world?" I heard Mom yell from the kitchen.

"Chase is cooking himself in the tub," Rick said, surely not distracted in the least.

With water beating off my turtle-shaped big toes, I filled the tub to my chin while a million thoughts bounced through my head. Many were ones I had suppressed for years: watching Dad drink and the poignant look on Mom's face being two of them. For whatever reason, Dad couldn't seem to break the hold alcoholism had on him during my pre-teen years. It was a daily struggle. Some days successful, some days not. I don't know why it had been so hard on him back then. Whatever it was, he'd sure seemed to keep it to himself. It had made life hard on us all, and I could see it wearing Mom down. As the years went by, Dad had won more and more of those battles.

We didn't discuss Dad's drinking problem. Once, Mom took us to a meeting for families of alcoholics. I had defended Dad and I wasn't sure why. I'd provided no support for Mom, and had felt guilty for years for not backing her, for not seeing how desperate she was to fix things.

I retrieved clean clothes from my room and returned to the kitchen. I couldn't hide my smile as I stood at the doorway, watching Mom putting the kitchen back in order. She contained a certain spirit of grace and a tenderness within her heart that showed, whether she was tending to the need of an elderly neighbor or wiping the stovetop with a soapy rag. Someone had told me once that she contained emotional intelligence. I think that was one attribute that enabled countless people to become drawn to her. She truly shared that most tender heart with all ages, and it made me want to be more like her.

I walked up from behind and leaned my head against her shoulders. I could feel her flinch a bit, as I'm sure she wasn't expecting someone coming up from behind. "Hey, Mom." I closed my eyes for a moment, trying my best to transfer the love I felt for her from my heart to hers.

She turned toward me and kissed the top of my head. "Hello, my sweet child."

"Can I help you clean?"

"Thanks for the offer, but I'm about done. Why don't you go play with Ricky?"

"I'll do that in a minute." I took the milk carton and the glass butter dish from the table and returned them to the refrigerator. There truly wasn't much left to do, but I wanted to do something to help. I think I inherited a strong dose of wanting to help others from her. I looked around the countertop to see if anything else needed putting away, and she rubbed her fingers lightly through my hair. "You've always been my helper, haven't you? Hard to believe you're already twelve years old."

Mom, if you only knew.

I smiled, still in disbelief. I couldn't quite grasp how surreal it was. What was happening on the other side? In the future? Was I still sprawled out on the ball field? Was I in the hospital? The sound of the refrigerator opening snapped me back as Dad removed another beer.

"Ellen, we got any peanuts?" he asked.

Dad's dinner that evening looked to be liquids with some light snacks. On really bad days, it had been liquids only. Dad returned to the den. I heard Ricky rummaging through the closet floor in the bedroom, certain that a spare Lego piece was being hunted.

In the living room I stared out the picture window into the moonless night. Shadows danced across the front yard as the breeze blew the slender pines beside the streetlight. The family stereo was located on the bottom of the bookcase so I crouched, located the silver 'ON' switch, and flipped it upward. Green LCD lights on the black metal panel illuminated the bookcase as Don McLean strummed 'American Pie.' A.M. radio never sounded so clear. I wondered if that song truly was about the plane crash that took the lives of Buddy Holly, Ritchie Valens, and The Big Bopper. I heard Dad's voice rise in the den and I turned up the volume to drown him out. Mom's voice was barely audible as she tried to restore order with whispers instead of shouts.

"I don't have a problem," I heard him declare as Creedence Clearwater Revival sang 'Have You Ever Seen the Rain?' It was an appropriate song for the turmoil raining down in the den.

"Please lower your voice, for the boys' sake," Mom whispered.

"This is my house and I'll talk as loud as I dang well please. You know, you would drive any man to drink." Surely no words cut her deeper. How could he not know that? I moved to the bedroom to escape the conflict in the den, though I should have gone in to help diffuse the situation.

Ricky walked in the bedroom and shook his head.

"Where's Bobby?" I asked.

"He left. He doesn't hang around home much, does he?"

"No. I just think he hates to be around when Dad's drinking."

I lay on my bed, staring at the strands of box-spring fuzz above me that seemed to grow like a Chia pet. I pulled on a few of the cotton candy-like strands, pondering the craziness of the situation, unable to find a reason that would cause Dad to struggle through this time of his life. It made no sense. He was as kind-hearted a man as ever lived, and would lend a hand to friend and stranger alike. He loved his family and, later, would become an adoring grandfather.

My thoughts turned to Lauren and Brett, and what they must have gone through to stand over my lifeless body. I thought about my wife, Blake, and my oldest daughter Sara, who hadn't been able to fly home from college in time for the funeral. She had been spending the semester in Europe, and her flight had been cancelled, tearing her apart for not being there when her Grandma was buried. I began to wonder if I would wake up 'back' in the future, my incredible dream complete. *Just give me another day or two*, I prayed. I decided that, if I woke tomorrow in my boyhood bunk bed, I would cling to Mom like a static-filled sock and do my best to help Dad through his dark days. It was the least I could do.

"Night, Rick," I said after turning off the desk lamp.

"Night, turtle turd," echoed from the top bunk.

Feelin' the love.

Chapter Three

Morning's light roused me from a deep sleep. I rolled to my left to check the time on the clock-radio beside the bed. Instead of the clock, I spotted a poster of John Kay and Steppenwolf on the wall. The dream was still on.

I placed my arms behind my head on the pillow and looked up at the bottom of Ricky's bunk. If it was a dream, it was the longest in history. I pondered what had happened on that ball field, and what my family would be going through. At that point, I wondered if I was destined to repeat my childhood.

I closed my eyes, trying not to think about it. It wasn't as if I could blink my eyes and beam myself back to the future, so I slipped back off to sleep, surrounded by the warmth of childhood. I hadn't been asleep long when memories of long ago returned.

"Wake up, slacker," I heard Bobby say. His hands firmly clutched my sheet, blanket, and bedspread, and he yanked them from my bed.

"What the...?" With unfocused eyes, I swept my arm towards Bobby in hopes of recapturing my covers.

"I'm going to work," he said. "Have a nice day." He tossed the glob of linen to the floor.

Welcome back.

I had forgotten what a pain Bobby could be in those days, especially when I was sleeping. I guess he figured if he had to be up, so should I.

I remembered the day only had so many hours, and I climbed out of bed. To the window I walked, arms stretched upward to get the blood flowing. Parting the blue-and-white linen drapes, I noticed the dew on the thick centipede, a glistening shawl laid by God. The morning shadows stretched long and deep, as if the sun was locked in the sky, never to reach the pinnacle ever again.

It was in the Carolina of my youth where invincibility ran stronger than at any time in my life. I was a boy lost in a world where boundaries between fantasy and reality were blurred by pursuit of freedom. By freedom I mean the ability to harness all that was good while blocking anything that could hurt me. Serious matters had no place in the summer days of childhood. A disheartened mother, a father crying out for help in the bottom of a bottle, were circumstances that could fade away whenever I grabbed hold of a baseball bat or ran barefoot through the cool grass, or whenever the dew shone between the morning shadows.

I walked into the kitchen and spotted Ricky's head buried in a bowl of Kellogg's Frosted Flakes, wearing nothing but his underpants. Nostalgia rang out in the ticking of an old black-and-white wall clock and the occasional gulp of air rushing through Ricky's mouth, along with giant spoonfuls of sugar-coated flakes swimming in milk. I got cold chills from the sight and sounds. The days of being a kid—I had missed it terribly.

Reaching for the kitchen phone, I wanted to call Lauren to describe Ricky's attire, or lack thereof, but remembered she hadn't been born yet. She would have cracked up. A dwarfish James Dean he was. All he needed was a pack of cigarettes wrapped in his Fruit of the Loom t-shirt. Of course, he would have to put the t-shirt on first.

"Hey Captain Limpwrist," I said, "you wanna play some ball?"

"Forget it. Johnny Quest is getting ready to come on."

Any child of the 70's remembers the Saturday morning cartoon lineup, and ending up, by lunchtime, with scuffed elbows from lying on the shag carpet on our stomachs with our face resting on our hands. Johnny Quest was the coolest cartoon character of them all.

"Well, can you at least put some pants on before we watch it?" I asked while plucking a strawberry Pop Tart from the pantry.

"Bite me."

I followed Ricky and his red-and-blue Superman undershorts to the den. He plunked down on that dark-green shag carpet and I turned the brown-and-silver knob of the bulky television. The set was eighty percent wood, twenty percent picture tube, and was the first color set for the Watson household. Unfortunately, it was the pre-remote days. Of course, when Dad was watching TV, we were the remote.

Speaking of Dad, he walked in the den. "I want you boys outside to help clean the yard. You got fifteen minutes!"

So much for Johnny Quest.

The Watson backyard was perfect for playing outdoor sports of various categories, including some that were made up. The 'Plastic Golf Ball Homerun Derby using a Squash Racquet for a Bat' game was one of my favorites. Though the yard offered much in the way of sporting events, it was a bear to clean. From time to time, I schemed ways to avoid yard duty, such as the time I had pried off one of the wheels of the mower with a claw hammer. The problem with that was Dad had a knack for quick repair work, so I'd stopped trying.

Bobby avoided yard work like The Plague. When asked why he wouldn't help clean the yard, Bobby would say, "I only work when I get paid for it."

"Well, you better become a landscaper," I remember telling him, "and pay yourself."

"That's what children'll be for," he told me. *Always planning ahead.*

Ricky went to the bedroom and put on blue denim shorts and a red shirt with 'The Kid' emblazoned across the chest. I followed behind to put on my sneakers — Chuck Taylor high tops. Black, of course.

"Morning, boys," Mom said as we walked single file through the kitchen. She was busy folding clothes on the countertop.

"I love you, Mom." I hugged her, so amazed that I was seeing her alive and well again. I couldn't shake the still-fresh memory of her frail body during her final days in the hospital.

"Don't chop off any arms or legs out there."

We opened the back door to a huge yard filled with rope-thick pine straw, melon-size pinecones laced with tips a porcupine would envy, and thick grass that could test the finest of lawnmower blades. All that faded away when I looked toward the tool shed. I knelt, and I squeezed her tightly when she leapt into my arms. The impact knocked me onto the grass. She licked my face, and it was the best slobbery kiss in the world. It was Mandy, my Golden Retriever, my gift for my tenth birthday. I had forgotten all about her in my short time in the past, which made me feel guilty. Her coat was deep red, much like that of an Irish Setter. She was the smartest dog in the whole world. Had to be, and not just because I trained her. I really had trained her. All by

47

myself, thanks to a book given to me on how to train Retrievers.

We rumbled and tumbled, rolling over in the grass for several minutes. I noticed Rick watching us wrestle.

"Don't think I'm going to do the yard work while you play with the dog," he said.

"Come on, girl." I patted Mandy on the head. "You can be my supervisor."

I ran for the mower, shouting at Ricky over my shoulder, "You take the rake. Dad says you're too young to mow."

"You better pick up the pinecones first," Ricky yelled. Rick apparently didn't realize mowing over pinecones sped up the yard cleaning process. And it didn't just apply to pine cones. The same pertained to small sticks, wild flowers, rocks, and small animals.

I jerked twice on the pull cord, and the mower sputtered to life. *Let's get it on.*

I attacked the yard with a vengeance, smiling while the aroma of freshly mown grass filled my head. Mandy ran along side me, barking at the mower and crossing back and forth in front of it, as though it were some metal beast that needed to be stopped. Yard work had never seemed so much fun. I stopped about every thirty seconds to wrestle Mandy to the ground, rub under her ears, and give her slobbery kisses of my own.

The roar of the mower drowned out most of the profanity flowing from Ricky's mouth as he voiced his displeasure of having to rake. I laughed. *Quit your bellyaching.*

Dad, pulling weeds in the garden, checked periodically on us to make sure the yard work was going smoothly and, at the same time, doing inventory on arms and legs. Sometimes kids and mowers mixed along the lines of oil and vinegar. I recall a time, while mowing a neighbor's yard, coming across a stick that wouldn't fit under the mower. Putting creativity to action, I decided to give the stick a nudge with my foot and pushed it under the blade. Not only had the mower shred the stick, it had removed the top half of my sneaker, turning it into a sandal. It had taken me most of the day to create a lie that kept my backside from getting blistered.

The heat from the Carolina sun, combined with oppressive humidity, turned the yard into an outdoor furnace. I plodded along, however, pushing the red handle of the roaring Briggs and Stratton. Mandy stayed close by, seemingly tired of barking at the mower. My hands tingled from the vibration that the five-horsepower hog cranked out. Ricky tried to rake piles quickly so he could carry them to the trash pile, but the devil in me made me scatter the piles each time I rumbled by with the mower. I received a strange sense of satisfaction watching the angst on Rick's face as his piles kept getting destroyed.

I shredded many pinecones and other objects with my trusty mower. I spied a rubber 'super ball' the size of a golf ball ahead in the thick grass. When I rolled over it, I heard a loud thump as the mower hurled the mangled projectile. The thump was quickly followed by the yelp of Mr. Marbles, the neighbor's cat, as it struck the animal's backside as he walked along our fence railing. Mandy gave chase once he tumbled off the fence. Life was grand.

I completed my task in record time and pulled the On/Off lever located on the side of the handle, silencing the metal machine. I pushed it slowly to the tin storage shed as sweat trickled down my peach fuzz sideburns. It was nice not to worry about shaving, by the way. I gave Mandy another bear hug and led her to the kennel that was adjacent to the shed. She went straight for her water bowl, and I figured a large glass of iced tea was waiting in the kitchen with my name on it.

"Another satisfied customer," I said aloud as I surveyed the yard before going inside.

I had spent many days mowing for elderly neighbors in my early years. Mom had wanted us to lend a helping hand to those in mowing need, and for the gratification it brought. It certainly hadn't been for the pay. The ladies might offer up fifty cents, and sometimes tomatoes or squash from their garden. There'd been nothing like a yellow vegetable to make my day complete. Couldn't they have at least given us candy?

Ricky was finishing his glass at the kitchen table when I, shirt dripping with sweat, came in. I glared at him. "How'd you finish before me?"

"Because I didn't stop to pet the dog every twelve seconds."

The doorbell rang.

"Can one of you boys get the door?" Mom called out from the bedroom.

I volunteered. It was Joe.

"Hey," Joe said, "some of the guys are headin' to the field. Can you come?"

Baseball. Are you kidding? No hard decision there.

A pickup game was a chance to hit and field like Mickey Mantle and Willie Mays. It was a chance to pitch like Don Drysdale and Bob Gibbons. Mom gave me the green light, and I gathered my bat, glove, and ball cap. Amazingly, I, and the boys of my generation, had survived without a bat bag in which to carry our baseball gear. At the time, it seemed a fairly simple process for us. We placed our ball cap on our head, and we placed the bat handle through the hand strap of our glove. Finally, we held our bat over our shoulder. As I performed the routine, I thought of the equipment bags Brett and Lauren *had* to have. Bags so big they could hardly fit in the back of the SUV. Bags so heavy that they required a back brace to carry.

I hopped on my shiny banana bike, so named for the long, curved seat. My left hand gripped the handlebar that was shaped like the horn of a yak. With my right hand resting the bat on my shoulder, I maneuvered my cheeks perfectly in the seat. My canvas tennis shoes pushed the ridged pedals in perfect rhythm as the ride began. The trip was all downhill on the way to the field which, combined with the excitement of playing the game, made it a joy ride. The combination of playing for hours, and the punishing heat, would make the ride home feel like a Navy Seal obstacle course. The harsh heat of a Carolina summer had not been lost on me when I'd become an adult. I'd often talked about how I was certain we'd lived in the hottest part of the world. But, as kids, the heat had just meant that it wasn't too cold to play baseball.

Joe and I flew down the rough asphalt towards our 'field of dreams.' The strife of life on a young boy disappeared when a baseball game was played. When we arrived, there were eight boys throwing to each other in pairs on the field. Eight bikes, some shiny, but most faded, formed a line behind the bleachers, resembling a milquetoast version of a motorcycle gang. After hopping off our bikes, we pulled down our kickstands with our feet and placed them in line with the others.

"Alright, who the captains gonna be?" Joe asked. "Chase, how 'bout you and Davy?"

I seemed to be chosen as captain quite often, and felt proud to be held in such high regard by my friends. I looked at the faces of my childhood buddies, rattling off their names in my head. I wanted to tell them I had missed them, curious as to what they had become. Perry was there, and I walked up to him and shook his hand. He gave me an odd look. Twelve-year old boys didn't shake hands.

"What are you doing, running for Office?" he said with a laugh.

"President. I guess I need to start kissing babies' foreheads too. Would you be interested in putting a sign in your front yard? A vote for Chase is a vote for insanity."

As Davy began the player selection, a boy, not part of the baseball fraternity, walked on the field. I didn't recognize him at first, but when he spoke, I whispered, "Michael." A quiet, lanky boy with pasty, pale skin, Michael was an effeminate kid with blond hair so light that it was almost white which, combined with his skin color, gave him a Casper-esque look.

"You guys mind if I play?" he asked.

"I've told you before you can't play with us," Joe said. "You're no good."

Joe, a type-A personality, was tall and strong. He had little tolerance for boys who weren't good in sports. I hadn't stood up for Michael, or other boys lacking in athletic skills, who'd wanted to play when I was a boy, mostly because it just wasn't cool to come to the defense of a kid who wasn't good. Why was that the case? I had been taught to look after the meek and those who couldn't defend themselves. And yet I had chosen to keep quiet, more concerned with being cool than looking out for a boy who meant no harm to anyone. I remembered watching Michael grow up emotionally insecure. A kindhearted kid, he'd lacked the social and athletic skills to be a part of 'the crowd.' I felt ashamed for not standing up for him. But, here I was with another chance.

"Let him play," I said.

"Are you kiddin'?" Joe asked. "He's terrible."

"Well, I'll take him. Come on, Michael." I took him by his sleeve so that he stood beside me. The expression of joy on Michael's face doubled the disappointment I had for not coming to Michael's aid in my former life. I was ashamed of myself.

Joe murmured, "Suit yourself."

Davy and I picked our teams, and I somehow managed to pick Joe and Perry. A coup. We realized, by me picking Michael, one team would have six boys and the other team five. Bart Evens stood waiting for one of us to pick him. He looked uneasy being the last man standing without a team.

"Davy, you take Bart," I said.

Game time.

I tossed my bat upside down to Davy, who caught it one-handed, midway up. I squeezed the bat, placing my hand just above his. We took turns alternating hands, working our way up to the handle. This ritual was performed to decide which team got to bat first. The hand of the captain that ended up closest to the handle hit first. Davy's hand just barely fit under the handle to claim honors.

My four teammates and I took the field. Aside from Michael, the boys knew where to position themselves. They were quite adept at strategically placing themselves about the field in an attempt to cover what the regulation nine players covered. First off, no catcher was used. Obviously, each team had to have a pitcher and somebody to play first base. Since some players batted left-handed, the teams shifted from left to right like human windshield wipers. For righties, I normally played between shortstop and third, with a guy in leftfield and another in center. On occasion, games were played with just three on a team, making creativity extremely important. In those situations, the pitcher's mound shared double duty as first base, so fielded ground balls could be thrown back to the pitcher. If the ball arrived at the mound before the batter got to first base, he was out. Now, the amount of time arguing whether balls arrived to the mound before base runners touched first base had caused some games to last for days. However, it had taught us great debating skills, as we'd always felt certain our unbiased and unobstructed view was absolutely the correct one.

Michael looked confused when he took the field. I decided to play left field and told Michael to play center. That way I could help him if he struggled, and I knew he would struggle. Michael lacked hand and eye coordination, meaning any hard liners coming his way might result in a black eye or an extremely sore crotch. Joe, who I wisely picked, was our pitcher. As Joe took warm-up throws, I looked at Michael and noticed a look of contentment at finally being selected for a team. The contentment almost masked his nervousness…almost. Michael smiled at me. I smiled back.

"Don't worry. I'll help you if you need it."

Michael nodded. I rubbed the back of my soft leather glove against my cheek. I had missed that part of life so much. Why was it so hard to recapture that feeling in the adult world? Was it possible?

As play began, pale shadows of gray moved across the field like floating amoeba as bloated, ashen clouds drifted northeastward. The short bursts of sunshine magnified the contrast of the sandy infield and the deep green, manicured outfield bordering it. A pair of chubby wrens chattered away on top of the wooden scoreboard behind the outfield fence, as if debating which team would win.

Game on.

Davy's team got off to a good start as they loaded the bases with well-placed hits through the infield. When Rusty stepped to the plate, I figured we were in trouble. Joe brought some heat with a low fastball. Rusty wasted no time and hacked at the first pitch, mashing a line drive to center. Michael performed his 'deer in the headlights' impression while I made a beeline toward the center field fence. Michael, his knees shaking, raised his glove above his head and closed his eyes. Like a homing device, the ball somehow managed to find the web of his glove. Michael's grip, or lack thereof, allowed the impact of the ball to knock the glove completely off his retreating hand. As the ball and glove fell behind him, it tumbled towards the ground while he lowered his head and closed his eyes. I could hear Joe and the others groan as the glove and ball approached the soft grass. I dived head first across the ground, sliding behind Michael, cradling the rotating glove into my own. I quickly rose to my knees and held up the glove, revealing the ball inside. It had been about twenty-five years since I'd made a play like that, and it felt indescribable. I checked my elbows for scuff marks.

Michael clasped his hands around his face. "That was unbelievable."

"If you hadn't slowed down the ball, I wouldn't have been able to get to it in time." Removing the ball, I tossed Michael his glove and threw the ball to Joe.

"Man, that was awesome."

"It was easier than it looked." Compared to catching balls while ducking pine limbs and holly trees in my back yard, it was a breeze. "You did the hard part. I just cradled it in."

Michael's face lit up like a Christmas tree. After a pair of groundouts, we ran off the field to take our turn at bat. I watched the other team run onto the field. Even though we were opponents, we shared a common bond. I truly loved those guys. They played the game for the pure love of it. I know that sounds corny and cliché, but it was true. We treated the game as something reverent. We took care of our bats and our gloves. We'd comb the woods for homerun balls. We didn't have much, but what we had we wouldn't trade for the world.

"You guys wanna let Michael bat first?" I suggested as we congregated outside the first base dugout. The other guys reluctantly agreed. Michael snatched the first bat he saw and stepped to the plate. "Okay, Michael, take a good cut. Get something started."

Michael tried unsuccessfully to hide his nervousness.

"Geez, he doesn't even know how to hold the bat," Perry said as he noticed Michael's hands separated several inches apart. I called time and ran to the plate.

"Slide your hands together so they touch." As Michael did, I lifted the bat by placing my open palm under the handle. I raised Michael's hands, which clenched the bat tightly, until they were chest high, and lightly pushed the end of the bat until it touched his right shoulder. "Now stay like this, and when the ball comes across the plate, knock the cover off of it."

Rusty delivered the pitch and Michael swung, his body spinning like a top. The ball clanged against the chain link backstop. He looked toward the dugout, in need of moral support. I smiled and said, "Try it again. But this time just swing the bat, not your body."

The second pitch was soon on its way. Michael swung with all his might, and the ball hit the bat just above his bony fists, sending a dribbler five feet in front of the plate. We yelled for Michael to run. Lumbering like a man carrying a dead cow, he waddled down the first base line. With no catcher, Rusty had to make the play. Fortunately, it was too much ground to cover, and Michael stepped on first base just before Rusty's throw reached the first baseman's glove.

"Safe!" Joe screamed.

Michael looked so excited he could hardly stand on the base. I thought he was going to pee in his pants. I never knew a five-foot base hit could mean so much. The game continued and eleven boys, with me leading the way, became lost in our baseball world. Doing our best to imitate our baseball heroes, Brooks Robinson-like stops were made at third, Willie Mays-like shoestring grabs were made in the outfield and Sandy Koufax-like pitches were delivered from the mound. The game went on for two glorious hours and the heat began to take its toll. Steam radiated off the sand and my shoes were baking. We mutually agreed to make the inning the last one.

The game was over and we said our goodbyes. Michael, who lived across the street, walked happily to his house. I think he had the best time of us all.

"I guess I'll see you on Monday," Joe told me as he jumped on his bike. Would he? Would I be there?

"Okay. Hey, thanks for letting Michael play. You know, he's a good kid. He can't help that he's not a good ball player. Did you see the look on his face when he got that base hit?"

"Yeah, he was pretty keyed up. He's a little spastic, but he is a pretty nice guy."

"See you, dipwad."

"So long, butthead."

I stayed behind for a few minutes to look at the empty field. A quiet presence, it promised more games and more dreams to chase. It was the quiet part of the day, the time when the afternoon heat built to a crest, chasing us into the comforts of our homes. The streets were empty, not in a solemn or sad way, but something in the way of a neighborhood siesta. I headed home, making it two blocks up Harry Truman Street, where I stopped at the edge of the Simpson yard. Old man Simpson's yard was one of the few with Bermuda grass, which was ideal for shade-seeking boys like me. I placed my bike down carefully on its side, just at the edge where the grass met the road, and found a spot in the shadows of four lofty pines. The shade was quite perfect for keeping the manicured Bermuda soft and cool.

Hands behind my head, I lay on my back as the soothing grass tickled my parched neck. The pine limbs, encased in thick needles resembling green steel wool, ran helter-skelter like bark-lined barb wire. As I watched the treetops swaying lazily against the backdrop of the eastern sky, I realized I was seeing it in a way I never imagined possible. Though the scene unfolded through the eyes of my youth, my middle-aged soul filtered the beauty of it, sending the brain into an unknown state of nirvana. It was hard to explain, since it was something I had never experienced. I soon heard laughter and slowly raised my head, spotting two girls on bikes riding towards me. As they got closer, I recognized one of them. "What have we here?" I mumbled. "It's Vicki."

Vicki was my childhood sweetheart, only I was too shy to let her know that. Whenever she was near, I completely lost what social skills I had. And, between you and me, there hadn't been a lot of social skills to begin with as far as talking to girls was concerned. Vicki's personality and demeanor had been years ahead of other girls her age. Cute as a bug's ear, she couldn't have cared less about baseball. That had been a trait I'd been willing to overlook. Many nights I had lain in bed and imagined holding her hand on a fall afternoon, hugging her gently in the moonlight or stealing a kiss at her doorstep. For me, playing ball in front of the entire neighborhood had been a breeze. Talking to Vicki was another matter. I'd stammered and stumbled, and I'm sure she'd felt I was mentally challenged. At least that's the way it had been when I was a boy. Now, after twenty years of dating and marriage, I knew the second go around would go much smoother.

"Hey, Chase," Vicki said, flashing her angelic smile as she applied the brakes to her bike. "What are you doing on the ground?"

Vicki's friend, a portly, cold-hearted gal named Celeste, shook her head as if sensing a 'boy-girl' conversation was about to unfold. "I'm going home," she said to Vicki in a slightly irritated tone. I gave Celeste a quick 'quit whining and just go' look.

"Wow, you look great," I said with no sense of pretense. "Come lay on the grass with me. It feels great under the trees." Vicki placed her bike gently on the grass. As she lay beside me, the fragrance of lavender from her long, light brown hair permeated the muggy air.

"Check out the view," I said, as I pointed skyward. Massive clouds, gray on their underbelly, lifted skyward in countless bundles of white, standing in sharp contrast to the light-blue ceiling above it. "Isn't it awesome? I think God's showing off a little bit."

Vicki, both arms behind her head, focused her caramel-brown eyes on the clouds. "I never pegged you as a cloud watcher. Kinda thought there had to be a ball involved for you to want to watch."

"In the old days, maybe. Now I see things in a way I never thought possible."

Vicki turned her head cock-eyed at me. "The old days? What old days?"

My mind raced for an answer. "I just meant I see things differently these days. Learning to appreciate stuff now that I'm gettin' older." *Shut up stupid.*

Vicki said with a slight laugh, "You're not *that* old."

"I can't believe I'm getting to see you again. This is unbelievable."

"What's so odd about that? We live two blocks apart." Vicki looked at me with confusion. "Are you okay?"

"If I was any better, I'd be twins." My attempt to talk away her perplexity was only digging me a deeper hole. "So, how have you been? What have you been up to? I have to tell you, your eyes are even prettier than I remember."

I could tell she thought I was out of my mind. "I think the sun may have fried your brain," she said.

Heck, yes, it's fried. And I can't do a thing to stop it, at least lying next to you. "You're crazy," I said with a shrug while I gently touched her elbow with mine. Unfortunately, I was as goofy around her as I ever was. *Get a grip.* I tried to act cool. "You want to go for a ride? Can I buy you a drink at Frank's Market?"

"I can't. I have to be home in about a half-hour to babysit my brother."

"What are you doing tonight? Wanna hang out?"

"Hang out?" she said slowly while pulling herself into a sitting position. "You sure you're okay?"

"I'm just excited to see you."

"Okaaay," she said, and it was easy to tell I was trying too hard. "I think maybe I should just head on home."

I'd blown it, again. "Well, maybe I'll see you tomorrow." I stood at the edge of Simpson's yard while Vicki hopped on her bike, feeling like a complete idiot. "Way to go, Mr. Smooth," I whispered to myself through a painted-on smile. As she pedaled away, she turned and gave me another puzzled look.

I reached for the handle of my bike. "I suck."

Chapter Four

I parked my bike on the red brick patio that bordered the kitchen and back porch. Underneath my shoes, I felt the smoothness of the perfectly lined clay blocks of the patio. Each row of the L-shaped patio was arrow straight, just the way Dad had painstakingly laid them in the spring of my seventh year. I thought of how the passage of time had slowly altered the delicate brickwork to where, in later years, it had developed the callousness of a cobblestone street.

I smiled at the vision of Mom's silhouette at the kitchen table. Just the sight of her sent adrenaline through the veins of my skinny body. It was scary to think of how time had aged her and how fragile she would become. But, for now, she was as young as hope itself. I entered the kitchen and placed my hand on her shoulder as she chatted on the phone. She spun the long black cord around her fingers as she talked. She let go of it and reached her hand to mine with probably no clue how magical that felt.

"He just walked in, Katherine. He'll appreciate you asking. Thanks for calling. You too. Goodbye." Mom returned the black receiver to the base of the phone. "That was Katherine Hancock."

"Who?"

"Joe's mother," she said, looking at me curiously as though my memory had been erased. Well, it had been a while since I'd heard that name, so you can't blame me for not recalling it instantaneously. "Anyway, she called to invite you to go camping next weekend. But I told her we had company coming."

"Who's coming?"

"Uncle Doc, remember? You've been talking for weeks about his trip."

"Sorry, I guess I just lost track of time," I grossly understated. If she knew the distance I'd traveled, the track of time lost, she'd have hit the floor like a frozen Pekinese.

My uncle was one of the all time greats. Tall and silver-haired, with forearms like Popeye, Doc's day had always centered on charming the ladies, young and old. Sadly, the last two years of his life had found him in a nursing home, a victim of Alzheimer's. His mind had faded like a winter sunset, but the twinkle in his patented Watson baby-blues never left him. Even in his last days, as he would sit, quiet and alone in his room, there had been warmth emanating from his eyes when I'd come to visit.

In the den, Dad watched a Braves game.

"Who's winning?" I asked. I jumped at the chance to watch the greatest pastime with my father, something I had taken for granted years ago. Again, it was that feeling that youth was eternal. Why did I have to have it taken away from me to truly appreciate what I had?

"Certainly not the Braves," Dad said with disgust. "They get worse every year. I think your Little League team could beat 'em." The Braves had been a struggling organization, even though they had Hank Aaron. Being the only professional team close to the Carolinas, we'd pulled for them by default. I reclined on the couch, my head propped up by two yellow, velvet pillows. The hum of the air conditioner battled the volume of the hulking television set. The steady flow of air from the window unit quickly cooled my tired body. I

63

could have used a nap, but no way was I going to miss this chance. Dad's recliner faced the television set straight on, allowing him to use his feet to frame the action on the television set. From Walter Cronkite to Andy Griffith, the nightly parade of stars he had viewed between his big toes was endless. I reached and tickled his foot that dangled slightly over the edge of the footrest of the soft recliner.

"Cut that out," he joked, while pulling his foot away. "I'll knock you into the middle of next week."

"I'm really, really scared."

The Braves game was the only show in town that day, as the influx of wall-to-wall ball games offered by cable television had not begun yet. It was 'Saturday Afternoon Baseball' and, for years, had offered the only opportunity for me to watch my heroes on the diamond. The Braves were playing the Mets, and it was great to watch Willie Mays roam center field, even if it was the twilight of his career. No one could cover center field like Willie. Curt Gowdy's golden voice painted the scene of the game unfolding at Shea Stadium. I had been so enamored with baseball as a boy, I could name the starting lineup of every team in both the National and American Leagues. When I became an adult, free agency sent players from team to team in pursuit of million dollar salaries. Loyalty to teams was lost, and with it my passion for the professional game.

The Braves were batting and Hank Aaron stepped on deck. "There's the homerun king of baseball," I said.

"Since when? Somebody better let Babe Ruth in on it."

I realized I was speaking of future events, as Aaron wouldn't become the home run champ for several more years. "I meant the homerun king of guys still playing," I said, covering my tracks.

Lying back on the couch, my mind turned to the invitation extended by Joe's mother, and it got me to thinking. "Where is Joe going next weekend?" Comfortably situated on the couch, the pillows behind my head, I felt shouting to Mom made much more sense than walking through the house to ask her. It also required so much less energy.

"Flat Rock," Mom responded from the kitchen.

My head rose quickly off the pillows as I remembered Joe had died in Flat Rock after tumbling three-hundred feet over the falls of the Tyger River. His death had tormented me for years.

"He can't go," I said.

"Why not?" Dad asked.

"Because he's gonna d..." I couldn't finish the sentence.

"He's going to what?" Mom asked as she entered the den, a dishrag in her hands.

"He's going to, um..." I had no clue how to finish the sentence.

"Spit it out, son," Dad said.

"It's just that it's dangerous up there, you know, with the waterfalls."

"Surely they'll stay away from the falls," Mom said. "I wouldn't worry about it."

It's man's desire to assume the role of God that has led to his demise since Adam and Eve roamed the garden. And yet, the thought that I could alter the future of a friend's life stirred my soul. The power of knowing the future could allow me to take the jigsaw puzzle of life and make it regain wholeness, become a complete picture just like it looks like on the box. But this was not just a box — it was the heartstrings of man I could make complete.

Ricky walked dejectedly through the front door, and I removed my feet from the couch so he could sit.

"Where've you been?" I asked.

"Trying to make some cash. David and I bought some candles with our allowance and we tried selling them to the moms on the block."

"Why would they buy candles from you?"

"To save them from having to go the store. We are called 'middlemen'."

"So, are you reeling in the big bucks?"

"Are you kidding? We haven't sold a one." Rick's first venture as an entrepreneur was off to a shaky start. He shook his head in disgust and went to the kitchen to drown his business sorrows in a bowl of ice cream.

Speaking of food. "What's for supper?"

She sipped on a glass of tea while taking a break from the kitchen chores, attempting to work on a crossword puzzle. Drinking tea was as common as breathing in the South. "We're going to Robert's for dinner."

Mom's brother, Robert, was a one of the most impressive men that I'd ever known. He was a decorated war hero, had survived the jungles of the Philippines in WWII, and fought on the battlefields of Korea. A true man's man, an avid hunter and marksman, Daniel Boone had nothing on this guy. Dinner was sure to be an entertaining one.

But first, back to the ballgame. The Braves came from behind to win by a run, and Dad commented, "Well, sometimes even a blind sow finds mud in the barnyard."

The game was completed, and now it was my turn. I walked out the front door and panned the street. With the sun sinking in the sky and temperatures relenting, I knew a game of some sort awaited. Ah, so nice to be back in the days when the hard decisions involved trying to find which game to play. I walked to the back yard, and Mandy sat at the gate, her tail sweeping across the ground as she saw me approach. The closer I got to the kennel, the more excited she got. When I opened the gate she took off like a bull coming out of the shoot at a rodeo. She zigged and zagged across the yard, no doubt releasing built up energy that the kennel wouldn't allow her to burn. After a few minutes of me watching her go, she returned and sat by my side. She gave me that, 'okay, you can pet me now' look. So I did.

"Let's go for a walk."

We went to the street, and the neighborhood was alive with activity. Across the street, four boys, six-shooters on each hip, roamed the plains on imaginary horses, looking anxious to tame the Wild West. A pair of pre-teen girls rode down Brennan on shiny bikes, giggling, surely, over newfound 'boy' secrets. Three doors down, the Adams sisters played hopscotch in the driveway, doing their best to keep their toes inside pink chalk boxes. I noticed Mrs. Jacobs chatting with Mrs. Foster over an ivy-covered fence post. Across the street, Granny Wiggins squinted at a Reader's Digest while moving gently on a porch rocker. I'd stepped into a Norman Rockwell painting.

It was the era of stay-at-home moms, when mothers were gatekeepers of the neighborhood, at least by day. At night, the fathers took over, because the dark brought on totally separate issues. The daily goings on were taken care of so well by the mothers that the fathers rarely requested the details of the day. Unless someone ended up in the hospital, or in jail, dads didn't need be bothered. If it took a village to raise a child, Belmont was the village to live in. If a child misbehaved, he didn't need his mother there to dole out discipline. Any mother would do. An unwritten pact gave each mother that right. So, if one was one foolish enough to cause trouble while out of sight of his mother, he would inevitably feel the wrath of not one mom, but two, as the news would quickly pass down the mother 'hotline.'

The heat of the afternoon sun relented a bit as shadows stretched across the lawns. Abundant pines and hardwoods slowed the sun's rays, enough to cover most of the front lawns on the block. I spotted some of the neighborhood gang playing kick ball on Allan Johnson's front lawn.

"Chase, come play with us," yelled Allan, a tall teenager with a blonde crew cut and small, Curious George shaped ears.

Unfortunately, Allan was a link to a past event that belonged on the hall of shame wall.

It was a warm, spring afternoon. I was six years old. Bored, in search of something to do, I walked out in my back yard. Spotting Allan and his pal, Woody, at the white wood fence at the back of our yard, I slipped quietly behind them.

"What are you guys doing?" I asked.

"Throwing persimmons at cars," Allan replied. "Go home, junior."

"It's my yard. I can stay if I wanna." I was a tough kid. Can't you tell?

"You just stay out of the way."

I watched as the boys threw persimmons at cars moving down the two-lane road running parallel to my back yard fence. Maybe they were having a bad day, accuracy-wise, or perhaps they just sucked at throwing. Cars ambled up and down the highway, and persimmons fell harmlessly in front, behind, or beside the vehicles. The boys stood thirty feet from the road, using holly bushes as cover.

"You guys are terrible," I told them.

The boys looked at each other with frowns upon their tough-guy faces.

"Listen to this little punk," Woody said. "I guess you could do better?"

"Heck, yeah. But I don't wanna get in trouble."

"Waaaaaaaah," Allan said. "You baby. Go home and get your diaper changed."

Diaper? That struck a nerve. I had the right to remain silent, but I didn't have the ability. "I can throw better than you left-handed."

"Well, we'll give you a sporting chance and let you do it right-handed," Woody said. "Come on, Mr. Expert. Step right up." Woody swept his hand in front of him as though he were turning the show over to me. "Though I know a squirt like you won't come close to hitting a moving car."

I was being challenged and my athletic skills questioned, though, at age six, how many skills had I really acquired? Still, I buckled to the challenge. Surveying the ground, I found a plump, light yellow-and-green persimmon, slightly larger than a golf ball. I rolled the persimmon in my hand to get a feel for how to release it from my fingers when the time was right. I looked both ways for a target and saw nothing. I hoped that no cars would come, eliminating the need for me to follow through with my boast. Soon, the sound of a truck turned my head to the right. A blue pickup, with gray wood boards surrounding the bed, chugged forward. Its engine sputtered as the rickety truck rambled towards me while I crouched behind a holly shrub. Slowly, I stood, eyes focused intently on the truck. Too late to turn back now. The driver's side window, rolled down to draw cool air into the vehicle, really should have been up that day.

I uncorked a bullet and the persimmon flew into the driver's window, striking the man behind the wheel in the left cheek. A lit cigar, which looked like it was clenched tightly in the man's mouth, fell onto his lap. The man pulled the steering wheel sharply to his right and the truck exited the highway onto the right shoulder, the brakes squealing like a stuck pig.

Allan and Woody dropped their persimmons and took off for home. The back yard was about three-quarters of an acre and, with all the trees, it seemed like my house was a mile away. I thought it best to run alongside Woody's house, which bordered mine, and slip around the front yard, hopefully putting the angry driver on the scent of other game. I took off, high-tailing it as fast as my skinny legs could carry me. Safely inside my den, I locked the door and crouched low, trying not to blink or breathe. For close to a minute I felt that I'd escaped. That was until I heard footsteps on the concrete steps. My heart stopped when a firm knock on the door killed the silence.

Get out of here, mister.

My first thought was to stay perfectly still and hope the shadow from the other side of the door would leave. The knocking persisted, becoming louder and more forceful. I knew Mom would eventually hear the knocking, so I took a deep breath, and opened the door slightly.

"Your parents home?" the gruff voice asked.

Parents? What parents? I'm an orphan.

Peeking through the narrow opening, I saw, standing before me, one angry man with persimmon peel hanging from his chin. I shook my head quietly.

"Chase," the soft voice from behind asked. "Who's at the door?"

"Oh, fudge." Perhaps fudge wasn't the exact word used. My recollection of that statement remains cloudy to this day.

After minutes of humbling apologies, I was ordered to my bedroom. Mom apologized to the man, whose pride, surely, was hurt as much as his chin, and she promised swift punishment to the young perpetrator. When I made it to the bedroom, I sat on my bed, tears already mounting, knowing full well I was getting ready to get a whipping of monumental proportions. On the bright side, I realized I had a future as a baseball pitcher.

The spanking Mom doled out that day with the rubber spatula stayed with me for a long, long time. The first forty or fifty whacks didn't hurt so much, because the rubber was soft. But the next two hundred helped me understand the importance of never tossing anything at cars again.

"You're on our team," Allan yelled to me, snapping me back to the kick ball game.

I did a quick head count. "Both teams have five players."

"Yeah, but Luther plays like a girl, so we need another guy." Luther looked mad. Timid, but mad.

I instructed Mandy to sit, although she looked as though she'd prefer to play on my team. I set up beside a yellow sprinkler that represented third base, ready for action. Allan's older brother, Toby, sat on the front steps, his pale green transistor playing Top Forty tunes. Jennifer, a diminutive girl with curly brunette hair, was up to bat—or kick, in this case. Kick ball was a game that girls struggled to play well when I was a boy, but they played nevertheless. They lacked leg strength and rarely kicked it out of the infield—an infield that was never that big to begin with. Sure enough, Jennifer tapped it softly back to Ben and ran towards a spindly dogwood that was custom-built for first base. Ben tossed the rubber ball towards Jennifer's back as we awaited Jennifer's scream. I calculated that girls screamed about a second and a half prior to the ball making contact with their body. It was nothing scientific and I'm sure the theory could be disproven. But it was as if girls had an internal radar system that sounded an alarm just before a spherical object was about to make impact. As if on cue, Jennifer screamed and the ball pegged her in the back. She walked bitterly around the parked car in the road to the dugout, which was two folding chairs, a beige trashcan turned upside down, and a Big Wheel.

The game played on and the pale, red ball was kicked, thrown, and knocked around the yard. Kick ball, unlike baseball, was fast paced, and a fifteen, twenty inning game was common.

Eventually, the aroma of country fried steak and macaroni pie drifting from nearby kitchens turned our attention away from the game to our stomachs, and the kids began to migrate home. The game, called on account of hunger, sent me to the high concrete steps of Allan's front porch where I sat beside Toby. I motioned for

Mandy, and she ran to the steps, sitting below me. Toby and I petted her. He was a quiet boy who had dropped out of high school, and was the only boy I knew who had built his own car. He worked at a nearby garage, and the owner helped him rebuild an old Chevy Impala.

"What's shakin', Chase?"

"Not much. How ya been?"

"Other than my old man ridin' me, I can't complain."

"How's the Impala holdin' up?"

"Outta sight. Want to take her for a spin?"

"Sure." *Can I drive?*

The transistor made a loud click as Toby turned the volume dial to 'Off.'

"Give me two minutes while I take Mandy to her pen." She and I flew to my back yard. "See you in a bit, girl." I hurried back to Toby's house.

Bright royal blue, the Chevy sat under a large, mushroom-shaped Bradford pear tree in the driveway. I opened the passenger door, and felt the softness of the shiny cream leather seats against my legs.

"Where to?" Toby asked, backing out onto the road.

"Nowhere in particular. Let's just ride."

Windows down, radio blaring, two guys lost in their youth took to the street—Toby, into his first venture into adolescence, and me, my second. Toby drove down each road in the neighborhood, and I realized how much it had changed. Well-kept lawns, with driveways cluttered only by bikes and tricycles, would become yards covered with knee-high weeds, the driveways filled with old furniture and broken-down cars. Neighbors who had welcomed friends into their homes would be replaced by untrusting eyes hid tightly behind closed doors, afraid of the outside world. The wind pushed through the Impala's windows, and I reflected on the sad passage of time.

"Man, this was a nice place," I said.

"What do you mean *was*? This ain't a bad place to live at all. Don't tell anyone I said that."

"I just think this was a great place to grow up. Everyone was so nice. They were always there when help was needed. Good times or bad. Great people."

"Man, you're talkin' weird."

"Sorry." I struggled, remembering I was twelve again.

"It's cool," Toby said, giving a slight wink. "Let's ride."

We traveled down each street with little conversation, as Toby seemed to be preoccupied with the purr of his Impala's engine. I was busy looking at the homes and people of the neighborhood. I felt as if I had jumped into the pages of a yearbook. Toby wheeled up in front of my driveway, the joyride complete.

"Thanks for the spin," I said as I gripped the shiny chrome door handle.

"Anytime," Toby replied, adjusting his rearview mirror to make sure the wind hadn't tussled his brown hair styled a la Ringo and John. "You're alright for a little dude."

"Thanks. You're alright for a big dude." I waved as the Impala pulled away.

Dad drove up when I walked into the yard. He exited the car holding a bottle of liquor in a brown paper bag. The brown bag again. How I hated the sight of that bag. I watched him hide it in the trunk of the car. The hiding places were anything but. The trunk, under the sink, in the bushes outside my bedroom window, the tool box in the storage house—I knew them all. They were holding cells for the drink that had chained his being and self-worth, which, during that time, surely was not much. And yet I had let those hiding places stand unaltered, continuously crumbling what self-worth was left.

I wept inside for our weakness—his for the inability to stop, and mine for hiding in the shadows letting it unfold. Shame on me.

Chapter Five

Ricky and I washed our hands and combed what little hair we had, and the family headed to the car. We assumed our designated spots in the back seat. I started to roll up my window so the air conditioner could ease the heat that had built up in the car, when the grim reality hit that there was no air conditioner. To make matters worse, the plastic seat covers pressing against my legs immediately stuck to my thighs. What exactly were those seat covers for? The raised bubbles gave our bare legs the look of a leper. The ride lasted an excruciating twenty minutes, though I'd been through much worse. We pulled in the driveway, peeled our sweaty skin off the plastic seat covers, and exited the car.

Uncle Robert's house, constructed of large gray stones, sat high on the hill of a two-acre lot bordering a small creek and thick woods. The yard was like a mini-version of Wild Kingdom. It began with Skipper, the pet Collie. From there it expanded to the neighbors' pets, including dogs that had been abandoned or had simply run away. Cats moved about the driveway like a band of indignant hunters. Fighting gamecocks were housed in pens at the bottom of the long, sloping back yard, perpetually confused that dawn just might be an all day, and night, event.

The smell of venison filled the kitchen when we entered through the side porch door. Robert, lifting a black iron skillet from the stove, removed the coarse butterfly-shaped meat, piece by piece, with a long steel fork. Joanna slid fluffy biscuits off a baking pan, a touch of flour on her chin. She had passed away from cancer two years before Mom. A striking, refined woman, she stood in stark contrast to Robert's gamesman ways. They made a most handsome couple.

"Come in, come in," she said, placing the pan on the countertop. She looked at me, probably because I was thrilled to be there in that moment. "That's some smile you got there, Chase."

"Just happy to see you, that's all," I said.

Rebecca entered the kitchen. "Hey cousin." She surely noticed the gleam in my smile.

"You got that moon pie mug, sweet cuz," she said. "What's up with that?"

"Well, I just flew thirty years to see you."

"Thirty what?"

"Nothing." *Thirty years, my adorable cousin.*

"Dinner's ready," Joanna called out. Rebecca laughed and grabbed a plate. Dad came in from the carport, trying to slide in unnoticed. The brown bag in the trunk would be sought after often that night, that liquid demon, the great deceiver. He flashed a smile, as though to say he'd only been outside to smell the evening breeze. Mom's disappointment showed, and I could tell Robert and Joanna knew full well what was going on. Dad was the only one who didn't realize we all knew.

The supper line formed, and I jockeyed for position ahead of Ricky. Biscuits, hidden under linen, filled a wicker basket. Venison sat in a large, white porcelain bowl next to a metal bowl of thick gravy. Cholesterol hovered in the air, arteries clogging at just the thought of what would soon enter our mouths. I listened to the laughter and love passed around with the basket of biscuits. If only the scene were possible in the present. Growing older, losing parents, relatives, and childhood friends, was absolutely a bitch to take. At that moment, though, death was a million miles away.

I couldn't stop smiling at Rebecca. Conversation was light and I coaxed Robert to tell us stories about his younger days. The poster child for devilishness, he'd been legendary in the little mountain town where he and Mom had grown up.

My favorite tale was the time Robert had got revenge on Ollie Matthews, who had poisoned his prized coon dog. Robert was a teenager at the time, and had trained his dog from a pup. As the story went, Ollie had ridden his prize saddle horse to Luke's General Store one Saturday. Robert and two of his buddies had sat outside the store, eating licorice they had just purchased. Ollie had cut a smirk at Robert as he'd entered the store. As if the smirk had added insult to injury, Robert had taken his pocket knife and cut a slice out of the barbed wire fence that bordered the back of the store.

Slowly balling the wire, he'd lifted the tail of the horse, shoving the wire into the animal's backside. The animal had stirred a bit from the discomfort. When Ollie came outside, again looking at Robert like he was just a tad bit beneath him, he'd climbed aboard the big animal. Proudly, he'd taken off, high in the saddle. After only a few gallops, the wire had began to cut into the animal. Apparently the pain had worsened with each step, and it'd scared the horse so that it took off, surely not knowing what else to do. From what Robert was later told, the horse had carried Ollie seven miles into the mountains before Ollie jumped off. The horse had never been heard from again.

After supper was finished, Dad slipped outside to smoke a cigarette, as well as have himself another drink. Ricky, Rebecca, and I walked out the back door to catch fireflies. For some reason, fireflies had disappeared by the time my children came along. They never got to experience the fun of wandering through the darkness, waiting to catch flies in empty prescription medicine bottles. Timing was the key, as the fly's light faded in and out like a distant tower.

"Hold still," Rebecca said to me as we stood beside a massive magnolia. "I see one rising behind you. It's coming up above your shoulder." I froze as Beck reached up slowly beside my head. "Don't move. He's right here." The tiny plastic bottle in her right hand, the cap in her left, she slowly closed in, reaching outward.

"Oww!" I cried.

Rebecca giggled. "I just wanted a little bit of your lobe."

"I'll get you for that one." I managed a smile as I rubbed my aching ear. Mischief and beauty—what a powerful combination.

Ricky quickly looked frustrated, unable to take any fireflies captive. Not one for patience, after a few tries, he threw his bottle to the ground. "Trying to catch fireflies is the dumbest thing ever," he mumbled in disgust before heading indoors.

"Come back, Ricky," I called out. "Let me show you how to do it."

Ricky's fly catching was done. The fireflies we caught that night would be returned safely to the night air due to Rebecca's insistence. She was the Ellie Mae Clampett of the family. She protected man, beast, and even winged insects.

I looked out into the summer darkness as a warm breeze caressed my face. The carefree feeling of a childhood summer night had quietly returned, and a warmer feeling there could never be. We shimmied onto the hood of Robert's Delta 88, where I placed my feet on the front bumper for support. Rebecca slipped into an Indian-style position. My forearm brushed against the soft, olive-toned skin of her leg. I watched the light from the porch dance across her soft brown eyes.

"Hey, Beck." I glanced at the crescent moon fading in the western sky. "Have you ever thought about time travel?"

"Like H.G. Wells kind of thing?"

"Well, not a time machine, necessarily. But travelling back in time. You think it's possible?"

"Well," she said after a brief pause. "I've never really thought about it. Why, do you?"

"I'd never given it much thought until recently. But I have a feeling it's possible."

"Be great if we could, huh?"

I scratched my chin. "If I could go back, I think I'd pick this time of my life. Right here, right now."

"That would be something. Especially if we could do it when we're old. Could you imagine?"

"I think I can. It might not be all fun and games though. In some ways, it might be sad."

"I don't see how."

"I wish we didn't have to grow up."

"I'm looking forward to it."

"It's not all it's cracked up to be."

"Why do you say that?"

"And I wish our parents didn't have to grow old. Didn't have to die."

"Chase! Don't talk about those things. That won't happen for a long, long time."

"Maybe, maybe not. All I know is, we need to count every day, every minute, as a blessing. So when your mama kisses you tonight, you hold onto her with all your might. Never take her for granted."

The feeling of somberness dropped over us like a net and we decided to release the fireflies and walk back inside. Dad's speech was slurred and slow. It was time to go.

Hugs were exchanged and we walked to the car. I looked at Joanna, wondering if I would see her again. I waved at Rebecca from the back seat of the car as Dad backed shakily out the driveway. Mom glanced slightly toward him and she wore a look of concern. Looking over her left shoulder at me, she nodded in a not too convincing manner that the ride home would be okay. That attitude changed quickly as the car crossed the yellow double line when we took off for home.

"Why don't you let Mom drive?" I asked.

"'Cause I'm driving."

"Well, we're swerving all over the road. This is ridiculous."

"Don't give me any lip, son. I'm driving and that's that."

"Chase, sit back and be quiet," Mom said.

Even with Dad losing a fight with sobriety, Mom was quick to make sure we showed respect. I shook my head in disgust as Ricky somehow managed to drift into a coma-like state.

The ride home wasn't dull, as Dad barely missed a phone pole and lost a hubcap when the passenger side struck the curb. Ricky slept through the entire roller coaster ride.

The car came slowly to a halt in the driveway. Ricky, like a human slug, lay slumped in Mom's arms as she carried him to bed.

Once inside, I brushed my teeth and went to the kitchen for a drink of water.

"Get your ass in the bed," Dad said as he kicked my backside with his right foot.

The physical pain paled in comparison to the pain that slammed my heart. Part of me wanted to turn and hit him. Part of me wanted to hug him and tell him I was there to help. "Yes, sir," was all I said, looking downward, biting my lower lip to fight the pain, physical and spiritual.

Lying still in the lower bunk, I stared at the box spring above my head, unable to sleep. I wiped tears from my eyes. The minutes ticked away as I lay in the quiet darkness. A faint train whistle blew in the distance as the 12:50 from Camden rolled down the tracks a half-mile from our home. Many sleepless nights, in my boyhood days, I had lain in bed, sometimes wishing I was on that train. I never knew the destination of the locomotive, but I had often wondered who was on board, and where they were going. Were they watching the world roll by, or were they fast asleep in their cars?

The whistle slowly faded into the night as the train rolled down its steel highway. Like the whistle, I faded off to sleep.

Chapter Six

In the dim morning light, I lay in bed. Rain beat softly on the shrubbery outside my window, a peaceful murmur that made the world seem far off in the distance, as though the house had become its own entity in its own galaxy. Ricky's breathing was steady above me, and I knew he was dead to the world. Wrapped up in the secureness of my bed, I dozed off, and dreams began to run through my mind in black-and-white, reel-to-reel fashion. The dream seemed more like a series of dreams where rooms and the floor below me shifted constantly, each turn bringing a new cast of characters and, with them, confusing conversation. It was the kind of deep sleep where it appeared I might never awaken. At least it was, until cold water rushed into my eardrum.

Thoughts of water boarding came to mind, and I was hoping I could surface in time to fill my lungs with air. I looked around and realized I was safe in my bed, though water ran from my ear.

"Wake up, dumbass," I heard Bobby say. Of the torturous ways he used to awaken me, water in the ear was the worst.

"Son of a…" I shouted, leaping from bed. Bobby bolted for the door, headed for another day at the grocery store. "Your day's coming," I mumbled. I made a mental note to punch his lights out when I returned to the future.

I must confess that even Bobby's water torture brought comfort in some strange way, as it was just another realization that I was somehow locked into my childhood. Lying wet ear side down, I closed my eyes and thought of my family. I couldn't help but worry that they sat bedside in some hospital room, waiting helplessly for me to awaken.

The hardwood floor whispered familiar creaks when I tiptoed in bare feet to the kitchen. Opening the pantry, I was tempted to hide the cereal boxes to aggravate Ricky. I decided instead to fix breakfast. I removed a white bag, bulging with corn meal grits, from the pantry. I moved on to the fridge and took the food supplies I would need. Turning on the gray box-radio on the counter, I heard Three Dog Night singing 'Pieces of April.'

How old are those guys now? Older than me, I know that.

Eggshells cracked, pork sizzled in the pan, and I whipped up a feast. A pot of coffee brewed on the back burner, and the aroma of roasted beans filled the air. I was the best twelve-year old cook in the world. The wonder boy, spawned from Emeril and Julia Child.

Glancing out the kitchen window, I spied a budding yellow rose in the garden by the patio. It reminded me of the flower I had bought Mom in the final hours in the hospital, only to arrive too late. I walked into her bedroom and gently rubbed her arm.

"Morning, sleepy head. Thought you should have breakfast in bed."

Mom fumbled for her glasses on the nightstand, obviously caught off guard by her eager-to-please middle child.

"What in the world?" She looked at the food on her plate. "You made this?"

"Yes, ma'am." I slid the tray on her lap. "Hang on, Dad, yours is next." I returned to the kitchen and pulled another tray from the cabinet. I fixed Dad's plate and carried it to the bedroom. While fixing Ricky's plate, I heard Mom and Dad laughing. Ricky shuffled in, wearing nothing but his tighty-whities. "Here, underwear boy. I fixed your breakfast."

"Riiiiiight," Rick said as he reached for the giant box of *Cap'n Crunch* in the pantry.

The day was off to a great start. I looked out the window to the beautiful morning. Life seemed so new, so full of possibilities. It reminded me of those days when the future had been so far in the distance. The last thing on my mind would be what was waiting down the road. I would always be young, and never ever would I have to worry about experiencing death and thoughts of my own mortality. I was decades removed from the day when I had realized that life wasn't an endless highway. I was young again, but I understood that moments were meant to be treasured, to be tucked away so I could pull them back out one day to be dusted off and relived.

"Thanks for that wonderful breakfast," Mom said as she placed the dirty plates in the sink. The gentle aroma of lilac drifted across the room when Mom squirted some lotion from a pink bottle on the counter. We stacked one sink with the dirty dishes and stood side-by-side as we cleaned the mess I'd made. I leaned my head and touched her arm. Ricky placed his empty bowl on the counter and headed to the den. He was in no mood to clean. Big surprise.

Scraping uneaten scraps into a milk carton, I asked, "Mom, you think Joe could spend next weekend with us?"

"He's going to the mountains, remember? He wanted you to go with him."

"He can't go on that trip." I couldn't let my best friend die. Time to play God.

"Again with the 'he can't go' talk. Why are you so intent on keeping him from going to Flat Rock?"

I rubbed my forehead with my hand. "I can't tell you."

"You can't tell me? Why not?"

"I just can't. All I can tell you is he can't go to Flat Rock."

"You have to have some reason. Why won't you tell me?"

I paused, closed my eyes, head tilted downward, and breathed deeply. "'He's going to die if he goes."

"That's it. I'm taking you to the doctor. You haven't been the same since that ball smacked your head."

"Mom, I don't need to go to the doctor." I quickly realized I'd made a mistake. Time to change directions. "It's just that I've been having dreams about Joe going over the falls in Flat Rock. The dreams are so real. I'm telling you he's not coming back if he goes on that trip. You just have to trust me."

"Dreams can certainly seem so real. But I'm sure you have nothing to worry about."

I was living proof of that. Mom pulled me gently to her chest. Inside her arms was the safest place in the world.

"Boys, it's time to get ready for church," Mom called out from the kitchen.

"Dang it, I wanted to stay home and watch TV," Ricky responded.

We went to church most every Sunday, but didn't mind sitting one out on occasion. On the Sundays we did stay home, we were faced with the worst television lineup imaginable. *Meet The Press*? No thank you. *Southern Home Party*? We would rather have had our eyelids scraped. *The Pastor Robinson Gospel Hour*? We may as well have gone to church.

The only thing worthwhile on Sunday mornings took place in the fall when Notre Dame football games were replayed. Ricky thought the games were live broadcasts. I would 'magically' predict the score of the games after convincing Rick to wager some form of a bet. I acquired quite a few of his possessions thanks to those Notre Dame replays.

And so, that morning, we put on our Sunday bests, resolved to the fact that television was not on our Sunday morning schedule. Our dress clothes were always clean, but not exactly something out of GQ magazine. It didn't matter. I smiled, shaking my head while selecting baby-blue gabardine pants and a blue-and-green plaid shirt from the closet. It was a good thing my children weren't there to see me sheathed in polyester and rayon. Dad fetched the paper and sat down at the kitchen table.

We were ready for another dose of Baptist therapy.

"Bye, Dad," I said as we converged at the front door. As we got close to the car, I turned and yelled, "Be right back." I walked back into the kitchen. "Dad, will you come to church with us someday soon?"

Startled, he responded, "Yeah, I'll go someday."

"Promise?"

"I promise." Dad smiled, and I smiled back.

"I love you."

Those three words had rarely flowed from my lips as a child, and the same could be said about the rest of the family. The Watson philosophy had been to show it instead of verbalizing it. That had all changed when

Lauren was seven. We'd been on the way home from a family dinner at Mom and Dad's one evening. She'd shared her disappointment in the family's failure to use those words. She had said them every day to me since she was old enough to talk. Thanks to my child, we had become a family intent on saying 'I love you' on a daily basis.

Mom pulled the massive Plymouth out of the driveway and drove down bumpy Brennan Road. Once outside the neighborhood, I saw restaurants and shops that had long disappeared. Passing the A & W, I asked, "Can we eat at A & W after church?"

"No," Mom responded. "They aren't open on Sundays, remember? Besides, I promised Rene we'd eat with her."

"Aw, Mom," Ricky moaned.

Aunt Rene was as sweet as the day was long, but her house was not 'boy friendly.' It was decorated with ornate paintings, silk flowers, and fine china. Her only child, Caroline, was totally unfamiliar with the word tomboy. Consequently, there wasn't a baseball, football, or anything sports-related to be found.

The front yard was the size of a patio, and nothing more than a hardened dirt floor. Roots from a fat oak stretched across it like giant gray tentacles waiting to snatch unsuspecting children. The back yard was much larger but was overrun with ivy, making it more suitable for lizards and snakes. The neighbors were all card-carrying AARP members, so finding other kids to play with was out of the question.

A few minutes later, we arrived at our Southern house of worship. The church, built in the 1920's, was located in a sleepy section of the oldest neighborhood in town. Two oaks, which looked to me as if they'd been around since George Washington was in preschool, flanked the sides of the ashen cement steps. The trunks of the oaks looked like gnarly smoke stacks, their limbs stretching helter-skelter. The steps were twelve in number, starting wide at the base and narrowing as they rose to the white front doors. The sanctuary was open and airy with mahogany pews. Two windows on either side of the room contained paintings of Jesus in pastel blues and wine. It was a peaceful haven for the flock.

Sunday mornings in a Southern Baptist church had been a bit tight and constricting when I was a child. The boys in my Sunday school class were diverse, and that had made me a bit uneasy. My pals from my neighborhood had shared many interests—read sports— and it had been easy to be around them. But the boys from church were different. They'd had interests in music, camping, and making trips to the museum. It wasn't so much that I hadn't cared for these activities, but I'd thought boys should only have a passing interest in them. How could a boy have interests outside of sports? It'd made no sense.

Mom walked Rick to class and I walked to mine alone. Though I felt out of place with the boys in Sunday school, I felt at peace when I entered my class. The best part of Sunday school was our teacher: an older gentleman named Pete Chandler, six-foot-five if he was an inch and a man in love with God.

"Good morning, Chase," Mr. Chandler said with a huge grin as I entered the room.

"Good morning, sir."

"It's a great day to be in the Lord's house, isn't it?"

"I've never known there to be a better one."

Mr. Chandler extended his hand, and I watched mine disappear inside his massive, wrinkled fingers. I took the seat next to Mr. Chandler as other boys filtered in. Most of the faces looked unfamiliar. Since I had only seen them on Sundays, it was hard to remember much about them.

Mr. Chandler turned his Bible to the book of John and he began to discuss how the Pharisees tried to trick Jesus into condemning a woman who had committed a great sin, a sin that the Law of Moses required stoning. Jesus told them that those that were free from sin should cast the first stone. Mr. Chandler read the verse where Jesus told the woman he wasn't there to condemn her, and for her to leave and sin no more. Mr. Chandler's voice was full of spirit and excitement as he talked of the events that occurred on that day.

By the look in the eyes of the other boys, their thoughts were on things other than the Gospel. I normally would have been daydreaming the hour away, hitting bombs off of Juan Marichal, turning double plays with Brooks Robinson, and scaling outfield walls, stealing home runs away from Hammerin' Hank. But on that day, my mind soaked in Mr. Chandler's words like sausage gravy on one of Mom's biscuits.

"What is the Bible saying to us in these verses?" Mr. Chandler asked.

I am one of those types that tend to sit back, a silent observer, when it comes to any kind of classroom setting. But on that day I felt compelled to participate.

"That we shouldn't judge others," I said.

"That's correct," Mr. Chandler responded, and he seemed a bit surprised that I actually was a participant.

"We shouldn't judge each other, but what about Judgment Day?" Roger Ravenel asked. "Won't we be judged then? You think that stuff is real? I've done some things I'm not proud of, and I wonder if God's gonna have my name already stamped with 'Don't even think about it.'"

Mr. Chandler looked enthused that he had class participation going. As he began to speak, Ronald Gibbs raised his hand.

"If Roger's got his name stamped out, there's no way Jerry here is getting in," Ronald said.

"Hey," Jerry said, "you just worry about yourself, weasel neck."

"Easy now, boys," Mr. Chandler said.

The class had just livened up.

"You know you got no chance, Jerry," Ronald said. "I saw you take those apples from Phillips' Garden Center last week."

Jerry's eyes got big, as though telling Ronald to shut his mouth on the apple thievery. "You don't know what you're talking about, Ronald. I didn't steal anything."

"Don't get upset," I said. "Roger was just messing with you."

"Shut up, Chase. You're nothin' but the son of a sorry drunk. My daddy told me so."

Rage surged through me, and I leapt across the table, grabbing Ronald by his shirt. I pulled back with all my might, dragging him across the wooden table. The others scrambled out of the way as I slugged him in the jaw, knocking him into my chair. His feet were sticking skyward and I flipped them so that he was flat on his back. As I was about to land another blow, Mr. Chandler's powerful hand grabbed my wrist.

"That's enough," Mr. Chandler said.

"You talk about my father again and I'll beat you senseless," I said while trying to get loose of the stronghold grip on my wrist.

Mr. Chandler pulled me back, and Ronald scrambled to his feet.

"I'm gonna kill you," he said as he yanked the chair I'd been sitting in so he could charge at me. "Your old man's nothing but an alkie."

He lunged at me with his fist, and Mr. Chandler stopped the blow with his forearm. "I *said* that's enough," he said sternly. He took Ronald by the wrist, and we tried to find a way to go at each other one-handed.

I somehow managed to maneuver around Mr. Chandler's side and landed another blow to Ronald's face, snapping his head back so that Mr. Chandler had to hold tightly to prevent Ronald from falling into the wall heater.

Tears filled my eyes, and the anger within me grew to where I felt at that moment that I could truly beat that boy to death. How dare he talk about my father? How dare his father say that to him?

I broke free from Mr. Chandler and bolted out of the room. I took off down the hall and down the stairs. Through the years, I'd heard people talk about my dad's drinking problem, making it sound as though he was the scum of the earth. They didn't understand. Neither did I, but they had no right to cast those stones.

There was an alleyway behind the church and I took shelter there. I fell to my knees, and all the emotions poured out of me. Rage, pity, embarrassment—I had pushed those to the furthest corners of my mind as time passed. But, at that moment, they came rushing back.

Mr. Chandler found me, and he knelt, placing his large hand on my shoulder. "Son, I'm sorry you had to go through that."

I nodded, wiping tears from my face. "I'm sorry too. I shouldn't have hit Ronald and disrupted your class. I don't know what got into me. I should've been more in control."

"Chase, you don't have to apologize. I'm speaking as a man with experience in growing up with an alcoholic parent. It's not an easy thing."

Mr. Chandler stayed with me in that alley for quite some time. He told me about his father, and how alcohol drained the life from his father. I wanted to tell him I had experienced the same for far longer than what he assumed was twelve years, but I thought it more important to talk about the effects it had on us. It felt as if he knew he was talking to a grown man, the kindred spirit we shared. In those moments, I remembered why I had loved that man. His soothing voice and gentle demeanor had a calming peace that made Ronald's comments fade away.

"Remember, Chase," he said, "it's not your fault. And remember that your father doesn't want to be addicted to the bottle. There's something inside him, his own demons, that push him to drink."

"I know. And before my time is up, I'm going to help run those demons out of him."

Mr. Chandler looked at me a bit peculiarly. "Hopefully, your time won't be up for a long, long time."

I shook his hand. "You will never know the impact you've had on me."

"Thanks," he replied. "That means a lot. I hope my words each Sunday help you as you go through life."

"They already have."

"See you next week."

How real was the possibility? "I hope so," was all I said.

I had regained my composure and hoped no one noticed my red eyes. I walked to the car and spotted Ricky standing behind a fence, obviously agitated by a barking dog.

"What are you doin'?" I asked.

"This stupid dog acts like he's going to jump the fence and rip my head off."

"From the look of him, I think he could do it." The German Shepherd continued to bark, his snout pointed at Rick's feet. "Just ignore him and keep walking. Make sure you keep the fence in between you."

Rick snarled at the dog. "But he won't shut up. Pipe down, you dumb dog."

"You think he understands you? Who are you, Dr. Doolittle?"

"I ain't takin' crud from a dog."

"Yelling will only make him madder."

"Oh, what do you know?"

The conversation was going nowhere fast.

"You boys ready to go to your Aunt Rene's?" Mom asked as she walked up the sidewalk.

"Can we leave as soon as we eat?" Ricky asked.

"Absolutely not."

"Well, I just hope she doesn't try to make us sing. No way am I doing that."

For some reason, Rene had thought we could sing, which we couldn't. My daughter, Sara, could sing like the angels, but she inherited that from Blake, not me. So, to please Rene and appease Mom, sometimes we had been forced to belt out a tune or two. And they were always goofy songs. We hated it. Didn't she know we were athletic studs with no time for Puff the Magic Dragon?

"Well, if I have to sing 'Michael Row Your Boat Ashore' one more time, I'm gonna throw up on her carpet," Ricky said.

"Ricky, Aunt Rene loves when you sing," Mom said unconvincingly. "It doesn't hurt you one bit to bring some happiness into her day."

We followed Mom into the house with the enthusiasm of a beakless buzzard at a roadside kill. Rene hugged us in the warm fashion sweet aunts are supposed to use. Mom set her purse on the kitchen counter and immediately began to assist with food preparation.

"Chase, honey, will you do me a favor?" Rene asked.

"Yes, ma'am."

"How about you walk down to Margaret's and tell Caroline to come home. I can't get an answer at the house, so they must be out in the yard."

"Sure, I don't mind."

"Let me come too," Ricky suggested.

"No, you stay with us," Mom said. "You can help us stir the waffle batter."

Rick shook his head in obvious disgust at being forced to stay behind and hang with the women folk. I patted him on the head before I walked out the door. "Don't forget to wear your apron, Alice."

"Up yours."

I scooted across the root-infested yard and into the street. The walk was a short one, as Margaret lived only seven houses away. The midday sun was hidden above me, veiled behind a blanket of a haze of cloud that made the afternoon's heat seem sourceless. It was like walking through a greenhouse. The street was quiet except for the distant hum of vehicles two blocks away, speeding down four-lane Rosewood Drive.

Three doors down, I noticed a woman standing at her front door.

"Joplin? C'mon girl. Where are you? It's time to eat." The woman stepped out of her doorway and onto a tiny porch with an aluminum overhang. "Here girl. C'mon sweetie."

Across the street, a chocolate dachshund emerged from behind a row of holly bushes. The wiener-shaped dog's stubby legs hobbled along like some Fisher Price toy that you had to pull on a string for it to run. As it entered the street, a large Buick approached. It was one of those cars that was as wide as the entire road, like something that should have a Wide Load sign on the hood. I raised my right hand and began sprinting toward the car.

"Whoa," I said.

Joplin paid me no mind at all and continued running, coming to the edge of the road as the oncoming car made its way up the street. I waved both arms and rushed toward the lumbering pup. The woman on the porch began to scream as she, too, sprinted to the road. I scooped up the dog just as a tiny, white haired lady brought the car to a stop.

"Joplin, you silly pooch," the woman said as she took the dog from my arms. "Thank you. Thank you so much."

"You're welcome."

"I don't know what I'd do if something happened to Joplin. She's the sweetest dog in the world. The absolute sweetest."

I stepped into the woman's yard as the Buick resumed its path down the street. "My name's Libby."

She placed Joplin in her left arm and extended her right hand to me.

"Hi. I'm Chase."

"Well, Chase, you must come in and let me fix you something to drink."

"Thanks, but I have…"

"You'll love my herbal tea," she interjected. She turned toward her house and walked onto the porch. I glanced towards Margaret's house and saw no one. *Oh, what the heck.* And so I followed Libby inside the house.

Libby looked like she had just pulled in from Woodstock. Her hair was long and sandy-blonde. It was parted down the middle, and she wore a headband made of lilac petals. Her dress was long and flowing. It was cream-colored and had a gauze look to it.

She was barefoot and wore a choker with a silver pendant shaped like a marijuana plant. She appeared to be around the age of forty. There was a natural beauty to her face—high cheekbones, hazel eyes, and not a trace of makeup. Her skin looked smooth and fresh, liked she'd been soaking her head in a vat of delicate creams and lotions all day.

Her dress hid the curves of her body, but she wore no bra and seemed quite adequate to feed a newborn if the need arose. I tried not to stare but buckled under the pressure.

I followed Libby into the den and the smell of raspberry incense draped the room. The only furniture in the den was a pair of beanbags and a short-legged coffee table with a purple lava lamp. A brown-and-tan acoustic guitar leaned against the panel wall. An ashtray made of metal pipe with a tambourine on top stood beside a beaded doorway that looked to open up into the kitchen.

Libby sat Joplin on the floor and the stubby dog ran to the kitchen. Libby followed, saying, "Wait here. Be right back with your tea." She slid through the pink-and-blue beaded door. I plopped down on a beanbag, and my backside disappeared into the green vinyl upholstery. Libby returned with two mugs, a string hanging over the side of each. Steam danced above the mugs.

"Here you go, Chase. I like that name. Chase." She seemed to enjoy saying it. "This tea will not only bring your body to life, it will set you free."

Free from what? was my first thought.

Libby handed me the drink and sat on the other beanbag.

"Drink up," she said.

"I won't go schitzo, will I?"

"There's always the possibility." She smiled and took a slow sip.

"Interesting place you got. Have you lived here long?" What a smooth way to start the conversation. If you'd seen the chest on this gal you'd understand my struggle.

"No. I never stay in the same place for long. You might say I'm a free spirit. I love to wander."

"What do you do?"

"What does anyone 'do?' I'll tell you what I do. I read people's minds. I tell their fortunes. I give people my herbal tea and let them take a magic carpet ride to the land of hallucination. I grow pot in the back yard and sell it to pay the rent."

So much for sampling the tea.

"So, you read minds, huh? How does that work?"

"I just hold their hands, look into their eyes, and my soul talks with theirs. In an instant, I know their life's journey, and I know what their future holds."

"Just like that, your soul talks to theirs."

"Absolutely. Do you not believe me?"

Looking into her beautiful green eyes, I sensed that, in her heart, whether or not she could, she truly believed it. "It's not easy to believe something like that, but I have a feeling you can convince me."

She placed her mug on a purple canvas rug beside her bean bag. "Give me your hands."

I set my mug on the floor and wrapped my fingers around hers. Libby rose up on her knees, and so I did the same. I was a bit hesitant to stare deeply into the eyes of someone I'd met five minutes earlier. After a few seconds, I took a deep breath and focused on the explosion of green, yellow, and gray before me. Libby squinted gently, nibbling her bottom lip with her two top teeth. Within a matter of seconds, her eyes widened and she pulled back.

"Oh, my," she said. She squeezed my fingers tightly while her eyes cut right through me. "Oh, myyyyyy."

"What? What do you see?" I had never been so anxious to hear someone's reply.

"You've come from another time dimension. You're from another place and time."

"You think?"

"You've come back for something...no, for somebody. You've come back to fill a void in your heart. A void someone caused by leaving you."

I was as dumbfounded with Libby's unearthly abilities as she appeared to be with talking with a time traveller. She reached her hands behind my head and pulled me to her chest. I momentarily struggled to breathe as she held me close to her bosoms.

"Take me with you," she said.

"Huh?" my muffled voice said, my lips pressed to her breastbone. I couldn't breathe, but I wasn't complaining.

"Let me come with you. We'll travel through all dimensions of time. We'll watch Marc Antony kiss Cleopatra. We'll sip wine with Aristotle. We'll...."

"Whoa, whoa, whoa," I said as I broke Libby's vice grip on my head. "I'm not looking to do this for a living. I just want to spend some time here and go home."

"You don't understand. We can travel the galaxy. We'll never grow old. We'll learn the secrets of the universe."

"I think your tea has already got you headed down that course." I rose from my beanbag. "Look, this has been swell, but I've got to go."

"Don't leave. Teach me your secrets. Show me how to travel. Let me bear your children. Keep the seed going." She reached to hug me, but I backed away towards the door.

"Lady, you're scaring me. I gotta go."

I opened the door and stepped off Libby's porch. I heard the faint cries of "Please don't go" as I jogged towards Margaret's house. I might not have been anxious to spend time at Aunt Rene's house earlier but, after spending time in Psychoville with Libby being the mayor, I was ready for some sanity.

Caroline sat on the brick steps on the carport leading up to the kitchen of Margaret's house. Her hair was long and dark and curved along the edge of her soft face. Her dark blue eyes stood out like jewels. She wore a flowery shirt, and her bell-bottom jeans covered all but the toes of her bare feet.

"Hey, Chase," Caroline said and I hugged her.

"It's so good to see you." I pulled away and stared into those young eyes. Caroline had endured some hard times down the road, losing her father when she was six, and her husband when she was middle-aged. Her eyes were full of youth and hope and I hugged her again.

"We were about to go inside and listen to the new James Taylor album. Want to come?"

"I would, but your mom says it's time to eat."

When we walked home, I used Caroline as a bit of a shield between Libby's house and me. She was taller than me. It seemed like forever ago since that had been the case.

"Who's ready for some waffles?" Aunt Rene asked as we entered the front porch door.

Rene made unbelievable waffles, and they were the size of tractor tires. It required an entire bottle of syrup to cover one. Our sugar level would be off the charts in minutes.

"Aunt Rene?" I asked. My desire to be the best big brother in the world forced me to make the next statement. "Ricky wants to know if he can sing for you after we finish eating. It's really all he's talked about today."

"That's a wonderful idea."

Ricky steamed. Oh, did he look ticked off.

"I'll get the mop ready," I whispered. I was ready to test his barf promise, made earlier.

"The what?" Rene asked.

"Oh, nothing," I said, burying my head in my waffle. After we cleaned our plates, we excused ourselves to the kitchen to rinse them in the sink.

"What are you doing, dip wad?" Ricky said. "I'm not singing any stupid song."

"You don't want to disappoint Aunt Rene," I said sarcastically. I glanced out the back door, looking unsuccessfully for something, anything, that we could play with. Since there wasn't anything, I figured I might as well watch Ricky make a spectacle of himself.

"Okay, Ricky, are you ready?" Rene called out from the dining room table. "Come stand in the living room where we can hear you."

Ricky was one unhappy camper. Rene, Caroline, and Mom moved to the couch, and I positioned myself behind them so they couldn't see me laughing.

"Why don't you sing 'Michael Row Your Boat Ashore'for us?" Rene said.

Bingo!

Ricky shook his head, cursing under his breath. Mom cut her eyes at him, telling him in no uncertain terms that he better start singing. He slowly began to croon, but he looked anything but happy. He completed the first verse and, as he began to sing the chorus, his face took on a greenish hue. By the middle of the second verse, he struggled to enunciate. As he began the final verse, he fell to his knees and puked on Rene's beige carpet.

I was stunned. Mom was livid. Aunt Rene was speechless, and poor Ricky, looking at the expelled mess, commented, "I don't remember eating that." He ran to the bathroom and closed the door. Well, I had no choice but to grab the mop like I promised.

"Oh, my goodness," Rene said. "I hope he's okay." Mom assisted Rick on the bathroom floor.

I pulled my shirt above my nose to mask the smell. "You know," I said to Rene, "he mentioned something earlier about throwing up. I guess he's either got a bug or he's psychic."

The visit was cut short thanks to Ricky's sudden illness. I helped him to the car. I couldn't leave a wounded man in the trenches, right? Rick lay spread-eagled across the back seat of the car. Mom rolled down the back windows.

"Rick, I hope you feel better soon," Rene said, looking through the window.

"Yes, ma'am, me too," he responded pitifully.

Mom pulled the Plymouth onto the street, shaking her head.

"I'll get you," was heard from the back seat several times on the ride home. What a fun time we all had. Wonder if Libby still wanted to travel the universe?

Chapter Seven

Rick, still a light shade of green, walked slowly up the driveway as Mom guided him toward the front door. I was still sporting a smile from Ricky's projectile singing when I spied Vicki riding up the street on her bike.

"Mom, can I ride my bike for a while?"

"Don't you want to change clothes first?" Mom asked.

"No, ma'am," I said as I ran to the porch for my bike. I would have preferred to shed my polyester garb, but I didn't want to miss another chance with Vicki. My legs pushed hard on the pedals and I flew down the street like a mouse on a spin wheel.

"Vicki!"

Her pretty head turned as she sought the source of my voice. "Hey," she said, while pulling her bike to the side of the road.

"Where you going?" I brought my bike to a stop beside hers. She looked even cuter than the day before.

"To the woods. Wanna go?"

Duh. I pulled alongside her, trying to look at her while simultaneously keeping my bike from crashing. Dressed in snug, khaki shorts, a yellow short-sleeve knit top, and white Keds, she sat upright and erect as if riding a pony. Graceful and smooth, her long hair danced in the wind.

We rode to the edge of the woods behind the centerfield fence and leaned our bikes against a plump, knobby oak tree. I remember spotting Vicki walking into the woods from time to time during ball games, causing me to momentarily shift my focus from the game to the woods. For someone to take my attention away during a game had been no easy task.

We walked through dense pines and maples sheathed sleepily by thick underbrush. The natural canopy offered us a welcome relief from the heat. A shallow, serpentine-shaped creek, filled with crawfish and salamanders, flowed at a snail's pace. The tiny stream was no more than a foot deep, no wider than five, and cut a jagged path through the woods. I never knew where the creek originated, or where it led. It looked like it had existed since the beginning of time, hiding from the suburbia that had been built around it.

Vicki strolled to the edge of the cool water.

"Look," she said, spotting a slender rat snake under a fallen oak limb. "Want me to catch it?"

"It looks like a biter."

"It's not poisonous, silly. Walk behind him and chase him my way."

Great. It was time for Wild Kingdom and my role was to play Jim, the one assigned the task of giving the enema to the gorilla while Marlin hangs close to camp, sipping coffee.

I slowly moved towards the black-and-gray serpent and it tried to retreat to the murky water. Vicki reached down, wrapping her petite fingers around its neck. She lifted it up so that it was no more than a foot in front of my face. "Feel how slimy his skin is."

Snakes ranked near the top of my 'do not touch' list, right behind vampire bats. I nervously touched it. "Okay, that's good. You can put him down now." I had seen enough of the coldblooded creature.

"He'd make a good pet."

"No, no, he wouldn't."

"I'm not kidding. He'd be great to keep in my empty fish tank."

"What part of no didn't you pick up on?"

Vicki smiled and reluctantly placed the snake in the water, watching it swim away. "Isn't the creek beautiful?"

I had never thought so until that very moment. Vicki, standing at the creek's edge, made it so, as she did anything fortunate enough to have her in its presence. Man, she was so cute, so inquisitive about the world around her. As she looked at the stream and the woods surrounding it, I moved beside her and placed my hand to just where it touched hers.

Tucked away in the avenues of my youth are memories of that first touch, the excitement of that first kiss, the innocent tenderness revealed in a warm smile. All those memories returned in that moment. She was the embodiment of every girl, and the epitome of why boys drop their shield of toughness and let their hearts become ripe for the taking. She was the essence of all that boys were not.

"You sure seem different, Chase. You have a look that says there's more on your mind than hitting or throwing a baseball."

"You are very perceptive." The world had dismantled this boy's ball field, day by day, to where the only part of the game remaining were the memories. Life couldn't take that from me. "Vicki, I found out years ago that what takes place outside the chalk lines consumes the game going on between them."

"Years ago, huh? Well, since you're twelve, how many years back are we talking?"

"It's complicated. You wouldn't understand."

"Try me," she said, taking me by the hand. Her soft fingers fit perfectly inside mine.

"What do you want to be when you grow up?" I asked as I pointed to a fallen pine tree that looked like it would suffice as a park bench.

"Don't change the subject."

"I'm not."

"You tell me you learned there's more to baseball years ago and then you go into asking me what I want to be when I grow up?"

"The future is something I've become pretty knowledgeable with."

"Oh, really. Then tell me about mine," she said as she sat on the make shift bench.

"I don't know if I should."

She stared at me intently. "What has gotten into you?"

"There's something I need to tell you, but you gotta promise not to tell anyone."

"What is it?"

Craning my head skyward, I began to speak, but hesitated. She squeezed my hand. "What's going on?"

The urge to unload was too much. I had to tell somebody.

"I'm not twelve years old."

"Okay? How old are you?"

"I'm forty-four. I'm married with three children." I couldn't tell if the look in her eyes showed distrust or disbelief.

"That's fascinating. You want to know why? Because I talk with people about once a week who are three times their age."

"I'm not kidding. Two days ago, I was a middle-aged man, and my mom had just passed away. Today

107

I'm twelve, Mom's alive, and I'm sitting next to the girl who made my heart melt when I was a boy." My eyes welled. "I don't know if I'm dreaming, or if I'm in a coma. I'm scared my children watched me pass away on that baseball field." I pointed over my shoulder. "You want to talk about the spectrum of emotions. It's been great to see my mom who, by the way, was just laid in her final resting place. I've seen my aunt who passed away a couple of years ago. I got to play a baseball game again. How cool is that? But what about the future—I mean the present. Will I see my family again?" I drew in the sand with a stick. "You ready to take me to the nut house?"

"Oh, Chase, I don't know what to say." She brushed my bangs with her fingers, looking at me as though she was searching for sincerity.

"It's okay if you think I'm crazy."

"I don't think you're crazy," she answered quickly. "I can tell from your eyes you're serious. I just don't know what to say."

I shook my head. "I just need you to believe me."

"Then that's all you have to say."

"Promise me you won't tell anyone. I can't let others know. Not yet, anyway."

"I won't tell. What are you gonna do?"

"Make the most of every second, that's what."

"That's what I'd do. You need to take advantage of the chance to be with your family again. Especially your mother. I wish I could travel back in time."

"I know of a traveling partner, if you're interested."

"What?"

"Never mind." I wanted to tell her about Libby but passed on the notion.

"What's it like in the future? Do we stay in touch?"

"No. Our paths haven't crossed since high school."

"Do you know what I become when I grow up? Do I still live here?"

"I know a little. I heard you traveled throughout Europe. You studied marine biology or wildlife biology. Something like that. It definitely had something to do with animals. Your mother is doing well from what I've heard." Vicki's father had passed away when she was seven. "I think your brother moved away, too. I don't want to say too much."

Vicki shook her head in disbelief. "Amazing. I really want to know more, but I think you're right--it's best not knowing. I hope we see each other again in the future. If we do, you think we'll remember this conversation?"

"I'd bet money on it."

Vicki glanced at the pink pseudo-leather band encasing her Timex.

"Thank you for today, Chase," she said before giving me a soft kiss on the cheek. "I will never forget it. I'll never forget you."

"And I won't forget you."

Vicki straddled her bike. "Bye. Thanks for telling me your secret. I won't tell a soul."

"I know you won't."

Vicki rode away as I stood beside my bike. The ride home was a lonely one.

Chapter Eight

The Carolina humidity lay heavy, suffocating, a haze above that dimmed the sky, as though God had grown tired of the baby-blue, whitewashing it from the heavens. The temperature was well above ninety, and though the shade eased the extreme heat, it did nothing to chase the uncomfortable humidity. As I walked my bike to the patio, I spotted Mom sitting at the edge of the patio under the shade of a maple tree. She wore a sleeveless white blouse and hunter-green shorts. Her delicate legs were pressed together, and a brown paper bag sat on her lap. I parked my bike beside the white back porch wall and slid a metal lounge chair beside her. I spied a metal pot beside her feet, filled with plump pole beans.

"Let me help you," I said.

"Good idea." She pointed to a brown plastic bucket on the faded red picnic table a few feet away. "Snap the beans in half, break off the tips, and toss them in the pot beside your chair."

There is nothing like the taste of fresh pole beans, and they made canned beans at the market taste like rubber bands. "Mom?"

"What, dear?" Her eyes looked downward at the six-inch bean pressed between her thumbs and forefingers.

"Are you happy?"

Breaking the bean in half, a puzzled look quickly surfaced. "Why are you asking me that?"

"I just want to know. You've always taken such great care of us, but I'm not sure we've done the same for you." Silence. "So, are you?"

"Yes, I'm happy. Why, you think I'm not?"

I shrugged my shoulders. "Well, it isn't easy raising us. Course, I know I'm a joy. But rearing Ricky and Bobby must be tough." I smiled and Mom chuckled. "And I know Dad's having a tough go of it." The laughter stopped.

"You needn't worry about me."

"Well, I do. I want you to be happy, more so than us. You've spent your whole life making other people's lives better. You taught us what love is all about." She really had.

"Chase, take this bucket of beans and put them in the sink, will you?" she said in an obvious attempt to change the subject.

"Do you ever blame yourself for Dad's problems?"

Her eyes again focused on the bean in her slender fingers.

"I *don't* want to talk about it."

"Why not?" I had tip-toed around the subject my entire life, but I wasn't going to anymore.

Her eyes begin to tear, making me wonder if I should back off. I'd rather eat nails than hurt her. But I couldn't let the question go unanswered. "Do you blame yourself?"

Looking skyward, the tears rolled down her cheeks.

"Mom, you're the last person in the world responsible. If it wasn't for you, we wouldn't be a family."

"I don't know. Sometimes I feel like I've failed."

"That couldn't be further from the truth. We are so blessed to have you as our mom, and I thank God every night for you. And I know Dad feels the same way."

"If that's the case, he has a strange way of showing it. There must be more I can do."

"You can only do so much. I should have helped more."

"It's not something a child should have to deal with."

"Maybe Dad's trying to reach out, but doesn't know how."

"It sure doesn't appear that way."

"No matter what we do, he's got to be the one to realize what he's doing to himself. What he's doing to us."

"I never knew you felt this way. I've never heard you express yourself like this."

"It's been inside me for a long time."

"But you're just a child."

"Well." I shrugged my shoulders. "Anyway, I want you to know you're the last person responsible for this, and we all love you. More than you'll ever, ever begin to understand." When I hugged her, the beans fell on the patio.

"I love you, son."

Ricky opened the back porch door and broke up the hug-fest. "Mom, when are we gonna eat?" Food was a priority for Rick, though his slender body said otherwise.

"Soon," Mom replied. "You can try one of my biscuits just to make sure they're edible."

Ricky shut the porch door and retreated to the kitchen. The smell of yeast rolls rising slowly on a metal

112

baking pan on the back porch has always been one of my fondest memories.

The last bean was snapped, and the batch was ready for washing and placement in the mason jars.

"Thanks for the help. And thank you for sharing what's on your heart and letting me know how you feel. It lifted my heart."

"You're welcome," I replied. I hated that I made her cry, but she needed to know she wasn't alone in the battle.

Entering through the kitchen's back door, Mom noticed Ricky had finished his first biscuit and was reaching for more.

"Hey, stop that," Mom said. "You don't need to fill up on bread before the meal."

The phone rang.

"I'll get it," I said as I lifted the heavy black rotary phone. I'd forgotten how much the old phone weighed. "Hello."

"Hey, Chase. It's Joe. Mom said you wanted me to call."

"Hey, buddy. How it's going?"

"Good, I guess. How about you?"

"Well, I was wonderin' if you wanted to spend next weekend with me."

"That would be great, but I'm going camping," Joe replied. "My family's been planning it for weeks."

"I know," I said, determined to keep Joe from taking his fateful trip. "But I was hoping you'd stay with me. My uncle is coming down from Ohio, and I really want you to meet him."

"My parents would kill me if I missed this trip. I'll have to meet your uncle next time."

"No, that won't work. You have to stay with me." I didn't know what else to say.

"Well, like I said, the trip's been planned for a long time, and I can't back out now." I sensed agitation in Joe's voice, but it was a small price to pay to save his life. "Gotta run." The dial tone rang in my ear.

I had five days to keep my best friend from dying. I decided if I couldn't come up with a plan, I'd just tell him what would happen if he went.

I turned on the radio in the living room, staring out the picture window as Jackson Browne sang, 'Doctor My Eyes.' At that time I wished I didn't know the future. Mom and Dad were watching television in the den, and I stood at the doorway.

"What time's Bobby coming home?" I asked.

"He should be here any minute," Mom said. "That boy works too many hours," she said, a bit of melancholy in her voice. She loved being around her boys. I regretted that I hadn't spent more time at home with her when I had been in high school and college.

The den windows began to rattle. Earthquake? Jet? UFO?

"Bobby's home," Ricky said.

I had forgotten how loud Bobby's car was--in more ways than one. A bright orange Dodge Charger with a white roof, its engine was suited more for NASCAR than the peaceful avenue of Belmont. Neighborhood dogs cowered in prone position when Bobby rumbled home.

He turned off the turbo engines. I stepped out onto the front steps and watched him exit the car.

"Hey, cissy boy, why you standing there looking goofy?" he asked. "You want to ride in my car, don't you?"

"I'm trying to remember why you were stupid enough to buy that piece of junk. Not only does it run ragged, it's plain old ugly."

"It's the pride of the neighborhood."

"It's the puke of the neighborhood."

"Chicks love it."

"You're delusional."

"You're an idiot."

"Pipe down, bag boy."

We called it a draw.

Mom rose from her recliner. She always did when Bobby walked in.

"Hey, sweetie," Mom said. "I have pimento cheese and sweet tea waiting on you. Change into something comfortable while I get it." Golden Boy had arrived.

"That'll work," Bobby replied, removing his polyester yellow-and black-tie.

I never could figure out why jeans, sneakers, and a dress tie were proper attire for a bag boy. Exactly what was the tie supposed to signify? Professionalism? Did it really emit an 'I'm an executive bagger' message? Especially when sporting the clip-on variety. I had the right to poke fun at it because, for three of my high school years, I had manned that same position. Oh, the countless Saturdays I spent lugging bags of groceries, some wild-colored polyester tie choking my skinny neck.

While Bobby changed, I hunted for Rick. On the bedroom floor, he lay on his stomach, his feet bent upward so the soles of his shoes look skyward. He hovered over a block of wood roughly the size of a square dinner plate.

"What are you doing?" I asked.

"Making a baseball game," he replied. "It's about finished. Let me show you how it works." Rick placed the block on the living room coffee table. "What I did was, I cut out a round piece of cardboard, and I sectioned it off like a pie with a pencil. Each slice is a different size. Doubles, triples, and home runs are the smallest." Inside each slice Rick had written the 'play description,' such as 'Ground Out' and 'Strike Out,' and hits like 'Single' and 'Homerun.'

"After I finished the cardboard," he continued, "I hammered a nail into the middle of it onto the wooden block, leaving about an inch of the nail exposed. I placed one of Mom's bobby pins around the nail and when I flick it with my finger, it spins around. Wherever it lands is the play. I got this notebook to keep the score."

It looked like a small version of a *Wheel of Fortune* device.

"Do you want to play a game?"

"You sure we come from the same gene pool?" I tried to think back whether the milkman or postman were extremely bright. Just a thought. "You want to bat first?"

"Okay," Ricky replied anxiously. He spun the bobby pin to start the game and I saw the look of excitement in his eyes. I just wanted to hug him. What a kid.

"Boys, it's time to eat," Mom shouted from the kitchen.

Our hunger pains took a back seat as the game played on. More fun than a video game, yet so primitive, we flicked away, forgetting about dinner. Several minutes went by and Dad walked in.

"Did you hear what your mom said?" Dad asked. "Supper is ready."

"Just a couple minutes, Dad," Rick said. "It's a close game."

Dad picked up the block of wood. "The game is over, boys. Didn't you hear me say dinner's ready?"

"Yes, sir," I said as Rick looked ready to tell Dad what was on his mind.

I told Rick with my eyes to keep quiet. The look of frustration was in Dad's eyes, as if the liquor inside him negated any rationality he had for treating us like we were idiots.

We walked to the kitchen table where Mom had already filled up a plate of food for Bobby. I wondered if she would try to spoon-feed him.

"You boys have a seat," she said as she carried the pitcher of tea to the table.

Dad filled his plate and turned towards the den.

"Dad, will you eat with us?" I asked. Dad usually ate alone when he was going through a drinking spell. It was as though he felt he didn't deserve to eat at the table with his family. "C'mon, let's eat together."

He placed his plate on the table, and Mom looked surprised but pleased.

"Will you hit us some baseballs after supper?" I asked. Small inroads.

He took a bite and chewed, as though chewing on the question as well. "I guess I can hit you a few." This would be fun, because even when Dad had a few belts inside him, he still could knock the crap out of a baseball.

"That's great, Dad," I said. "Hey Rick, you can play if you think you can avoid the trees."

"You just worry about yourself," Ricky said.

And in that moment the walls of tension came down, and we were a family of normalcy again.

"What's goin' on at the grocery store these days?" Dad asked Bobby.

"Who are the cashiers?" I asked. I remembered making out with Barbara Kathwood one night after we'd got off work from the store. I'd been fifteen at the time and she eighteen. An experienced, older woman to teach me the ropes.

"Amy. Barbara. I'm goin' out with her next weekend."

"With Barbara?" He couldn't. I'd cornered that market.

"Yep."

"You planning on kissing her?" Ricky asked.

"That's not exactly dinner table conversation," Mom said.

"Well if I kiss her, I won't tell you," Bobby said.

As the plate of country fried steak, the bowls of gravy, fresh pole beans, and mashed potatoes were passed, we filled our souls as well as our bellies. Dad appeared comfortable and relaxed.

"Hey, Dad," Ricky asked, 'want to see me blow a milk bubble with my nose?"

Dad, somehow combining both a smile and frown, looked at Mom. "Ellen, I told you, if you dropped this boy on his head too many times, he'd turn out goofy."

Mom, playing along, replied as she wiped the corners of her mouth with her napkin, "It's your fault. You're the one who tried to bounce him in the yard when he was a baby."

Ricky, unfazed by the comments, opened the refrigerator door and grabbed the carton of milk from the top shelf. He poured a half glass and returned the milk to its spot on the shelf. He sat and took a sip of cold homogenized. Expanding his cheeks like Louis Armstrong, he exhaled through his nose. A white bubble formed inside his right nostril. As he expended the air, the bubble exited the nose, making a loud pop.

"Wow, that's impressive," said Bobby.

"Ricky," Mom added, "that's disgusting."

Dad and I smiled at each other. I raised my glass of tea. "Here's to cheap entertainment."

After dinner, everyone except Bobby took their dirty plates to the sink. He waited on Mom to pick his up from the table while sipping on his third glass of tea.

"Can you hit us some balls now?" I asked while placing the butter dish on the top shelf of the refrigerator.

"Get the bat and a couple balls, and I'll meet you in the backyard," Dad said as he went to the den. He returned with his sunglasses in hand.

"Bobby, you want to catch a few?" I asked.

"Yeah. I could use the work. Colt League practice begins next week."

"I didn't think you needed practice."

"I don't. Just gonna show you how it's done by the big boys."

"I'm so lucky."

"Aren't you?"

We removed our gloves from a round, metal laundry basket on the back porch. The basket, two feet in diameter and two feet deep, served as a sports locker. It overflowed with baseballs, gloves, basketballs, footballs, tennis balls, and a plastic wiffle ball or two. The bat rack, built by Dad, was located behind the basket, next to the back porch door. The rack had slots for six bats, but never held more than four, mainly because Dad wasn't going to spend money on a bunch of bats.

I grabbed three balls from the basket, placing each into the pocket of my glove. Bobby grabbed a thirty-two inch bat, the largest on the rack. Rick placed his glove across his head, looking like a drunken pirate.

"I hope I don't run into the big knot oak again," Ricky said. "My head still hurts from that one."

"We'll yell if you get close to it," I said.

"Maybe we'll yell *after* you run into it," added Bobby.

I jogged to Mandy's kennel and I think, when she saw the balls and my glove, she knew it was time for some fun. She burst through the doorway when I opened the gate, getting her energy laps out of the way before baseball time. She zipped by me for a ceremonial pat on the back, and looped the yard several time before returning to me. She sat and waited for me to tell her how she was the best dog in the world. And that I did.

I think Dad had really enjoyed hitting line drives and pop flies to us, almost as much as we had running them down. He would stand at the side edge of the yard, just inside the fence adjoining Mrs. Mackie's back lot. The huge yard, almost an acre in size, had been shaped like a pork chop.

Dad would position himself in the bone-handle part of the pork chop to allow maximum hitting distance, making us cover as much ground as possible. Pines and oaks had generously populated the yard, turning it into a natural obstacle course. For me, the challenge of following the ball through the sky while skirting jagged tree trunks had been as much fun as making the catch itself. We would catch them for as long as Dad would hit them.

Dad picked up the khaki-colored Louisville Slugger and well-worn balls lying beside the picnic table on the patio. He was dressed in gray slacks, a short-sleeve beige dress shirt, and black leather shoes. He removed his shirt and draped it across the back of a tin-framed lounge chair, removing a cigarette from a half-empty pack in his shirt pocket. The tank-top tee-shirt accentuated his broad shoulders.

Pulling a lighter from his pocket, he surrounded the cigarette, already clenched tightly in his mouth, with his left hand to prevent the light breeze from extinguishing the flame. He made it to his designated spot, resting the bat on his left shoulder. There we stood, gloves ready, waiting anxiously across the yard in front of an oak tree with low-bending limbs.

Mom, dishrag in hand, the last dish washed, sat on the picnic table to watch. She was an audience of one, but she was always there, pulling for her children to do well.

Mandy sat at my foot, waiting for her time to participate.

"Who's first?" Dad yelled.

"Let's let Ricky take the first one," I said.

"Rick's first!" Bobby shouted as he tapped his glove on Ricky's head.

Rick walked forward two steps, his right hand balled up into a fist, hidden in his glove. He looked so determined, his knees slightly bent. Dad, a lefty, tossed a ball skyward, cresting a foot above his head, and hit it as it dropped to belly button level. The crack of the bat echoed across the yard. A high fly sent Ricky to his left, intently following the flight of the ball. He scurried around a slender pine into an open space of grass, increasing his speed as he watched the ball make its descent. As the ball skirted through a pine-cone laden limb, Rick zoomed in for the catch. He extended his glove in front of his left thigh, focused on the scuffed rawhide sphere falling rapidly to Earth. He didn't notice the knotty oak tree in his wake.

"Look out!" I shouted.

My warning was not delivered in time. Rick's chin made direct contact with a macaroni-shaped limb, knocking him sharply on his backside. Bobby and I dropped our gloves and ran towards our little brother. Mom leapt off the picnic table and scrambled to her youngest. Mandy was the first one there, and she circled him as though she were pointing out to us that he needed assistance.

"Ricky!" Mom shouted as she knelt beside him. We stood over him as Dad trotted across the yard.

"Rick," I said, "are you okay?"

"Can't believe I did it again," he said, looking skyward, obviously ticked off that he'd run into the one tree he'd set out to avoid. Shaken but not hurt, he sported a small cut on his upper chin, causing a small amount of blood to ooze towards his Adams apple. We decided to do our part and offer assistance.

"How many fingers am I holdin' up?" Bobby asked, extending the index, middle, and ring fingers.

"What day is it?" I asked.

"What's the square root of eleven?" Bobby inquired.

"I wouldn't know that if I hadn't hit the tree, dummy."

Mom lifted Ricky to a sitting position. "Let me take you to the picnic table and clean that cut."

"Stick a band-aid on it and come back out," I said, patting Ricky on the shoulder.

"Your turn," Bobby said to me as we walked back to our spot. "Which tree you gonna hit?"

"Tree? Right. Let me give you a free lesson on concentration and pure athleticism."

Dad, bat again on his left shoulder and ball in hand, shouted, "Who's next?"

"Me!" I raised my glove, the exposed pocket facing Dad.

Dad tossed the ball in the air and ripped a high fly ball. I realized the ball was heading deep behind me, and I turned, side-stepping Mandy before ducking under the low oak limbs of the tree behind me. I followed the flight of the ball through an open patch of trees against the backdrop of the red velvet sky ushering in dusk. I jumped between the limbs of a v-shaped wisteria as the ball began to drop into the treetops.

The ball hit a pine limb, dropped, and hit another, pushing it straight down. Dad had hit a tough one, but I wouldn't want it any other way. I scrambled underneath the pine, softly extending my glove as a small limb and pinecone landed on my shoulder. The ball fell softly into the web of my glove. Turning towards Bobby, I raised my glove high.

"Luck-eee," Bobby said, shaking his head. I think he was impressed, but not surprised. I jogged back to where he stood.

"'Bout ate a pinecone on that one," I said. Mandy wagged her tail, her nose pointing straight ahead, eyes on me. I carefully placed the ball on her nose. "Wait for it. Wait for it." She didn't budge. "Catch it," I said and she snapped her nose upward, sending the ball several inches in the air. She softly caught it on its way down. "Take it to Dad."

Mandy flew toward Dad, and I could see his smile from across the yard, a cigarette held loosely in his mouth.

"Not bad," Bob said. "Not bad at all."

"Let's see what you can do," I said, stepping behind the oak to give him space.

Mandy dropped the ball at Dad's feet and bolted back to me. I loved watching that pretty dog run. It was art in motion, her sleek body sauntering like she was on parade.

Bobby raised his glove, signaling Dad he was ready. Dad cranked one towards the back corner. Bobby ran to his right, watching the screaming liner cruising just under tree top level. He bolted towards the fence that enclosed the back yard, almost to the spot where I had popped the truck driver with the persimmon years earlier. The ball somehow carried along an unimpeded path.

As I yelled, "It's outta here," Bobby, looking over his left shoulder, extended his left arm, thumb facing down. Leaping like a high hurdler on an Olympic track, he cleared the four-foot high cyclone fence, the ball popping into his glove.

"Whoa!" I yelled and I threw my glove in the air. "What a freakin' grab!"

Bobby stood behind the fence, holding the ball high with his right hand.

"Way ta go!" Dad yelled, sounding a bit uncertain that he had actually seen his oldest boy make the circus catch.

Bobby tossed the ball and his glove on the ground inside the fence, and, placing his hands on the top bar, leapt back into the yard. I jogged towards Bobby and fell to my knees.

"I'm not worthy," I said as I bowed, waving my arms up and down like a man waving palm branches. "I'm not worthy."

"Did you see that?" Bobby asked. "Barnum and Bailey should've been here."

I pushed my knees upward and stood. "High-five," I said, raising my hand, palm facing Bobby.

"High who?" Bobby asked with a confused look.

High-fives were still two decades away, so I was jumping the gun just a bit. "I can't believe you hurdled the fence and caught the ball."

"Numbnuts, I hurdled the fence *while* catching the ball."

Rick returned to the action, chin bandaged. Dad spent a solid hour mashing balls to us, looking himself a bit like a kid again. Feeding off our enthusiasm, he hit so many balls that both hands blistered. Mandy was surely going to sleep well that night. I knew she had had quite a workout when the baseballs had become quite slobbery.

The sinking sun finally chased us inside, where Mom had strawberry short cake and whipped cream waiting at the table.

"Thanks, Dad," I said while sliding into an empty kitchen chair. "That was great."

Dad, spoon in hand, lifted his eyes upward and away from his plate, staring directly into mine. "You're welcome." Glancing around the table, making eye contact with Bobby and Ricky, he said, "You boys aren't half-bad, you know that? I think we'll keep you around a while longer."

"You're not so bad yourself," I responded.

"No kidding," Bobby said. "You sure can smack the snot out a baseball."

"Yeah, almost as good as me," chimed in Ricky.

All was right with the world. But would it last?

Chapter Nine

A shard of light slipped through a gap in the curtains, pale blue from the streetlight outside. The soft gleam gave shape to my bedroom. I had just awakened from a dream, though I couldn't recall what I had dreamt about. My eyes tried to focus on my surroundings and, slowly, familiarity returned to the room. The house was silent except for the faint snoring of my father. The stillness cast a blanket of isolation, a feel that, although my family was asleep in their beds, I was totally alone.

Next to my chest of drawers, in front of the closet, I noticed a silhouette lurking in the shadows. She was tall and slender, her back slightly slumped, wearing a tall, pointed, black hat that looked to be on loan from the Wizard of Oz. Through the darkness I could see her green eyes squinting, as though she was straining to see if I was looking back at her in hopes she could steal my soul if she remained hidden. As if she could snatch me away once I fell back to sleep. The sight of her made my entire body flinch, and I reached for my covers to hide. She had appeared many times through my early years, watching me from the shadows. I had hoped she'd have moved on to another house by now. Maybe she was Libby in her natural state.

The frequent visits of the witch had been almost as nerve wracking as being a chronic sleepwalker. Most times had been harmless strolls, like stuffing my covers in the bottom drawer of my chest of drawers. At least that's what I remember. But other times things had got a bit dicey, and I'd been known to cause quite a stir. It seemed I'd done my best work when relatives or friends spent the night. I'd been known to run through the house, screaming as though my hair was on fire. I had been told that I'd rap on bedroom doors and announce that burglars were loose in the house.

A couple of times, Mom had caught me outside the house. When I was eight, on the night before my first baseball game of the season, she'd caught me at the mailbox. I'd been sound asleep, of course, walking with my glove on my hand and my cap on my head, and all I'd had on was a pair of cotton briefs. I thank God she'd woken up, because I could only imagine waking up at the ball field in my underwear. How would I have lived that one down?

At least I would have been the first one to arrive for the game. The odd thing was, Mom normally slept as though she'd been sedated with an elephant tranquilizer. But, somehow, she'd known when I was wandering about in my sleep. I'm just glad I had finally outgrown it.

I flipped my pillow over to the cool side, the witch now gone from my bedroom, surely off to terrorize some other kids. The house was quiet, yet alive and warm. I was sleepy, but I stayed awake to enjoy the quiet of a young boy's night.

That peace and quiet soon came to an end as a whippoorwill perched outside Mom and Dad's bedroom window and began to sing. I'm telling you, this bird sang as though it wanted to serenade the entire neighborhood. Dad was a solid sleeper too, but the bird was hitting decibel levels usually achieved by jets and rock concerts. I knew it wouldn't be long before the fireworks began. Literally.

"That bird!" I heard Dad shout from his bed. "He's back." I pictured him fumbling for his glasses on the nightstand, cussing under his breath. I walked to the doorway and watched him hastily slide on his green robe. The streetlight cut a straight path to Dad's room, and I watched him accessorize the thigh-length robe with a pair of black nylon socks, calf high, and blue slippers. I tip-toed behind him to the den, where he removed a twelve-gauge shotgun from the gun rack. He then filled his robe pocket with shells. What a hunter's outfit my father wore that night. I clung to the shadows, not letting him know I was watching, and I muted my laughs as I tracked him to the kitchen where he snatched a black rubber flashlight from the pantry.

Dad's surely skyrocketing blood pressure probably took an additional hit when he failed to realize the back door was bolted at the top. *My bad.* I had locked it before I went to bed. "What the…," he muttered as his head bumped against the glass window of the door. Finally he made it outside.

I ran into Bobby's room. "Wake up. Dad's outside trying to kill a whippoorwill."

Bobby jumped from his bed and followed me to the back porch door. Things were shaping up to make it a night to remember.

The night sky was an endless pattern of incandescent stars flung like glitter against its ebony ceiling. Underneath it, the neighborhood slept in undisturbed serenity, unaware that a battle was about to take place. Dad walked to the tree outside his bedroom window, his milky-white legs providing the only distinguishable light.

He positioned himself under the tree and the flashlight clicked to brightness. Boom! Limbs and leaves were ripped to shreds and Dad dipped his head briefly to prevent remains from hitting his face. On came the kitchen light next door at Mrs. Mackie's. I saw her cup her hands over the sides of her eyes, pushing her face up against the window to cut out the reflection of the kitchen light. She seemed to strain her eyes to see what was going on in our backyard.

"Take that, you feathery varmint!" Dad shined the light to the grass and began to follow its path to the back porch door. His gun rested on his shoulder, and he cut a silhouette of an infantryman. Well, except for the robe and fuzzy slippers. Silence had returned. Dad was strutting, and I could see the feeling of satisfaction in the way he walked, confident in knowing he'd eliminated the source of trouble. But, when he stepped onto the patio, the whippoorwill began singing in a tree twenty feet away.

"What the...?" Dad turned quickly toward the sound. "I know I filled that bird full of lead." He spoke as though he was trying to convince himself. He flipped the flashlight on, and the hunt resumed. Walking quietly to the tree, he shone the flashlight upward. The singing stopped, as if the whippoorwill was taunting Dad. Bam!

Again, leaves and limbs scattered everywhere. Dad stood motionless, his head craning upward for signs of life. Again, he shined the light toward the porch and walked toward Bobby and me. He nodded. *Way to go Dad*. When he walked by us on the back porch, the whippoorwill called out again, twenty feet further back.

For fifteen minutes, Dad blasted tree after tree, reloading like a man trying to single-handedly take the beach at Normandy. Mom had joined in watching the onslaught, peering over our shoulders, wrapped in her pink terry cloth robe. Ricky must have been in dreamland, because he never showed himself during the weapons demonstration. I couldn't see Mandy in her dark kennel, but I imagine she was one startled and confused pup.

The view of Dad's flashlight shining through each tree, the ensuing blast that followed, and the obliteration of limbs and leaves was side-splitting comedy. At least, it was to us. Maybe for the whippoorwill too. And, with each blast, our laughter grew louder. Even Mom couldn't help but snicker. After Dad had emptied the gun, and his robe pocket, he walked dejectedly to the back porch, and the clear crisp song of the whippoorwill echoed through the yard. So much for Normandy. He was a beaten man.

"Ellen, just shut the blasted bedroom window," he mumbled, placing the flashlight down on the kitchen counter.

I laughed myself back to sleep.

Morning came and, along with it, a new day of possibilities. Dad had left for work. I strolled to the kitchen and looked out the window facing the patio. Mom was talking with Mrs. Mackie. I remember that the slow pace of those mornings had given Mom a chance to build friendships of her own. It had been a chance to share stories, surely with a little gossip thrown in for good measure. I figured Mom was filling Mrs. Mackie in on Dad's hunting expedition the previous night.

I walked outside. "Mornin', Mom. Mornin', Mrs. Mackie." I wrapped my arms tightly around Mom.

"You look bright-eyed and bushy-tailed this morning," Mrs. Mackie said.

What did bushy-tailed mean? At that age I barely had enough tail to sit without falling off my chair.

"You sure look happy today," she said.

"Yes, ma'am," I said, the person I had my arms wrapped around the reason.

"Chase, honey, I've got instructions from your father," Mom said with a bit of a grin.

"Ma'am?"

"See the mess in the back yard?" She pointed over my shoulder.

"Aw, Mom. Are you kidding me?" Dad's seek-and-destroy mission looked much worse by the light of day.

"Do I get any help?"

"Your father can't 'cause he's working."

"What about Bobby? What about Ricky?"

"Bobby has to go to work in a few minutes, and Ricky might hurt himself with all those jagged limbs."

Odd man out again. Why did I have to be the middle child? I wish we could've been like Dad's family, with nine children. "Can I do it after breakfast?"

"Sure."

I scoured the kitchen for food. No need to work on an empty stomach. I smelled something, and I saw the Tupperware container on the counter. Cinnamon rolls, with white icing, still warm and drippy, huddled together in a circle under the plastic top. I carefully lifted a roll, icing sticking between my thumb and forefinger. It almost melted on my tongue, and it was so soft and warm I really didn't get a chance to chew it. It just slipped down the throat, and so I grabbed another to see if I could chew it. Same result. It was just too good to go down so fast. It would be nice if vegetables had that same taste. I reached in and snatched one more before returning the lid.

I took the roll and went to the bedroom, and I sat at the edge of Ricky's bed. I knew it wouldn't take long for the aroma to bring him to life. I waited patiently. Soon, Ricky's nostrils flared, and he opened his eyes.

131

"Mom made cinnamon rolls?" he asked as he rubbed the sleep from his eyes.

"She sure did." I bit into the roll. "But this is the last one. I told Mom you just wanted cereal anyway, so she told me to eat it."

"Give me that," Ricky yelled as he tried to wrestle it from my hand.

"I didn't think you liked 'em."

I slid to the floor on my stomach and he jumped on my back, reaching for the roll, which I made sure stayed just beyond the limit of his outstretched hand. He began pummeling me, and the more he hit me, the more I laughed. I managed to say in between the laughter, "I'm sure she'll make more soon." Ricky continued the beating.

Mom stuck her head in the door. "What's going on in here?"

"Chase just ate the last cinnamon roll," Ricky said, his face beet-red.

"Nonsense," Mom said with a laugh. "There's almost a dozen in the tin."

I bounced my eyebrows up and down a la Groucho Marx. "I've never been real good at counting."

"Moron." Ricky belted me in the arm one last time.

I was a one-man cleaning crew for the disaster area that had become the back yard. A mini-war zone, and I wasn't sure where to begin. It was a scene from the Apocalypse, a thick layer of limbs and pinecones covering the ground. But, I wasn't about to complain. By the time I threw the final wheelbarrow full on the trash pile by the road, Bobby was walking to the car, dressed for success. Grocery bags and little old ladies were calling his name.

"You missed a spot," Bobby told me. "Remember, perfection is something we should all aspire to achieve."

"Yea, thanks for all your help. Nice clip-on, by the way."

Bobby gave me a one-finger salute and opened the car door. The neighborhood pets scattered when Bobby fired up 'The Hog,' and the tires screeched as he peeled away.

"What a redneck," I said as I watched him drive away. If he only knew, in the not too distant future he'd be driving a Buick sedan, trading Dale Earnhardt for Mister Rogers.

Well, I had the yard as close to pre-whippoorwill state as I could, though it would take a while before the trees recovered.

I weighed the option of spending time with Mom, or hanging out with my buds. A knock on the door solved the dilemma. Robbie stood at the door.

"Hey man, what are you doing?"

"Waiting on you to tell me. You're the recreational planner around here."

"I've got no clue what you're talking about, but I do know this." He reached into his jean pocket and removed a small wad of change and two one-dollar bills. "I mowed Mrs. Culbert's yard and it's burning a hole in my pocket. Let's ride to Mr. Frank's and blow it on candy and soda."

Frank's was a mom-and-pop shop filled with all the good things that mothers despised. More importantly, it was the only store on the neighborhood side of the highway, and thus the only one we were allowed to patronize.

"Hang on a minute," I said. I remembered seeing my Babe Ruth bank in the bedroom. Maybe I could make

133

an early withdrawal. Or, in this case, would it be considered a late withdrawal?

I removed every penny, nickel, and dime from the brown ceramic glove, a grand total of one dollar and twelve cents. I wasn't exactly rolling in the dough, but in the 70's it would go a long ways.

It was great to spend time with Robbie again. He had been a good-natured kid. One of the true good guys of the neighborhood. He'd come from a long line of family blondes. Everyone in the family had been fair-haired, even the golden retriever. Rob's parents had passed away right after we had finished college. They had died within a year of each other. I can still remember the distraught look on his face after the second funeral that left him parentless.

We rode, side by side, along Brennan with no sense of urgency. I pointed to Rusty Richardson beside his porch railing, a paintbrush in his hand, and from his expression, it was clear to see he'd rather be doing something else. We waved and Rusty waved back by way of a head nod. The morning heat was building as the sun shrunk the shadows along the road. The sky was a canvas of baby-blue, with thin clouds of white floating lazy and low from the southeast. I watched a pair of mockingbirds chase a crow across the power lines, taking turns dive-bombing the slow-flapping bird.

Ten minutes later, we arrived. Mr. Frank had a metal bike rack out front, and we dismounted like cowboys from their thoroughbreds. The store was a wood structure with a slightly angled tin roof. There was a set of two front doors and one picture-style window with dusty blinds to the right of the doors. The first door was made of solid oak, painted pale brown. It opened into a tiny porch-like foyer that led to the second door, a glass entrance which opened up into the one-room store. I immediately noticed that the dark, hardwood floor smelled of cooked cherries, and it was an aroma that had stayed with me since childhood. Mr. Frank sat behind an eight-foot long counter, in a worn leather chair that had seen its better days. The counter was large enough to hold a metal display rack of pork skins, a 1972 calendar, and compliments of Mason's Pharmacy, and a fire-engine red National Cash Register with black keys.

The store was small but it was stocked. If he didn't have it, you didn't need it. The popcorn machine sat in the middle of the room and, by the smell, freshly popped corn waited behind the Plexiglas windows. A small set of shelves split the room into sections, with candy on one side and adult friendly items, such as bread and canned goods, on the other. The sight of the old open-air market opened a floodgate of memories for me.

The store had closed when I was seventeen. Mr. Frank, a kind and gentle soul who would cut us discounts on certain candy items when his wife wasn't around, had taken two shots to his ribs one afternoon from a wayward drifter searching for quick cash. His murder had been the first any of us kids had experienced. In a way, it had removed a veil from us, a sign that maybe the world wasn't always fun, games, and baseball. After the funeral, Mrs. Alberts, the neighborhood spinster, had hung flowers on the door of Mr. Frank's store.

I looked about the store to shelves filled with ancient goodies I hadn't seen in twenty-five years, and I wanted one of each. I picked up a tiny, two-inch wax Coke bottle filled with a liquid drink of usually flat soda. It was so small the liquid inside hardly filled a thimble. I selected a handful. Next, I grabbed bubblegum cigarettes.

Why they were popular is still a mystery. I wished my wallet had followed me on my journey to the past so I could really have stocked up.

The red tin drink cooler, positioned along the back wall, held cold bottles of R.C. Colas, Sundrop, Nehi, and Tahitian Treats. The drinks lay in stacks under ice-crusted elements. I chose the Tahitian Treat, and laughed when I realized it was bottled by Canada Dry. I must have forgotten that Canada and Tahiti were neighbors. The thick glass bottle chilled my fingers. Finally, I pulled a Nutty Buddy from the freezer that I knew would be the first casualty if I didn't want it to melt before I ate it.

My bill would have totaled ten to twelve dollars in today's world, but since I wasn't in today's world, I got it all for the bargain basement price of ninety-seven cents. I smiled at Mr. Frank when I gave him the handful of change. He returned the smile.

"Nice to see you again, Mr. Frank."

"You, too, young fella."

"This has always been my favorite store."

"Thank you, son. You taking all this candy home?"

"I might just eat it right here at the counter."

I started to walk away but turned back to the counter. "Mr. Frank, thanks for being so good to us through the years. You're a good man."

"You getting ready to leave town or something?"

"Well, you never know."

"You have a great day, young man."

"Yes, sir. You too."

We sat on the sidewalk beside our bikes. The heat of the day was building, but I didn't give it much thought. Instead of bills, college plans, meetings, and appointments, my only decision was whether the ice cream would melt if I drank the wax soda first. Sitting on the concrete walkway, I wondered why life had become so complicated. I decided we all needed to sit on the sidewalk of life every once in a while, chewing on a bubblegum cigarette. The innocence of it all had me in no hurry to return to the cruel reality of life.

"Chase, you gonna stare at the sky all day?" Robbie asked me.

"What?" Too much reflection on the current state of things had kept me from hearing Robbie talk.

"I asked you three times if you thought the Reds were going to win the pennant, and you sit there like you're in another world."

"Sorry about that. I was just, I mean, I was thinking...what was the question?"

"Do you think the Reds will win the pennant? They're loaded with pitchers, and with Pete Rose and Johnny Bench, they can't lose."

"I can't believe they didn't. To have that kind of talent and lose to the dang Oakland A's is unbelievable. It's almost as crazy as Pete Rose being banned from the Hall of Fame."

"What?" Robbie's eyes showed total confusion. I had tipped my hand on the future, big-time. "Oakland A's? Pete Rose banned? What are you talking about?"

I took a bite of ice cream, a stall tactic, to find a way to get out of the bind I'd put myself in. "Man, this ice cream has given me a major head freeze." I rubbed my forehead, trying to come up with something to say. "What I meant was, the Oakland A's are having such a good year too, something tells me they are going to win it all."

"I don't see that happening. And what about Pete Rose? You said he was banned from the Hall of Fame. He can't even be considered for the Hall until he retires."

A car rode by, and the Jackson Five's 'Stop the Love You Save' flowed from an eight-track tape player.

"Well, I've heard Pete likes to gamble. You know they don't want gamblers in the Hall. I think that might keep him out."

"You said he was banned."

"I did?" Confuse the mind. Make him doubt himself. "Why would I say something like that?" That was the best I could come up with.

"I don't know why. Doesn't make sense."

"It sure doesn't. Maybe the heat's getting to you."

"Me. You're the..." He shook his head. "Aw, never mind."

Whew. A close call, but I made it.

"You want to ride down where they're building the new interstate?" Robbie asked. "There's some good spots to ride. Just like motocross."

"I can't," I said, though it sounded like a worthwhile project. "But the sugar rush has been awesome. Maybe I'll see you at the ball field tonight."

"We play Long's Pharmacy. They've got no chance." Robbie wasn't blowing smoke. His team was loaded with good players. And it was always my team nipping at them from second place.

"See you tonight."

Robbie jumped on his bike and headed up Brennan. I hopped on mine, straddling it with both of my feet planted on the pavement. I watched Mr. Frank walk out the back door, taking a bag of trash to the dumpster. Beside the dumpster was an abandoned car. After Frank tossed the black plastic bag through the open door of the dumpster, he walked to the broken down vehicle. Rust had eaten away most of the paint off the old Ford. Faint traces of blue could be seen on the side doors, and there were small patches of white on the hood. As he leaned in the window, a silhouette of a man rose in the back seat. Frank handed him a small bag, talked briefly, and returned to the store. The frail black man opened the back door, stretching his bony legs out until they touched the ground. Only his badly stained navy pants and black canvas sneakers were visible from where I stood.

I watched as the man removed what looked like a sandwich and a soft drink. He moved to where he sat in the doorway. He wore a gray, felt fedora which tilted to the left side of his head. I watched the man turn the bottle up with his tiny wrist, and I peddled to the car, around the back door so that I could see him square in the eyes.

"Mawnin'," the raspy voice said.

"Morning, sir." The man looked to be at least seventy-years old. "You doing all right?"

"Doin' fine, young fella. Doin' fine." Sweat dripped along the sides of his slender face. His cheekbones were curved and pronounced. His eyes, though black as coal, contained an unexplainable innocence. He took a bite of his bologna sandwich.

"Do you live in this car?"

"Yessir. This ole' mind ain't as sharp as it once was, but I believe I been here two weeks. Maybe three."

"Do you have family nearby? Someone to give you a bed to sleep in?"

"Nawsir. Got a young'n in Charleston. Ain't sure how to reach her. I tried hitchin' a ride at the freight yard, but I'm too weak to climb up in a boxcar. My legs can't hardly hold me to standin' no mo'." He removed his hat

139

and wiped the sweat building on his forehead with the back of his brown and tan flannel shirt.

"If you made it to Charleston, how would you find her?"

"I know where she stay. Only thing, she ain't got no phone."

"We got to get you to Charleston, then." I rubbed my chin and placed my foot on the bike pedal.

"Reckon you got room on that sickle for an old man like me?" He cackled and took a sip of Pepsi.

"If I did, it'd take us till Christmas to get you there. That's a hundred and twenty five mile ride."

"I ain't worried. Jesus'll take care o' us."

"I don't doubt that. But let me talk to my mom and see if we can give Jesus a day off and get you to your daughter. My name's Chase."

"Clete." He extended his hand and, when I shook it, I noticed his fingers were frail and clammy, like dark tentacles. Clete smiled and nodded.

"I've got something for you." I reached into my bag of candy. "It's not much, but it's all I have."

He peered into the bag. "Candy? Ain't sure 'bout candy. They say it's bad fo' your teeth." Clete smiled, revealing a mouth with only four teeth.

"That's just an old wives' tale. Eat all you want."

"Thank ya kindly."

I hopped on my bike. "Don't you worry, Mr. Clete. We'll get you to your daughter.

"Bless you, young fella," he said as he raised his hand and waved.

As I peddled towards home, I couldn't stop thinking of Clete's situation and wondered how the old fellow could manage a smile when his home was the back seat of an abandoned car. Just the isolation and loneliness had to be hard. Not to mention no running water and no bathroom facilities. Seeing him all alone made me feel bad, and it reminded me of our neighbor, Mrs. Cutter, who had lived alone for as long as I could remember. Her husband had passed away many years ago, and they never had children. I would mow her grass and rake her yard, and Mom took her to the store, the doctor, or any place she needed to go. She always looked enthused to see us.

I rode towards home, but I decided to pull up into Mrs. Higgenbottom's driveway. She grew roses in her back yard, and she cared more for the roses than her neighbors. I figured it was time those roses should brighten someone's day besides her. I set my bike down quietly beside a bush and crouched when I walked by her kitchen window. I heard the television in the den, and I assumed that's where she was. I slipped my way to the rose bed, which ran along a wooden fence for fifty feet, where I snapped off a half dozen—three red and three yellow.

I took off around the far side of the house, circling back around to get my bike. As I ran around a fat magnolia tree, Mrs. Higgenbottom swung a broom at me. I'm talking a Paul Bunyon with an ax kind of swing. The straw came across my chest and knocked me on my backside.

"Get your scrawny fanny out of my yard," she said, and she swatted me on the back. "And give me back my roses."

I clung on tightly, the thorns digging into my fingers. No way was I letting go for that old broad. If she'd been a decent human being, I'd have walked up to her door and politely asked if I could clip off the flowers. But there I was, rolling on the ground, trying to find an opening. When she raised her broom high again, I gently placed the rose stems in my mouth and lifted my bike from the ground. The thorns cut my gums, but I rode until I pulled up in Mrs. Cutter's driveway.

I removed the stems slowly from my mouth and shook them a bit. I didn't think she would care much for spit-covered roses. Tapping on the door, I detected an aroma resembling tapioca pudding. Mrs. Cutter slowly opened the door.

"Well, hello there, Chase," she said to me with a smile. "My, what beautiful flowers. Where did you get them?"

"That's not important." Nor was the beating I'd just endured. "I thought they'd look good on your kitchen table."

The happiness in her face made me certain she had not received flowers in quite a while. She motioned me inside, and it was as I remembered. She looked as though she lived in an antique store. You know, the ones with fake rooms where they make it look like somebody actually lives in the store.

Her cherry coffee table was covered in trinkets and had a crystal candy dish of candy corn that looked long past their expiration date. The couch was eight feet long with high armrests, and the fabric had a look of gray corduroy. On either side were end tables with ornate lamps that sat on ivory doilies. Along the corner, towards the hallway, was a mahogany contraption, three feet high, on banana-shaped, tripod legs. Resting on the legs was a round, smooth table-top with a circular door which opened outward. Mrs. Cutter kept her romance books inside it.

"What did I do to deserve these?" she asked.

"Nothing in particular," I said. It was a true statement. I followed her to the kitchen.

"Let's find a vase."

The thick layers of dust on the sculpted glass vase she pulled from the pantry floor caused her to blush in embarrassment. "Let me clean this up a bit. We don't want to put flowers as beautiful as these in a dirty vase." She seemed excited as she filled the vase a third of the way with tap water. I handed the flowers to her one by one. As she arranged them, I noticed her wrinkled hands still possessed a refined gentleness. She placed the bouquet on the table beside an old radio, which I imagine provided companionship on lonely nights. As she looked at the arrangement, she did so with a look split between what seemed like joy and sentimental sadness. Maybe the flowers recalled younger days.

The light from the late morning sun shone brightly through her kitchen window, providing enough light that she didn't need to use the light hanging above the kitchen table.

"Would you like something to eat?" she asked.

"No, ma'am. I'm hopped up on sugar from Mr. Frank's candy."

While we sat at her table, she spent nearly an hour talking of her days with William, her late husband. On his deathbed, she had promised to meet him one day beside the weeping willow overhanging the pond at William's gravesite.

When I left her house, I realized the joy I brought her. Maybe I had piped a little sunshine into her world, even if only for a little while. If I did, great, though I felt as if I was the one receiving sunshine. I vowed to do more of the same to my elderly neighbors back home in the future.

Chapter Ten

The midday sun sat high and bold, and heat built like an incubator on our back porch. Strands of rays carved a path through the single-pane window. I walked into the small room and removed the black, plastic wiffle bat from the bat rack. Peering into the overflowing laundry basket that had been turned into a sports locker, I was hesitant to sort through the stack of equipment for the ball, as though a serpent waited to strike my exposed hand.

"You sure it's in here?" I asked as Ricky knelt to tie his black Chuck Taylor sneakers.

"Yeah, it's in there. But it ain't gonna jump out of the basket and into your hand. Keep looking, dummy."

"I see baseballs, a basketball, two footballs. Here's a tennis ball." I held it up and examined it. "Want to use that?"

"It's a little tough playing wiffle ball without a *wiffle* ball."

I fumbled around the basket again. "Here's a glove, a racquet, a...hey, here it is." Like a man pulling a prize lobster from a saltwater tank, I emerged with the white plastic ball. "Got it."

"Was that so hard?"

We walked across the patio and onto the side yard, a manicured spot of ground custom-made for a game of wiffle ball. Wiffle ball was a game best suited for a small playing field, and the dimensions of our side yard fit that description. The distance from home plate — which, on that day, was a paper plate lifted from the pantry — to the fence was a perfect 75 feet. Home plate was the only mobile base, and the only base which we would tag with our foot. The others required a touch of the hand. A twelve inch metal water spigot, rooted deep in plush centipede, served as first base. Second base was a side limb from a tender mulberry bush, and third was the scaly trunk of a slender maple. Shade from lofty pines and rotund oaks provided shelter from the baking sun, thus creating a dome effect and a climate-controlled field temperature of about 78 degrees on summer days.

The one snag to playing on the side yard was that Dad had strictly prohibited it. The back lot, and the back lot only, was reserved for ball games, as the clumps of sand and worn out grass would attest. The rest of the yard was to be revered like the Biltmore estate, and ball of any type was forbidden.

"Maybe we should just use the back lot," I said while swinging the ultra-light bat with my left hand. "Dad would be ticked."

"He won't be home for hours," Rick reasoned. "Stop being a baby."

"Sometimes he comes home for lunch."

"If he does, we do like we always do — run."

The Watson Wiffle Ball League had several rules, many similar to Little League. Three outs per inning, six innings per game. Nine inning games were played on occasion, but had to have prior approval before the game began from both teams. Since rosters were slim and us the only players, pre-game approval for a nine inning game went something like this: 'Hey, you want to play nine today?' followed by a response of, 'Sure, why not?'

There were three possible ways to make an out: the pop out, which was the least common, the ground out, and the strike out. Pop outs were rarely easy or routine, primarily because the multitude of tree limbs hovering above the playing field produced wicked ricochets. Ground outs, which required pegging the batter with the ball before he reached base, was fun for the defender as he was likely to inflict pain as the plastic ball was quite hard.

The strike out was the most interesting, and counted as two outs. A wiffle ball was, more than anything else, ultra light-weight. It also contained small, round holes throughout, giving it an appearance of Swiss cheese. The push of air through the holes during flight allowed even the worst pitcher to become a throwing wizard. Curveballs would bend like boomerangs, drop balls would flop downward like dying pigeons, and knuckle balls would dance across the plate like a space ship piloted by drunk aliens.

Rick batted first, as always, and the game began.

I began my pitching repertoire with a drop ball, and Rick's swing produced only air. Strike one.

"Thanks for the nice breeze," I said.

"Pipe down. Bring that pitch again and I'll send it off your chin."

My eyes peered over the top of the ball towards Ricky, whose feet were positioned next to home plate. With my left hand raised, nose high, ball cupped in my palm, I applied the grip with my right. Rick's curious eyes were denied access to the grip, rendering him clueless to the pitch coming his way.

I noticed Rick's fingers tighten around the bat and decided to toss him a slow knuckle ball. His over aggressiveness caused him to spring toward the ball well before it reached the plate as he whiffed air again for strike number two. As Ricky's upper row of teeth began to push down on his lower lip, I decided a submariner would finish him off. I stepped with my left foot towards the plate, lowering my throwing hand like a man trying to down the ten pin at a bowling alley, and released the ball beside my right knee cap. As Ricky swung, the ball dipped under the bat for strike number three. It was a beautiful pitch, if I do say so myself.

"You, sir, are out," I said, lifting my right hand, thumb extended. "Make that two outs."

"Shoot!" Rick said, smacking his forehead with the bat.

Having thoroughly enjoyed watching Rick strike out to start the game, I decided to let my little brother have some fun. And so I served up a meatball across the center of the plate, belt high. Rick crushed it right back at my head, and a quick duck allowed the ball to continue on a beeline for Mrs. Mackie's cyclone fence, which served double duty as the center field wall.

"Suck on that one," Rick yelled as he took off for the hook-shaped spigot. I motored to the fence, where I found the ball sitting on sun-dried pine straw behind a manicured row of azaleas. Turning, I saw Ricky rounding third. I straightened my body, lined up my left shoulder, hip, and foot towards home plate, and let fly a bullet. As Ricky's bent left leg began to step down on home plate, the hard plastic sphere smashed his calf, which was unfortunately exposed due to Rick's choice of wearing shorts. Rick tumbled across the paper plate and rolled on his side.

"Yes!" I shouted. "Out! O. U. T."

"No way!" Rick yelled while lying spread eagle on the soft grass. "My foot touched the plate first!" A deep red spot appeared quickly on his calf.

"You're crazy," I said as I jogged towards home. "Three outs. My turn to bat."

Rick grabbed the bat and tossed it on the roof above the back porch.

"Cheater," Rick said as he began walking to the back porch door.

"Ah, c'mon. Don't quit. We just started."

Rick refused, and the game was called on account of pouting. I returned the ball to the sports basket, and decided Rick could fetch the bat from the gutter in which it hung.

"Chase," Mom said when I entered the kitchen.

"Ma'am?"

"I need you to ride to Madge Jernigan's house. She has a Tupperware order form for me that has to be turned in today, and I have to wait here for the TV repairman."

"No problem."

"Thanks, sweetie."

"Mom, have you seen the old man who is living in the abandoned car behind Frank's Market?"

"Someone lives in that car?"

"Yes, ma'am. I talked with him today. He said he has a daughter in Charleston, but no way of getting there. She doesn't have a phone, so he can't call her to come get him. Think we could buy him a bus ticket, and take him to the station?"

"Do you think he is telling you the truth?"

"Yes, ma'am. I could see it in his eyes. I'll mow some yards to raise the money for the ticket."

Mom pulled down a blue porcelain jar from above the stove. From it she poured a mountain of change on to the counter. "Let's cash this in and buy him a ticket. I'll count it while you go to Mrs. Jernigan's."

I pushed hard on the black-ridged pedals and flew down Brennan. The breeze generated by the speed

148

of the bike tempered the steamy blacktop somewhat. My green denim shorts puckered a bit from the push of the air as I rode. The ride carried me past the schoolyard and the ball field. Turning onto Confederate Avenue, I heard the laughter of children playing on a red metal swing set at Bucky Jacob's house. They were familiar sounds of the neighborhood, and sounded great. Mrs. Jackson and Mrs. Swanson were chit-chatting beside the Jackson's mailbox, and they stopped their banter long enough to wave at me as I rode by.

"I heard she finally left the two-timing lush," Mrs. Swanson said within earshot. I was tempted to turn around to find out who left whom, but I pushed forward. Passing Joe's house, I sighed, knowing Joe's impending death was about to hit his family like a Texas tornado.

Mrs. Jernigan's house was one of the few cottage-style homes in the neighborhood. There were shades of violet and yellow peeking from underneath the top of the white porch in hanging baskets. Ivy-covered lattice enclosed the elbow curve of the porch. The unique home looked as if it was carried in from the countryside, a la Dorothy's house in the Wizard of Oz. Only, in this case, there was no flattened witch with curled up legs underneath the house. I wished it would flatten the witch that liked to appear in front of my closet at night.

Mr. Jernigan had assembled rows of pumpkin-colored gourds and hung them from a solid, white, metal pole in the front yard. Daisies lined the edges of the front walk, and a tiny lily pond that Mr. Jernigan had built in the 60's, was home to dozens of black-and-orange butterflies. Carolina wrens filled the yard, and yellow finches chased each other around the picture window. It was like the bird sanctuary at the local zoo.

I tapped on the stained glass window encased in the mahogany door.

"Hello, Chase," the soft voice said in the doorway.

"Hey, Mrs. Jernigan. How have you been? You're looking well." She had been placed in an assisted-living home three years before Mom had died as dementia had left her unable to take care of herself.

"Aren't you sweet?" she said. I think she actually blushed.

"Mom sent me to get the Tupperware form."

"I've got it on the kitchen table. Come in from the heat."

"Yes, ma'am."

The hardwood floor reflected soft beams of sunlight that slipped through the picture window of the den. The room was airy. A scent of burning vanilla candles wafted through the room. A bookshelf on either side of a marble fireplace contained shelves from floor to ceiling, filled with a lifetime collection of fiction novels and history books, though most were hidden by the multitude of picture frames. Mrs. Jernigan had five children, all of whom had grown up and moved away, and the pictures were ample evidence of a once-busy home.

"How's Mr. Jernigan?" I asked loudly while I glanced at a black-and-white family photo labeled, *Christmas 1957,* on the corner of the third shelf.

"Ornery as ever," she laughed. "He's on a charter fishing boat off Charleston. Probably tossing his lunch by now." Picking up the form, she ambled to the foyer. "Would you like some lemonade?"

"No, ma'am. You know, this is the coolest house."

"You think so?"

"It's like going to the country without leaving the neighborhood."

Smiling, she said, "I never heard it described quite that way."

I wanted to tell her I had a living room similar to it in the future but passed on the notion.

"Well, I better get going." I wanted to hug her but thought it would be too weird. "It was nice to see you again."

"It was nice seeing you too. Stop by anytime."

"I'll try. Have a good day."

I folded the order form in half and placed it in my back pocket. I turned my bike to the road and began to head home, but I heard loud voices coming from several doors down where the neighborhood was bordered by a busy highway. Curiosity led me to the commotion, and I spotted a large group of teenagers gathered in a circle beside the grease pit of Stubb's Service Station. I parked my bike against the faded brick wall and hurried around the side of the building to see what was going on.

"Hit him again," I heard someone yell.

"Yea, beat him good," another shouted.

I squeezed through the angry group, which I could tell were at least a dozen. Larry Jenkins, one of the meanest guys in the neighborhood, had his arm locked tight around a boy's neck. Larry was tall and lanky, with unkempt dirty blonde hair. He must have been at least a freshman in high school, though I remembered he'd failed at least two grades. His father was a machinist, strong and broad shouldered, and the word was that he liked to come home drunk and take out frustrations of the day on Larry's body. Larry's two older brothers had moved away from home to escape the rain of their father's blows. His mother had been a dark-haired beauty with soft, brown eyes, and I can remember her showing up at the ballpark. She had seemed to thrive off the stares of the men, and the slight wrinkles growing underneath her luscious eyes had only seemed to fuel her desire to turn their heads. From what I had been told, she'd spent much more time and energy on being the doll of the neighborhood than she had raising her three boys.

Larry bent the boy's head downward as his right knee drove upward into the boy's chin. The impact knocked the kid on his back and, as it did, I realized this wasn't a standard, run-of-the-mill neighborhood fight.

"Drag the asphalt with him," someone from the crowd shouted.

"Make him pay," said another.

The slender, dark-skinned boy looked to be no older than eleven or twelve. His round face and chubby cheeks showed an innocence that didn't seem capable of understanding the depths of why he was being attacked. He attempted to wipe the blood from his lip as he sat, stunned, on his backside among the grease of the gas station. His close-cropped afro was dotted with oily sand, and the pocket on his plaid short-sleeve shirt was ripped, exposing his chest. His shattered glasses lay behind him on the pavement. His eyes looked dazed and confused. As Larry grabbed the youth by the hair, I lunged forward, grabbing Larry's left wrist. Larry's head turned, his eyes sending flames through me.

"What are you doing?" I asked, most likely looking as confused as the boy Larry was beating.

Pain shot through my wrist as Larry's long fingers took hold of it. "Son, you better get on outta here."

"What did he do?" I asked.

"He came into our neighborhood, that's what. Any good black boy knows he ain't allowed in *our* neighborhood."

"Are you kidding me!?"

"Shut up and get outta here or you're gonna get whupped too."

"He's just a kid. No different than you and me, Larry. Just let him go."

My arms were quickly pinned to my side as Larry's buddy, Danny, squeezed my torso from behind. "Hit him, too," Danny yelled. Just because I could bench press nearly three-hundred pounds in the present did me no good in the past. I was again that slender kid with limited muscle capacity. That fact only made having my arms strapped worse. The claustrophobic side of me had me ready to bite Danny's arms.

Larry stepped in front of me and punched me in the jaw. As my knees buckled, Larry's backhand jolted me across the face, and blood squirted from the side of my mouth. As Larry raised his hand for another blow, he was tackled by the black youth. I lifted the right heel of my black sneakers into Danny's testicles, hoping he'd need pliers to pull them back down. Danny's certain immense pain allowed me to free myself from the stronghold. Backing away from the mob, I stood in front of the innocent boy.

"What is wrong with you?" Blood sprayed from my tongue. "This boy has done nothing to any of you."

"Shut up, Chase!" a voice yelled from the crowd. "Leave him to us."

"He's just a kid," I pleaded. "Let him go."

A fist landed against my left cheek, and the crowd closed in. We were pushed to the greasy pavement and pummeled with kicks and taunts from the crowd.

As the kicks rained in, I could hear Charlie Stubbs, the owner of the gas station, yelling. "Break it up!" he screamed.

A strapping man of sixty, his white, wavy hair told his age though his thick forearms said otherwise. Stubbs had invested his whole life keeping the modest one-pump gas station afloat. Grabbing Larry forcibly by the arm, he shouted, "Did you hear me, son? That's enough!"

Larry landed one last blow to the ribs of the boy who'd wandered into the neighborhood.

"What in the *world* is going on here?" Stubbs shouted.

"This boy here has come where he don't belong, and we're teaching him a lesson," Larry said, his fists still balled tightly.

I rose slowly on my hands and knees as the kid rolled on his back, gingerly touching his damaged ribs.

"All you boys get off my property," Stubbs said. "Go on now, before I call the police."

Larry, teeth clenched, said, "Let's go fellas. That colored kid will know better next time."

Standing guard over us, Stubbs watched the crowd slowly move away. Crouching, he asked, "You boys okay?"

I was still on hands and knees, and I turned my aching head to look at the wounded lad. "Are you okay?"

Tears streamed from the corners of the boy's eyes. Coughing, he rolled on his side to look for his glasses. Mr. Stubbs picked up the broken spectacles. Now sitting on my knees, I said, "Man, I'm sorry this happened. This is unbelievable."

"Leave me alone, white boy."

154

"I don't blame you for being ticked off."

"I only crossed the street to get a soda from the machine," he said, wiping the remaining tears from his face. "I made some money this mornin' collecting soda bottles from the roadside."

"Hey, you don't have to explain it to me."

"Let me get you boys something to drink and a wet rag to clean you up with," Mr. Stubbs said.

"You think your ribs are okay?" I asked.

"I been through worse."

"My name's Chase."

"I'm Reggie. Man, them boys got some hard fists." Reggie's forefinger touched the side of his cheek to slow the oozing of blood caused by the shattering lenses of his glasses.

Mr. Stubbs soon emerged from his shop with two bottles of Coke and two rags.

"Here," he said, "use these to clean yourselves up. I got you something cold to drink. I sure am sorry you boys had to go through this."

"My mama said to stay away from this side of the street. Now I know why." He held the remains of his crushed glasses. "Mama's gonna whup me for gettin' my glasses tore up. She paid good money for 'em."

"Young fella, I'll be happy to buy you a new pair of glasses," Mr. Stubbs said while handing Reggie his drink. "Reggie, where do you live?"

"On the back side of the tracks, 'bout a mile or so from here."

"Past the woods behind the school?" I asked.

"Yep."

"We heard that hobos lived there, and that we'd get killed if we ever went back there."

"What's a hobo?" Reggie asked.

I looked at him peculiarly for a minute, then had to think on how to answer the question. "I'm not really sure myself. I think it was men who were stowaways on the trains. You know, carrying their belongings over their shoulder with a stick and duffle bag."

"Why don't you boys get your keisters off my greasy pavement and out of the sun?" Mr. Stubbs asked. "It's a lot cooler in the chairs outside my office."

We hobbled to the two worn, vinyl chairs placed outside the front window of the station. The overhang of the roof shielded us from the mounting heat as the sun peeked out from behind soft, billowy clouds. As the clouds stretched across the sky, their dark bottoms gave hints of impending afternoon showers.

The carbonated water stung the cuts and abrasions in and around my mouth. I looked at Reggie's forearms that were lined with scars. One particular scar, five inches long, ran from Reggie's left wrist toward the elbow. He noticed me staring.

"I got that from my brother when I was six. I ate a pear he brought home from school. He sliced me with his blade. Mama beat him when she got home from work."

It didn't take me long to realize Reggie's home life was so much different, and more difficult, than mine. When I made Bobby mad, the results were a few smacks on the arm, or maybe a headlock. Getting sliced was never an option.

"Man, that's terrible. How many stitches did it take?"

"Stitches?" Reggie chuckled. "White boy, we didn't have money to pay for stitches. We just wrapped it up with an old rag soaked in iodine. That iodine set me on fire."

"What is it with parents that think the only way to heal a wound is to set it on fire?" I asked. "I just spread Neosporin or something on my kid's wounds." Feeling his stare, I cringed.

"You one strange white boy, ain't ya?"

"Stranger than you'll ever know."

"Why'd you help me? You took a bad beatin' just to help me."

"I couldn't sit back and watch them beat you. Besides, you'd a done the same for me." I turned my head and looked at Reggie's blank stare. "Wouldn't you?"

"Ain't no way I'm gonna get in the way of a gang of brothers beatin' up on a white boy." My stunned look was quickly dashed when a sly grin emerged from Reggie's face.

"Thanks a lot, Reggie."

"I'd a helped you. I'd a told 'em you'd pay 'em to leave you alone."

"Maybe I shoulda done the same for you. Told Larry and the guys you'd pay them to leave you alone."

"That wouldn't a worked."

"Why not?"

"'Ain't no white boy gonna think a brother carries pocket change," Reggie said with a laugh.

"You're killing me."

Our bruised and battered bodies strained to laugh. As we finished our drinks, customers who stopped by looked curiously at us. They seem drawn more to the fact two youths, one milky white and the other charcoal black, sat side by side in conversation, than the bruises and blood about our face and clothing.

"I think I better get on home," Reggie said. "It's been some kinda day, ain't it?"

"You ain't kiddin'. Sure the ribs are okay?"

"They're all right. I been through worse. You know, my brother ain't gonna believe me when I tell him your skinny, white butt jumped in to help me."

"All I did was get in the way of some of the blows. Mr. Stubbs is the one who saved you."

"I still don't understand why it happened."

"It's not gonna always be this way. I promise."

We stood, me from my black chair, Reggie from his white, and we shook hands.

"Thanks, man," Reggie said quietly.

"You bet."

"What's your last name?"

"Watson. Yours?"

"Roosevelt."

"So long, Reggie Roosevelt."

"See you, Chase Watson."

As Reggie walked to the road, anxious to cross the highway to his 'side of the street,' I shouted, "Be more careful next time you go bottle collecting, okay?"

"Ain't gonna be no next time. I'm retirin'."

As I mounted my bike, and began the long ride home, I smiled when it hit me that a few years after Lauren had been born, the town's first African American mayor, Reginald Roosevelt, had been sworn into office. Wonder what Larry thought about that?

Chapter Eleven

It was a rough ride home. It had been so many years since I'd been in a fight I'd forgotten how punishing it was on the body. Pain shot through my jaw when I tried to open my mouth, and my ribs ached when I pushed the pedals uphill. I finally rode into the yard, too sore to make it to the patio. I slid off the bike, leaving it on the ground beside the driveway. I noticed Dad's car parked crooked in the driveway. Slowly, I walked up the steps and into the front door. After slipping into the bathroom, I snatched a washrag from the towel rack. The shiny porcelain sink quickly turned dirty crimson as I gently rubbed the dried blood from my jaw. The water from the spigot washed away the blood as I held my mouth underneath the metal pipe.

I wondered why the color of a man's skin determines, to some people, the way he is to be treated. I had experienced racism through the years, so it wasn't like it was a novel experience and that I thought racism was one sided. I'd been on the receiving end of beatings and taunting when I had been in middle school, frequently jumped by a group of black youths in the schoolyard. The group had been led by a boy whose mother had cleaned our house on occasion when I was in elementary school. It had seemed obvious to me that his mother working for us had bothered him, as though we were perpetuating some southern ritual where blacks were subservient.

Mom walked past the bathroom, and I reached my leg outward to close the door. My attempt to hide the bloody mess from her was futile as she pushed the door open with her fingers.

"Goodness," she said. She walked to the sink and wrapped her soft fingers gently around my cheek. "What in the world happened?"

I rubbed my bottom lip delicately with my index finger. "It was crazy, Mom. Crazy."

"Let's get that cut fixed," she said, opening the medicine cabinet. "This iodine will do the trick."

Yes, let's burn that jaw right off. Why hadn't Neosporin been invented yet?

"Tell me what happened."

"Some boys were trying to beat up a kid at Stubb's Service Station. Let's just say I got in the way of some of the blows."

Mom dabbed the iodine-soaked cotton ball against my jaw, and the shooting pain made the blows from Larry's fist seem miniscule.

"Geez, that stings." My eyes began to water, but I regrouped. "Is Dad in bed?" I pulled the cotton away from my face.

"Yes. He's lying down. He says he's got a cold."

"He's drunk, isn't he?"

Mom rinsed a rag in the sink and dabbed the corner of my mouth. "Just a chest cold. He should be okay in a day or two."

"Mom, you don't have to protect him. He's passed out, isn't he?"

She nodded but tended to my wounds.

"We have to find a way to help him. Somehow, someway. And you don't have to do this alone. I'm going to help you."

When I was thirteen, Dad had been mired in a major struggle, and the bottle had knocked him to the canvas daily. For days, he slept and drank, slept and drank. Mom, down to her wit's end, had told Dad he had to make a choice—the bottle or the family. As Dad had attempted to muster enough energy to walk out the front door, I had foolishly stood in the way. Instead of supporting Mom that evening long ago, I had made her the bad guy. By me coming to Dad's rescue, it had reinforced his belief that the family wouldn't make him leave. The guilt had weighed heavy on me for years. And now, with a second chance, no way was I going to let Mom down again, or Dad.

"We gotta get to the core of what's making him do this to himself," I continued. "And if he doesn't accept our help, and you decide he has to leave, I won't get in the way this time."

"This time?" she asked. "What do you mean, *this* time?"

"Just listen to me, Mom. It's important we do this together. Our family's sanity is riding on it."

I could see part of her wanting to defend him and the other part begging for help. "I don't know if it's possible." She pulled me to her bosom.

"Yes, it is. Trust me. We just have to do it together."

Dad was asleep. The house was quiet. The lateness of the afternoon had softened the glare of the Carolina day, though the sun's rays ran bright and clear through the living room window. The doorbell rang.

"Get the door, would you?" Mom asked.

Herm Edwards, a stocky shoe salesman from down the street, stood at the door. "Hello, young man, are your folks home?"

"Hey, Mr. Edwards," I said at the door. "Would you like to come in?"

Walking through the doorway, he removed a corduroy Gatsby hat, revealing a shiny crown with thinning gray hair on the side.

"What's new?" I asked.

"Well, to be honest with you, I'm a little upset," he answered. "I prefer to discuss it with your parents."

Mr. Edward's only child, Buddy, had been a classmate of Ricky's. Their personalities had clashed like a golfer wearing a purple sweater and lime-green pants. The boys had fought constantly. Buddy had been huge for his age. He'd looked like he had spent his eight years as a taste tester for Willy Wonka. Nearly double the size of Rick, he'd often tried to push his weight around. Rick would have nothing of it. By the look on Mr. Edward's face, the boys had been at it again.

"Hello, Herm," Mom said, entering the den.

"Hello, Ellen," he responded. "This isn't a social call. I just wanted to talk to you about Ricky."

A social call? Neighbors in Belmont didn't make social calls. They dropped by, they checked in, they chewed the fat, or they passed the time. But social calls they did not make.

"What'd he do?" she asked, anticipating the worst of news.

"Well, this morning I looked out my living room window and saw Ricky hitting Buddy. As you know, Buddy is a tender child. I don't want him to develop a complex, and I think Ricky's bullying him isn't helping in that regard."

Maybe cutting back on the Twinkies would do the job. Perhaps some deep knee bends.

The visual of Rick punching a kid two feet taller than him made me laugh out loud, and I was proud of my younger brother.

"I apologize for my son's actions, and I'll send him down to do the same when he gets home." Mom had always been the mediator in times of conflict. She'd had the ability to calm the waters like no other. Well, except for Dad when he was drinking.

Mr. Edwards looked at me, puzzled as to why I found the situation funny. I should have told Mr. Edwards that, thanks to him, his son was going to grow up to be a major pain in the backside, but I didn't. I tell you, it was hard not to.

"Well, I guess I better be going," Mr. Edwards said as he turned the brass knob of the door.

"I'll send Ricky down to apologize as soon as he gets home," Mom said.

After the door shut behind Mr. Edwards, she looked at me. "What's so funny? Ricky shouldn't be picking on that poor child."

"Buddy's the size of Frankenstein, and he couldn't handle getting whipped by a kid that barely stands waist high to him. You ought to give Rick a friggin' medal."

"Friggin'?"

"It's a slang word for, well, I better not say."

"You surely have been acting peculiar since that blow to your head."

Again with the head.

I followed Mom to the kitchen. "Mom, what have we got going on this week?"

"We have your game tonight," she responded. "Your uniform is cleaned and ready on the dryer. If you'd rather do something else, we can skip it and stay

163

home." She knew those ball games were the center of my world.

"Well, I think there's a National Geographic special on about blonde-haired pygmies. Let's stay home and watch it."

Mom smiled. "Hey, don't make any plans for tomorrow morning. You boys have a dentist appointment at eleven." So much for fun and games.

Frank Belton had been the dentist from hell. Surely a former Nazi war criminal, he'd thrived on inflicting pain to children of all ages, and I think he'd most enjoyed giving it to me. His office had been on the second floor of what had to be the oldest office building in town. The front door had opened into a large foyer with giant ceilings and long, winding stairs that were akin to walking to a torture chamber. My knees had buckled just walking into the office as the smell of Novocain and drilled enamel hit me like a hippo jack-knifing water.

"No way, Mom. Reschedule. We've got way too much going on." I was hoping to postpone until my regularly scheduled appointment after I went back to the future with my dentist—a dentist who was concerned for my comfort.

"We've had this scheduled for six months, and we aren't changing it."

"Crud," I whispered. Actually, I think I whispered something a bit stronger. I had to come up with a reason for postponement.

The afternoon passed like a backyard snail as I impatiently waited to step into my baseball uniform and take off to the ball field. Sitting on the kitchen counter, I closed my eyes to soak in the solitude of the slow summer afternoon as frigid air drifted in from the wall unit in the den.

Dad stumbled from the bedroom and I hopped from the counter to take a look down the hall. He fell into the doorway of the bathroom and ended up on his knees. He looked helpless as he fought to find the strength to pull himself off the floor. I rushed to his side and took hold of his left arm, steadying him.

With glassy eyes and a look of hopelessness, Dad seemed oblivious to the fact I was there. Mumbling, he slowly made his way through the kitchen, holding onto the counter until he reached the back porch. I froze in my moment of truth, remaining inside instead of following him outside and tossing that stupid bottle into the trees. I just couldn't watch him struggling to stand as he turned back the bottle. I couldn't. I had watched it too many times, and I couldn't bring myself to see it again. And so I stayed in the kitchen, weak and gutless, right after proclaiming to Mom that I was there to help. I didn't deserve to be called a son.

After he had gotten his fill of liquor from a bottle hidden behind the patio, Dad tried to make his way back to his bedroom, and he fell onto a small table on the foyer. Again, I ran to his side and helped him to his knees. I saw the agony in his blue eyes, and tears filled the corners. My heart broke. Why couldn't I help him?

"C'mon, Dad. I got you." I steered him to his bed, and he fell on top of it, unable to slip under the blanket. Blood trickled from his lip. I went to the bathroom and returned with a warm, soapy rag. He had passed out, and I don't think there was any way he felt me cleaning his wound. He looked like he was a million miles away. I touched his face with my fingers, and wanted God to tell me why he had become that way. I prayed for God to heal him, make him the man he used to be and, in my heart, the man I know he wanted to be.

Mom walked into the kitchen holding an armful of sheets freshly removed from the clothesline. She looked grimly at me, but she didn't seem to notice the guilt on my face. "Get dressed on the back porch and I'll take you to your game."

Mom didn't want Dad to know I had a game, as he was likely to get behind the wheel and drive to the ball field after he came to. I changed quickly and removed my glove from the metal laundry basket. I placed my blue ball cap on my short blond hair, and it conformed perfectly to my head. I wished Dad were able to come and sit in the stands with Mom. But that hadn't happened very often during my final season of Little League.

The ride to the ballpark contained little conversation. Fortunately, it was a short ride. I thought about what had just happened at home, and I did what I had done when I'd been a child—the first time—and put the situation out of my mind. I knew Dad needed help but, for now, there was a game to play. How's that for unselfishness? I didn't deserve to play, not after leaving Dad to fend for himself. The car rolled to a stop and I stepped out.

"I'll be back in a little bit," Mom said. "Have a good game."

"Yes, ma'am."

Mom waved and glanced at me in the rear view mirror. She deserved so much better. As she pulled out of the parking lot, turning towards home, I raised my hand and watched in silence.

Each step I took toward the field took me further and further back in time. The guilt slowly left my mind, and a feeling of excitement returned as I began to walk the same grassy path as I'd done years ago. The ballpark was situated between the school and the woods. The trek from the parking lot to the field was no more than fifty yards long, but it seemed shorter that day than I remembered. The school was eerily silent, as the last day of school had ushered in summer vacation weeks before.

I lifted the horseshoe-shaped handle on the metal gate beside third base, stepped on the field, and my troubles evaporated. My teammates were in left field, warming up. Two lines, five players in each, thirty feet apart, hugged the left field foul line. The pop of balls hitting leather pockets echoed across the field. Talk was low and minimal. I noticed the focus in their eyes as they prepared themselves for the game.

"'Bout time you got here," Joe said from the bench just inside the dugout. Flipping a ball from his glove into the air, he said, "Let's warm up." Joe and I had always warmed up together, for superstitious reasons as well as the fact that we had been the closest of friends for six years.

"I'm ready," I said, raising my left hand, palm exposed. Joe tossed me the ball.

The chalky white rawhide felt smooth, emitting a slightly salty aroma. A soft breeze blew and the honeysuckle, as if on cue, drifted delicately over the field. I felt so at ease, as though the game and my soul were intertwined. My black cleats pressed down on the soft green centipede and it stirred memories of games played long ago. Games of last inning victories, and heartbreaking defeats, still remain in the crevices and corners of my mind.

Joe was uncharacteristically quiet. His eyes, very solemn, made me wonder if he sensed his baseball days were coming to an end. Surely he didn't. I wanted to tell him the fate that awaited him, to warn him that he would soon be dead if he didn't back out on the trip, but didn't feel qualified in playing God. Knowing it was the last time I'd warm up with my best friend, the last time we'd share the diamond, made it hard for me to throw with him. It would be the last chance to share the game that had brought more joy to us than anything we had experienced in our short lives.

"Think we'll ever find anything as much fun as playing baseball?" Joe asked as he cradled a toss from me in his tan Spalding glove.

"It will be hard to beat this." I struggled to focus on warming up. Should I tell him? What kind of friend was I? No different than standing in the kitchen while watching Dad walk outside for a drink, I reasoned.

The memory of Joe's funeral was a burdensome one.

Horrified by the thought of viewing a dead body, I certainly hadn't wanted to see my best friend stretched out in a coffin. Yet, there he was, lying on display in the room of the funeral home where the family was accepting visitors. I walked up to hug Joe's mother, and she took me by the hand to the eternal bed in which Joe slept.

"He looks so peaceful, doesn't he?" she said, choking into a deep sob. My knees buckled when I saw Joe's face, swollen from the river water that filled his lungs when he tumbled over Linville Falls. She told me the youth director had volunteered to take a few of the boys in the group for a hike. Three miles into it, they'd come upon a tree that had fallen across a narrow part of the river. The director, unsure as to the safety of crossing the river on the fallen tree, said it wasn't safe to cross. But Joe jumped on the root of the tree as the director glanced downstream, anxious to lead the way across the tree to the other side.

As the director called out for Joe to back off the tree, he slipped, unsuccessfully reaching for a limb to stop himself from falling in the swift-moving water. The river had pulled him downstream and, as he'd tried to swim to the edge, the church director and the others had frantically given chase along the bank. Unable to maneuver close to the side, Joe had been sucked under by the rapids and flung two hundred feet off the waterfall.

Joe had looked like a stranger lying in the morbid box, with a look of a defeated athlete, a sight so dispiriting that I hadn't slept a wink that night, and it made me unable to look at another dead body from that day forward.

When a group had approached to offer condolences to Joe's parents, I quickly left the room and ran outside. Mom, who had been quietly chatting with a neighbor, had noticed my quick exit, and followed me.

"Let's go home," I remember saying.

"I'm so sorry," Mom had said, placing her hand on my shoulder as we walked through the parking lot. "Sometimes things happen that we can't explain. It's times like this where we have to lean on God."

"Or wonder if God has forsaken us."

"What's a matter with you guys?" Randy shouted to Joe and me as we finished warming up. "Y'all look like your dog just got run over."

"Just worry about yourself, cissy boy," Joe said.

Coach Cooper walked down the foul line. "Chase." He tossed the game ball to me. "You're on the mound today. Get ready." I tossed the ball Joe and I had been warming up with back to Joe and rubbed the smooth, white game ball Coach had just given me. Artie Catoe jogged to the dugout to put on his catcher's gear.

While the team finished warm-ups, I walked to the corner of the field, to a rubber mound placed in front of the foul pole. I toed the cream-colored mound, rubbing the ball back and forth in my fingers. The role of the pitcher is different to that of any position on the field. To be certain, every position is important, and it takes a team effort to be successful.

However, the game revolves around the pitcher. He is the one player who can control the game, good or bad. Defensively, he carries the weight of the team on his shoulders. Some guys can handle the pressure, some guys can't. To me, being on the mound meant that, not only the coaches, but also the team, were putting their faith in my ability. I thrived on it. It's what made me tick.

As I rubbed my fingers along the seams of the ball, I heard the whack of a plastic bat. I looked to the grassy area outside the left field fence in the schoolyard and watched a boy with sandy blond hair run across the grass. He looked no more than three, and his khaki shorts covered his tiny legs down to his calf. He wore a Yankees t-shirt, white with blue pin stripes. A man slowly ran after a white, plastic ball that rolled to a stop fifty feet from where the boy had hit it.

The child carved a crooked path to his left, running toward what I assumed was second base. He passed by the ball that lay still on the grass, his face wearing a look of both determination and jubilation. The little guy was running as fast as his legs would carry him, and when he turned again, heading to a make-believe third base, he looked like the fate of the world rested on him making it back to home plate, which looked to be a small baseball glove.

The man picked up the ball as if in slow motion, and it was easy to see that he was going as slowly as possible to ensure that the boy got a home run. With ball in hand, he jogged slowly toward home plate and, when the boy slid into the glove on his back, the man touched him on his shoulder.

"Wow," the man shouted. "Another home run, Jake!"

I smiled as the boy lay on his back, eyes looking skyward as if thanking God for giving him the ability to hit what surely was the greatest home run of all time. The man lifted the child from the ground and placed him on his shoulder.

"Way to go," the man said.

"Thanks, Dad. It was a masher, wasn't it?"

"It sure was, Jake. A masher."

Watching the man and his son gave me chills. When the dad removed Jake from his shoulder, the boy turned and hugged his father. I knew their hearts were joined by the simple game that was baseball, a bond shared by father and son that surely they'd remember for the rest of their lives. It seemed, in some ways, a million years ago when I had been that little boy, hitting imaginary home runs with Dad. And yet it seemed like yesterday when I was doing the same with Brett.

After warming up with Artie, we returned to the dugout for pre-game instruction from Coach Cooper. All twelve of us sat tightly together with anxious faces, waiting to hear our roles for the day's game.

"Okay boys, here's the startin' lineup..."

As the lineup was read, I watched the expression on each player as his name was called. Did they look

171

back as fondly on their time at the ball field as I did? For the couple of guys who rarely got to be a starter, did they have fun playing the game? Guys like Bennie and Dickey, who stopped playing after Little League because they knew they weren't good enough to make the next jump — did they think back on their days with disdain, or did they think back on them at all? Whether they did or didn't wasn't important at that moment, because excitement surely grew in the dugout as game time approached.

I rubbed the sleeve of my jersey. My cotton uniform was soft to the touch. The guy who would later invent polyester uniforms in the mid 70's should have been hung up by his Buster Browns. The fabric had itched. It had been hot. And it had been ugly. It'd been like joining Disco and baseball in holy matrimony. A shotgun wedding.

My team, Phillip's Garden Center, was first up to bat.

Joe batted leadoff, and he stepped in the on-deck circle, swinging two bats. For some reason it was 'big league' to swing two bats in the on-deck circle. The idea was that, after swinging two bats, swinging one at the plate would feel much lighter and, consequently, more bat speed would be generated. I had never been sure if it helped. All I knew was that grasping two bats at the same time wasn't easy.

The bleachers soon filled with family members, friends who came for the love of the game, and the neighborhood bad boys who liked to hang out at the field. The tough guys were the ones who were probably good enough to play but, for some reason, thought it cool not to. Perhaps it was because playing on a team required the ability to follow orders from the coach.

A baseball team symbolized all that was right with athletics. A group of guys setting aside individual goals to be the best they could be for the good of the team. Weeks of practice, endless instruction, and a steady balance of encouragement and discipline was all part of the process. I don't know about the others, but I loved to practice. To me, it was just another chance to field, throw, and hit.

For me, wearing a baseball uniform had been a privilege, not a right. It had given me an internal pride unlike anything I'd ever experienced in my youth. When I'd been in uniform, it had been only fitting that I give heart, soul, and body for my teammates. There'd been nothing quite like the feeling of walking off the field after a game, tired, and sometimes bloody, especially when it resulted in victory.

Of all the tough guys who hung out at the field, Sylvester Derringer was the toughest. And the meanest. During one game, Sylvester had yelled from the bleachers to me while I was taking practice swings in the on-deck circle, demanding a home run. He had probably been fourteen, and had a girl on either side of him on the bleacher. What kind of guy demands a home run? Sylvester, that's who. I don't have to tell you, that's a lot of pressure to put on a Little Leaguer.

So, I'd tipped my helmet and stepped into the batter's box, figuring if I didn't hit one out of the park there would be a butt-kicking after the game, with my butt being the guest of honor. To avoid a post-game beating, I had crushed the first pitch over the left field fence. After I'd crossed home plate and received pats on my helmet from my teammates, I remember glancing at Sylvester, who had offered up a devilish smirk, seemingly impressing himself with the ability to coax a homerun from me through pure fear.

Sylvester had returned each game, making the same demand. The funny thing about it was I had hit homeruns in six consecutive games and had started to view the boy as a good luck charm. When the streak finally ended, I had worried about the consequences. When my last at-bat of the game had resulted in no homerun and I'd returned to the dugout, Sylvester had shrugged his shoulders slightly, letting me know my backside was safe. I guess six homeruns had been a worthy sacrifice to him.

And so it was game time. The smell of pinesap from the towering trees bordering the outfield fence competed with the enticing smell of hotdogs cooking in the concession stand, a true aroma of baseball. Bubblegum popped like soft balloons across the dugout, Bazooka Joe's the gum of choice. The late-afternoon sun began to disappear behind the trees beyond the right field fence, and the sky darkened to a royal blue.

Joe stepped up to the plate to start the game that would be his last on Earth. Eddie Roberson threw the first pitch for Buddy's Shell Station, and the game was under way. Joe lined a double to right center field. The dugout erupted. The bleachers cheered. I stepped on deck, swinging two bats. Cary Gilliam grounded out to the second baseman but advanced Joe to third. I walked to the plate, and a familiar voice called out.

"Chase!"

I turned slightly towards the bleachers and saw Sylvester sitting on the first row.

"Hit one out."

Not again!

I tipped my helmet and stepped in the box. With the fear of Sylvester emerging again, like that first time, I passed on the 'never swing at the first pitch, Pete Rose theory' and knocked the first pitch over the center field fence. Chills ran through my spine as I circled the bases. It felt like the first time all over again. There's something about hitting a homerun that is hard to match, on or off the ball field. When it happens, it's like a bolt of lightning where, in one swing, you've just brought the game to its knees, and the whole baseball world stands and watches you round the bases. The game becomes yours, for just a brief moment.

When I stepped on home plate, my teammates circled round me, smacking me on the shoulder and helmet. I raised my index and middle finger to the bill of my helmet, saluting Sylvester. I glanced to the top of the bleachers, spotting Vicki, cute as could be, flashing a quick wave at me. Caught off guard, I managed a semi-smile.

Seconds later, Vicki looked puzzled as she obviously noticed my smile disappear. Dad was on the hill behind the bleachers, struggling to maintain balance. He used the top row of the wooden bleachers for support, and his shaking hand pulled a lit match towards the cigarette barely hanging onto his lip. The game faded to gray as I watched Dad struggle to stand.

Mom turned around. She shifted nervously on the bleacher, as though pondering whether to escort Dad home or ignore him and hope he'd stand harmlessly behind the bleachers. She looked at me, motioning with her finger for me to turn around and focus on the game. Coach Cooper, as if realizing my frustration, walked up to me and gave me a slight tug on my cap. "It'll be okay, son."

My team finished our turn at bat with a two-run lead, and the guys sprinted to their positions. I sauntered confidently towards the mound. The pitcher was the only player who walked to his position, conserving energy, as he was likely to throw over 100 pitches through the course of a game. I threw every day as a kid, whether on the mound, at third base, pick-up games, or in my back yard.

My right arm was a human rubber band and I threw for years with no strain or pain. In high school, the years of constant throwing had caught up with me, and sometimes my elbow felt as if it were being probed by a carpenter's drill.

I struggled to clear my head from the off-field distractions. Circling the hill of the mound, I stepped to the rubber from behind. Both feet toeing the mound, I took a deep breath and looked across the busy bleachers. The umpire reached into a navy blue pouch looped on his belt, pulled out a shiny new ball, and tossed it to my outstretched glove. The heat of the June afternoon abated. Cotton clouds formed a soft red and purple curtain in the western sky as the sun disappeared for the night.

Artie was crouched and ready for warm-up throws.

I rocked back slightly, my glove in front of my chest, my right hand hidden in the glove, gripping the ball. Lifting my left leg, I rotated my body so my chest faced third base. I extended my left leg toward the plate, twisting my body as my right arm whipped forward, releasing the ball to Artie's waiting mitt. It felt as natural as breathing.

My first pitching experience, however, had been as natural as breathing dirt.

I was seven years old, the youngest boy on the team. Pitcher Lamar Swanson had struggled mightily, and the coach, whose name I can't recall, looked over at third and motioned for me to come to the mound. It had been my first chance to pitch in a game.

My first three warm up pitches had sailed over the catcher's head and hit the backstop. I remember being so jacked up I couldn't focus on throwing to the mitt. I had caught a glance of Mom in the stands with a terrified look on her face. She'd seemed to sense disaster. Where had her faith gone? After I had finished my warm up throws, I could tell the coach was having second thoughts, wanting to send me back to third and saving me the agony of looking like a fool. Who could blame him with the melon balls I had thrown? But I knew it was my chance, and I wasn't going to fail.

The batter had stepped to the plate on that late spring afternoon, taken a couple of nervous practice swings, undoubtedly concerned whether my first pitch was bound for his body. I reared back and let it fly. When the ball hummed across the plate, the batter had taken a huge cut, missing for strike one. The next eight pitches had had the same result and I struck out all three batters. As I'd run to the dugout, my coach and teammates had converged to congratulate me. I remember looking at the bleachers and the parents patting Mom on the back as well. At that moment, I had known what I was born to do.

"Batter up," yelled the umpire.

As I stood on the mound, I reflected on the great players who had stepped on the field before me. I was five when I began watching baseball games at Belmont. The players I watched, and later tried to emulate, to follow in their footsteps, were heroes to me. When I was six, the All-Star team from Belmont had made it the championship game of the World Series. They had been the epitome of what a ball players were all about. And, as I stood on the mound, preparing to throw the first pitch, I was doing it for Raymond, Hank, Bill, Jim, Bucky, and the rest of the boys that had made me want to be the best baseball player to ever play the game.

James O'Grady stepped into the batter's box, touching the center of the plate with the end of his thirty-one ounce, black-and-tan Louisville slugger. I challenged him, bringing high heat to the inside portion of the plate. James swung and missed.

"Steee-rike one," the umpire, Bert Canon, belted out. Bert drove a cement truck for a living, and some days his hands and neck looked like he was part statue.

My second pitch was a low fastball on the outside corner, dead-even with Artie's right kneecap. "Steee-rrrike two." James' fingers tightened around the handle of his bat, and I could see the tension in his eyes. I had him where I wanted him. He slid closer to the plate, looking for another fastball, low-and-away.

I slid the knuckle of my ring finger under the seam of the ball and aimed directly for James' head. He pulled his upper body away from the plate to avoid getting beaned. The curveball dipped downward and moved towards the center of the plate, popping into Artie's mitt. James shook his head, caught completely off guard by the breaking ball.

"Steee-rrrike three!" Bert shouted, holding his clenched right fist in the air.

The next batter, a slender lefty named Ray Greene, stepped to the plate. He fared no better, looking at a called third strike after fouling off the first two pitches. Like a gunslinger, I held my right hand at my side as I waited for the next batter to step in the box. Strong-hitting Roscoe Stillman popped the first pitch, a fastball on the inside corner, knee high, to shallow left for out number three. I walked off the mound stone-faced, eyes fixed on the dugout as my teammates jogged ahead. I walked off the field like I owned it.

After three innings, we led 3-0. I had held Buddy's to one hit, a single to right field in the bottom of the second. Dad was still behind the bleachers, leaning on them for support. I could see his eyes strain to focus on what was going on inside the white lines of the field.

Joe and I sat side-by-side in the dugout as the top half of the fourth inning began. Ricky sneaked up behind us, tapping the cyclone fence with a stick. "Chase," he said softly. "Want a piece of gum?" He opened his left hand and had four pieces of gum that were tiny baseballs the size of marbles. Each had a baseball term printed on it, such as 'Home Run', or 'Triple.'

"Yeah, thanks," I replied, reaching my thumb and forefinger through the rectangular opening of the fence. Ricky slipped two pieces into my fingers while popping a gigantic bubble. "Thanks little bro." We exchanged smiles.

"Give me some of that gum, you little turd," Rusty demanded from the corner of the dugout.

I gave Rusty a mean look. "Hey, shut your mouth."

"Whoa," Rusty said to me. "I was just having some fun."

I looked at Ricky. "He didn't mean anything by it."

"He better be glad I'm on this side of this fence," Rick said, "'cause I'd Kung Fu his ass."

The dugout broke into laughter, and even Rusty cracked a smile.

"Easy, Tiger," I said, and noticed Vicki looking towards the dugout. "Hey Rick, do me a favor. Take this piece of gum to that girl sitting on the fourth row, okay?"

Turning towards the bleachers, Rick said, "The one with the pink ribbon?"

"That's the one. Will you?"

"Sure. She's pretty. She your girlfriend?"

"A long time ago. Anyways, tell her the gum costs a kiss."

Rick, gum in hand, climbed the bleachers and sat next to Vicki. I watched from the dugout. Ricky placed the gum in Vicki's hand and they talked briefly. Opening the wrapper, she placed the gum in her mouth. She leaned towards Rick and kissed him lightly on the cheek. Rick smiled, giving me the thumbs up sign.

Talk about a major league backfire.

The game entered the bottom of the sixth with us leading 5-0. I was three outs away from throwing a one-hit shutout. While walking to the mound, I wondered if I would ever get an opportunity to pitch again.

I struck out the first two batters. Richie Gravino, the only boy to reach base for Buddy's, stepped into the box. I led off with a curveball down and away, which Richie hacked at unsuccessfully. My second pitch was low and on the inside corner, freezing Richie for strike two. Deciding on another curveball, Richie fouled it high and out of play. I took off towards the first base dugout as the ball drifted to the right side of the field. My eyes fixed on the ball, I moved closer to the dugout. As the ball made its way down, I realized it was heading straight to the tin roof of the dugout. In full stride, I leapt into the fence, pushing upward as the toe of my left cleat dug into the cyclone fence. I sprung up above the roof of the dugout, extended my left arm, twisting downward with my thumb and exposing the web of the glove. The ball landed in the pocket for out number three.

The bleachers erupted as I slid back down the fence. Joe was the first to reach me, and we embraced tightly. It would be our last.

"Great game, man," I said. "You're the best." I struggled to contain my emotions.

"Yeah, you too," Joe responded. "You'll always be my best friend."

Our eyes locked as our teammates patted us on our shoulders. When we separated, Joe nodded slightly. "It's okay, man. Everything's okay." At that moment I really felt as though he had returned from the grave to meet me on my journey back. It was if he knew it was time for me to return home and his soul to the heavens. I know, it's kind of creepy, but it sure felt that way to me.

We shook hands with the other team and walked down to the left field corner. Coach Cooper rehashed the game, again acknowledging all who contributed to victory.

We always received a free soda after the game from the concession stand. It was a great way to celebrate a win, and it felt good to stand in line at the back door of the concession stand for the paper cup full of fountain soda and crushed ice.

Usually, one of the concession workers would work the back door, serving us our hard-earned drinks. Concession workers were family members of the players and, occasionally, a volunteer who had no ties to the league, but who just wanted to help.

Mom had been coordinator of the concession stand for six years. I had assumed there would be perks from having her in charge of concessions—an occasional free hotdog, a couple of pieces of bubble gum, maybe a candy bar. But, sadly, fringe benefits hadn't come into play. If anything, it had been the other way around. Instead of receiving free food, I had to help clean the concession stand at the end of each week. The belief that it paid to know people in a position of power had held no weight. It hadn't been much of a position, and it came with little power.

We lined up, single-file, as the concession stand door swung open. The worker assigned to hand out drinks was Ralphie Mills, one of the goofiest boys in the neighborhood. He had no ties to the league but seemed to think he was a necessary cog in the concession stand wheel. He was our age yet carried on as if he were an adult. He had no time for frivolity.

Life was serious and demanded a take-charge kind of guy like him. An extremely chubby boy, with a flat top and thick, black, horn-rim glasses, Ralph would walk the streets of the neighborhood by day in his scout uniform, arms behind his back, his fingers entwined. He was constantly on patrol, keeping mayhem in check.

"Okay, here's the deal," Ralphie called out, his hand clutching the back door. "I want single-file, and I want it done in an orderly fashion. No pushing, no shoving, and no cutting in line. If I see you cutting, I'll move you to the back of the line so fast your head will spin."

"Pipe down, Ralphie, and don't spill our sodas," Rusty said.

We burst out laughing and Ralphie's pudgy face turned red.

"If I hear any more wisenheimer cracks like that, I'll shut the door and you'll get no refreshments."

"Aye, aye, sir," Cary said, extending a salute.

"You just earned yourself a spot at the back of the line," Ralphie said as he pointed in semi-circle fashion.

We were in stitches as Cary, teeth clenched, mumbled unknown words of kindness, and walked to the back of the line. "I'm gonna buy a snow cone just so I can shove it up his left nostril," Cary said. "It'd be worth the dime. His nose is big enough to handle it, that's for sure."

Ralphie distributed the drinks, giving Cary a disgusted look when he handed him his.

We took our drinks to the bleachers to rehash the game and solve the world's problems. I looked towards the parking lot, watching Dad struggle to make it to his car. My teammate's chatter faded. I couldn't change Joe's fate, but I could my father's. As emotions swirled through me, my thoughts were many: how to help Dad, wishing somehow Joe wasn't about to die, wanting Mom to enjoy life, spending more time with Bobby and Rick, and missing my family in the future.

Longing to stay at the ball field, I felt protected by its security. But I knew I was the one who needed to start providing security.

Chapter Twelve

I was in a deep sleep, caught in a dream unfolding in slow motion where I pursued a vision of Mom through a field of luminous purple daffodils and white tulips underneath a sky of gold. I had never given much thought to whether I dreamed in color, but in this dream, there was no doubt — colors I'd never seen before. In the dream, Mom stood in the middle of the knee-high flowers and, with her eyes, she was calling me to come to her. Though I ran as fast as I could, she drifted further and further away. She reached her hand to me but the distance between us grew by the second. Her age was that of her final days. Her hair was white as snow, and the wrinkles on her face told the tale of a lifelong journey. I cried out to her, and her smile invited me to join her in the distant land that waited. I reached my hand to her and, when I knew I couldn't catch her, I cried out. My heart ached as the distance grew between us, and she faded into the golden sky.

I awoke in a cold sweat and wiped my tears with the tip of my bed sheet. I tiptoed to Mom's bedroom and rubbed my fingers against her forearm. I leaned my head to her chin and felt her rhythmic breath against my cheek. My goodness, how I loved that precious woman. How was I going to make it when I returned to the future without her? I'm glad she didn't awaken to tears streaming down my face as I watched her sleep.

My time with her was not through just yet.

It was soon morning and the sun wrestled me from a deep sleep. I slowly rolled my lids back like a retreating ocean wave, my blue eyes trying to focus. My head perfectly still, my eyes began to glance about the room. I looked at the old felt pennants, in two rows of four, tacked onto the wall above the cherry desk. Many childhood nights, as I had read stories of the Revolutionary War, memorized multiplication tables, and written journals of summer vacations, the pennants would call my name. I would stare at them, fantasizing about the day I would play for one of those teams.

My wall covered a broad spectrum of colors, pennants from the bright red of Cincinnati to the pale brown-and-gold of Cleveland, from the royal blue of Los Angeles to the blue-and-white pin stripes of New York. I looked at the autographed baseball, perched high on the bookshelf, cradled by a gold-cased glove that Hank Aaron had penned one August day when I was eleven. Next to the ball lay the four ball caps I had worn through my Little League days. The bill on each cap was bent in the shape of a rainbow, perfectly symmetrical.

I slid the crumpled sheet and bedspread off my left leg and kicked the bed frame of the bunk above me. "Wake up Ricky." Silence from above. "Hey, wake up."

Sliding off the warm sheets, I stood slowly. Rick's bed lay empty, and I knew the cereal bandit was pilfering and pillaging the pantry. Known to put away an entire box if he had nothing better to do, Rick was the Great White of the breakfast table.

Passing by Bobby's room, I noticed Bob's limp body curled up underneath his covers, which meant he had a day off from the grocery store. Dad had already left for work and Mom no doubt was chatting somewhere down the street with a neighbor.

As I poured *Count Chocula* into my bowl, I schemed of a way to talk with Dad, somehow, someway, one-on-one. I decided a fishing trip would be the perfect setting, just me and him, side by side, stationary and away from obstacles. I picked up the black-handled receiver of the rotary phone in the dining room. Holding the phone was like holding an old, steel iron. It was better suited as a weapon. Of course, I couldn't remember Dad's number, but I did remember that Mom kept an index card taped under the base of the phone with important numbers. If you can still remember your father's work number after a quarter century, good for you.

"Hey, Dad. I'm sorry to bother you at work, but I was wondering if we could go fishing this evening. Just the two of us."

"Tonight? Let's wait till the weekend."

"Robbie told me that they caught two dozen rock bass last night." Okay, I lied. But if I had to resort to falsehoods, it was something I felt I had to do.

"Well, let's see how things are when I get home. But, yeah, I guess we can. I need to get back to work now."

"Great. See you tonight."

I looked in the storage room tucked away in the corner of the back porch to make sure the fishing rods and tackle box were accounted for. Dad kept them neatly tucked away in their own wooden casing. Removing two spin rods, I tugged on the hooks to make sure they were securely tied to the line. The rods and tackle box were placed carefully beside the back porch door.

The bait shop would supply the minnows, so the only other concern left to worry about was supper. Stopping at a restaurant would be out of the question for two reasons. First, it would cut into precious daylight, and second, it wasn't allowed. We only ate 'outdoorsman' food when we went on fishing expeditions. You know, the non-perishable crap that came in metal containers. My stomach began to churn, like I'd smelled a dead cat, as I recalled the dinner lineup we'd be eating. Wasn't fishing supposed to be fun? If so, who in the world decided Vienna sausages, potted meat, sardines, pickled pigs feet, and extra-dry soda crackers would make the trip worthwhile?

I remember the first time I had read the ingredients in potted meat and wondered why I hadn't developed a desire to bark and pee on fire hydrants. It had been bad enough reading the listed ingredients, but it had been really scary to wonder what the 'meat byproduct' category consisted of, and why that category was even needed. I'd just known it meant there was a testicle in there somewhere.

I walked back in the kitchen, praying that I could help Dad get a grip on his problem with the bottle. I was just beginning to feel good about the situation, that my trip back in time was for a higher purpose, when Mom walked in and burst my bubble big time.

"Brush your teeth, and comb your hair," she said. "We leave for the dentist in fifteen minutes."

Ricky looked up from what was most likely his fifth bowl of cereal, overtaken by fear. "That's bull crap," he whispered.

That was pretty dang funny, but the consequences of where we were headed killed the humor in Ricky's comment.

"Come on, Mom," I said. "Reschedule. Please don't make us go."

"Going to the dentist isn't that bad," she responded.

"Not bad?" I rhetorically asked. "It ranks up there with bamboo shoots in finger nails and unclogging prostate glands."

"You're so silly," she laughed.

I hoped my wit would be enough to change her mind, but she was too tough a nut to crack.

The ride to the dentist was deathly quiet. I looked out the window, wishing I could switch places with people we passed who were *not* on their way to the dentist. As a kid, I couldn't think of anything more traumatic. Growing up, I never had a broken bone, or the first stitch. I had several close calls, as all boys do, but had dodged just enough bullets to avoid hospital trips. In the big scheme of things, a trip to the dentist was insignificant, only not to us, since our dentist was Captain Pain.

"Mom, can you turn on the radio?" I asked, hoping some 70's music would ease my mind. I peeled my legs off the plastic seat cover and leaned forward from the back seat. The sounds of Benny Goodman weren't going to cut it.

"Aw, mom, do we have to listen to this garbage?" Ricky asked from the front seat.

There weren't many choices in those days. In our little town we had Big Band, Top Forty—bubblegum music as Dad called it—and Country. There was also just one station for each format. When Dad was behind the wheel, Big Band was the only choice.

"I guess we can change the station," Mom said. When I heard America sing 'Lonely People,' the ride became a little better.

Mom found an empty parking space in the first row of the small asphalt lot beside the dentist's office. Rick and I climbed out with little to no enthusiasm. The smell of Novocain brought instant nausea to the pit of my gut when Mom opened the creaky white door in the lobby. Slowly, we climbed the creepy, hardwood stairs to the second floor. Mom carried on small talk with the receptionist as she signed her precious boys up on the 'jolly good time' register. Ricky looked at me and shook his head.

"You go first," Ricky whispered.

"Oh, no. Age before beauty." I wanted to delay the inevitable for as long as possible, just in case I awoke from my journey first.

"Ricky Watson," the receptionist called out as she opened the door that would lead to 'The Chair.'

"Oh, joy," Ricky muttered, rising slowly, looking like a man being led away to a life sentence of hard prison labor. Within minutes, I heard the whirl of the drill. Poor Ricky was getting his, and I knew I wasn't far behind.

If only I had flossed more, I thought as Mom flipped through a copy of *Life* magazine.

I spied a cutie with long blonde hair smiling from across the room. Normally, the sight of a pretty gal would cause me to perk right up, but not then. Not on dentist day. She frowned and slowly shook her head at how my surely unpleasant expression broadcast a not too subtle message of 'leave me alone.'

Minutes seemed like days as I tried to occupy my mind with happy thoughts. Time flew like a lead balloon, as I was unable to block out the impending pain waiting like grim death on the other side of the door. Ricky eventually walked out, shoulders hunched, head lowered. He had survived, but knew he was only six short months away from coming back for more.

"Chase, you want to come on back?" the receptionist asked.

"Is this a trick question?" I responded.

Ricky shook his head when I walked by, unable to make eye contact. I patted him on the head as he sat down. No words were shared. What was there to say?

The receptionist placed her hand on my shoulder. I took a deep breath when I slipped into the chocolate, vinyl chair. On the tray beside the chair were the tools that would soon probe, pick, and yank on my choppers. The scariest weapon, uh, tool, was the syringe that contained the Novocain. It was long, made of cold steel, and required two hands to hold.

"Hello, Chase," said a deep-voiced Dr. Belton. "Have you been taking good care of your teeth?" I nodded, zombie-like. "Well, why don't we take a little peek just to be sure?" Dr. Belton snatched a handful of tools. With a gleam in his eyes, he slowly pulled down my lower lip, anxiously in search of a cavity.

I'm a grown man. This guy doesn't scare me anymore.

Within a couple of minutes Dr. Belton hit pay dirt.

"Hmmm," he said, poorly hiding his joy. "We got one. Let's just fix 'er right now."

He left the room, soon returning with his nurse, a stocky gal who looked more suited for playing linebacker in the NFL than tending to the delicate needs of dental patients. She picked up the syringe, squirted a tiny amount, and flicked the excess off the end of the needle with her thick, middle finger. I thought her only true duty was to hold me down so Dr. Belton could mine for gold. When he came in the room and took the syringe, he flashed some morbid grin. He yanked my lower lip and I tried to remain calm.

He can't hurt me. He can't hurt me.

The needle inched closer to the gum.

He can't hurt me.

The cold steel handle touched my lip. *He can't hurt...* I was telling myself when the needle penetrated deep inside the gum, driving downward towards my tonsils, and I mentally screamed *...youuuuuuu mother!*

My jaw, writhing in pain as if gored with a pick ax, throbbed with each beat of my heart as sweat surfaced along the edges of my hairline. Slowly, the needle was withdrawn. Very slowly.

Step one done.

The smell of burning enamel soon filled the air. I took two deep breaths. I wanted to tell Dr. Belton a well-known tip — Novocain worked best when given time to take effect. Once again, my lower lip was yanked and four pieces of gauze, each roughly the size of a ballpark hotdog, were forced inside my mouth, two on either side of my gum. Dr. Evil next inserted his silver-handled drill in my mouth, and smoke began to rise toward the rectangular light above the chair that burned a hole in my retina. Blinded and drilled. Insult to injury. I tried to clue in Dr. Belton that the Novocain sat dormant in my lower jaw, but was unable because the gauze, drill, and his chubby fingers filled my mouth.

Within seconds, the drill hit a major nerve and my body started to heave as if I was having a seizure. Like a scene out of *One Flew Over the Cuckoo's Nest*, Nurse Ratchett pushed down on my arms to prevent me from moving. She may have been female, but she was no lady. As she pinned me, I vowed to find her in the future.

After what seemed like hours, the nurse and Dr. Belton retreated. Sweating profusely, they wore a look of victory. The nurse left, quickly returning with a metal case.

"Here Chase, pick out a ring," she said. The ring was a 'prize' for surviving the pain and punishment. They were made of silver aluminum, containing a brightly colored 'stone.' Whoopty-do. The Hope diamond was more appropriate for what I'd endured.

I went back to the waiting room where Ricky sat, still teary-eyed.

"Now that wasn't so bad now, was it?" Mom asked.

"It was a thin slice of heaven," I answered. "Let's get out of here before they call us back for more."

We were relieved to have survived the ordeal. I'm glad I'd wised up enough to realize six months of half-ass tooth brushing made for a miserable time come dentist day, especially if Dr. Belton was the one holding the drill. Sometimes I wake in a cold sweat, dreaming that I'm back in that chocolate, vinyl chair.

As our old clunky Plymouth pulled into the driveway that day, Ricky touched his lower lip. "Oh, great. The Novocain just kicked in."

Too little, too late.

That reminds me—I need to track down Nurse Ratchett.

Chapter Thirteen

I removed my glove and a baseball from the sports basket on the back porch. I walked across the patio and stopped in the shade cast by a wisteria-laden pine. Gripping the seams of the scuffed ball, I looked carefully at the almond-colored rawhide, knowing it had seen its fair share of base hits and fastballs. No matter how old and battered a baseball was, it felt a part of me when I held it. I've always thought every ball had one more strike left to throw, one more homerun left to hit, one more double play to turn.

The sun was midway through its descent to the base of the western sky, and I knew Dad would soon be home. I rehearsed the things I wanted to say to him while we fished. I walked to the center of the back yard to a spot clear of the trees. I removed the ball from my glove. Lowering my right shoulder until it was almost perpendicular to the ground, like a javelin thrower aiming for the clouds, I threw the ball skyward with all my might. I positioned myself under the return flight of the ball, and when the ball found the bottom of my leather glove, a 'pop' echoed across the yard.

I repeated the process over and over into the quiet sky, going over the list of things I wanted to talk to Dad about. I came to realize the sole purpose of going back in time was not just to spend time with Mom again, but to right the wrong I'd committed by passively watching Dad, and Mom, struggle. And so, the success, or failure of the fishing trip, in my mind, might determine whether the journey back was more than just a chance to walk down memory lane.

I continued to throw the ball in the air, the only other sound competing with the pop of the rawhide in the yard a mockingbird perched atop a holly.

I looked about the yard, and it was stamped with Dad's caring touch. I looked at the shuffleboard game he'd made. I remember watching him meticulously measuring out the correct length, digging up the ground so that the concrete truck could fill the empty cavity bordered by 2 X 4's to make the surface just perfect. He'd painted the grids himself, and it had been so well crafted. I looked at both basketball goals and recollected the time he had taken to make the backboards and drill the goals into the backboards.

He'd carefully measured to make sure the first goal was regulation size, ten feet high. He had measured the second goal at 8'6" so that we could dunk the ball and feel like we were NBA players. And then I looked at Mandy in her kennel, lying in the shade, watching my every move, and I remembered the time and effort Dad had put into building the kennel for me so that Mandy would have a home and security so that she couldn't wander off at night. He had done so much for us. So very much, and there was no way he would have if he hadn't had a deep love for us.

I heard him pull up in the family wagon and I returned my glove and ball to the basket.

"Hey, Dad, everything's ready."

"Let me pack a few things in the cooler," Dad answered.

"It's ready."

Dad probably assumed that meant a six-pack, but he was wrong. He changed while I tried to convince Ricky he didn't need to make the trip.

"I'm going too," Rick pleaded while changing shoes in the bedroom. "I'll ask Dad. He'll let me go."

"I have to go alone with him. I can't explain why."

"You can't explain why because you're an idiot."

"Ease up, junior."

"I guess you're captain of the bass patrol. Where's your badge, captain?"

"Bend over and I'll show you."

"That's it. It's 'go' time."

Rick took a swipe at my chin. I ducked and lifted him off the ground by the waist. I flung him over my shoulder and walked to the closet, where I dropped him onto the closet floor and shut the door.

"Stay in there awhile," I said as I placed my foot against the door.

Rick kicked the door. "Let me out or I'll kick the door down!"

With one foot pressed against the door I reached and grabbed the desk chair, sliding it up against the doorknob at an angle. "That ought to hold you."

"Open this door or it will be the biggest mistake of your life." He shook that door like it was going to come off the hinges.

I walked outside the bedroom and met Dad in the kitchen. "We better get moving." Grabbing the bag of food, I said, "Mom, how about you let Ricky out of his closet in five minutes."

She looked at me peculiarly but I didn't have time to explain.

We were out the door and off to catch the big one. It was a thirty-minute ride to Lake Chapin. There was an odd stretch of silence as we left the neighborhood. I wanted it to be a great time, and was pressing hard on what to say to get the conversation going.

"Who taught you how to fish?" I finally asked. It was all I could come up with at the time.

Dad scratched his chin with one hand while his other held the wheel at twelve o'clock. "My dad."

"How old were you?"

"I guess I was about seven, maybe eight. You remember how close we lived to Spears Creek? It rolled below the farm a few hundred yards from the house."

"Must have been great to be able to fish in walking distance of the house."

"That creek was loaded with so many trout, all we had to do was stand by the water with a net. They'd literally leap onto the bank."

"Really?"

"If you didn't have a net all you had to do was hold your pant pockets open."

"Riiiight."

As far as fishing aesthetics went, Dad couldn't have had it any better. Spears Creek was a spring-fed stream that flowed through the heart of Doe Valley in the Blue Ridge Mountains of East Tennessee. I had got to walk the banks of the creek in my childhood with my father, and I still do so to this day.

Sometimes I walk it alone. And each time I do I feel a closeness to my dad and to my uncles, my grandfathers. I walk the banks they had walked many years ago, and I imagine what they felt, what they thought, when they'd walked those same steps. I know that who I am is, in part, because of who they were, and I wonder what they'd think of how I turned out. I had only got to know a few of them, and I knew them to be a tough but courageous bunch. Tough, but honest to a fault they were. And I sometimes wish I had more of their toughness, more of their courage. They were rugged mountain men, and I am not. But that doesn't stop me from feeling in my soul a deep kindred spirit.

Spears Creek ran fast and shallow, hugging the sloping mountainside, winding through plush valleys of saw grass. Brown and gray rocks lined the floor, scattered on the bottom like marbles. Large rocks looked strategically placed along the bank, and boulder-size rocks split the path of the rushing water in two. Though the water ran hard for the most part, there were certain elbows of the creek where slow, deep pools slipped over tiny waterfalls.

"Can you remember that first time when your dad took you?"

"I can't remember what I ate for dinner yesterday, but I remember everything about that day. It was early morning. Fall time of the year. I can still remember how warm the sun felt on my shoulders while my toes froze in the creek."

A certain excitement arose in Dad's voice as he recounted the tale, and I looked intently at the details of his face. His dark hair, parted razor straight on the left side, was neatly combed. A slight hint of Brylcreem ran along and above his temples. The lines under his eyes and upon his forehead were visible, but slight. His patented Watson blue eyes sparkled as the sun caught him without his sunglasses.

"Mom was mad at us because we were fishin' on Sunday morning," Dad continued. "'How can your mind be on God when your bait's in the creek?' she would ask. Anyway, the fog was rising off the water, hovering like a blanket. The sun was trying to make its way over the top of Iron Mountain. Dad had an old fly rod, and I stood beside him in overgrown waders watching him work it back and forth. He was aiming at the water under a willow tree on the far side of the creek. I tried a couple of times, but couldn't get the fly line to cast. So Dad would cast for me, and I'd hold the pole as the fly would float downstream."

"I sure wish I could have been there to experience it. How'd you do?"

"I had a few bites, but couldn't snag the fish's mouth when he bit. My waders felt like they were gonna fall down, but I held the pole tight with both hands. Dad kept his hands on my shoulder to make sure I didn't float downstream with the fly."

I had never seen Dad so animated while telling a story.

"So did you catch one?"

"Eventually. Dad put his hands around mine on the pole and, finally, was able to help me jerk the line when the fish took the bait. When that fish dug in, it felt like I had Moby Dick on the other end. Dad held me, and I held the pole, and between the two of us I caught my first trout. I was so excited after I caught it that I made Dad take me home to show it to my family."

"That's' a great story. Did you get to fish a lot with Papa?"

"Not like I would have liked. He was a school principal, and he had to ride by horse and buggy several miles to the school. He'd ride off on Sunday afternoons, not long after Sunday dinner, and wouldn't come home till Friday. So, I didn't get to spend a lot of time with him. I fished more with Danny and Doc than I did with Dad."

"What was it like growing up there?"

The youngest of nine, Dad had grown up in the shadows of six brothers. He was the only one of the children who had lived on the farm throughout the Great Depression.

"It sure wasn't easy," Dad began. "But we didn't know any different. We grew or raised most of the food we ate. We had to get up way before the sun."

I smiled as Dad spoke of chopping wood and trudging through the snow to school each day, as it was a story repeated often to my brothers and me so we'd realize how easy we had it. Interestingly enough, Mom hadn't endured as grueling a daily schedule, even though she'd grown up just three miles away from Dad. Could it be that he was fudging just a hair? Surely not. I had actually tried to use Dad's story on my children, but they hadn't bought it. They knew my school was only five blocks from my house, and that snow fell in our town along the same frequency as an Elvis sighting.

By the time he'd finished his fishing story, we arrived at the bait shop, located a couple miles from the lake. Minnows were our bait of choice for catching rock bass, and I carried the metal minnow bucket inside the tiny store. The dark, dank shop was stocked with worms, crickets, minnows, soft drinks, chips, and beer.

On the wall behind the register was a calendar of June 1972. It had a picture of a pretty woman wearing overalls and holding an oil can. Rembert's Auto Parts was written under her picture. June 1972. It was as if each and every month had blown off the calendar from the present backwards before my eyes. What day was it? I tried to calculate it as I'd not given thought to the exact day that I was in at that moment. It didn't really matter, I guess.

The owner, short, with a pot belly, was old and crusty. His face was tanned and weathered, with deep wrinkles intertwined like a road map. His hands smelled like discarded fish heads.

The minnows were kept in a small pond beside the shop, and I followed behind the old man like a new puppy. "How 'bout you hold that bucket for me," he said. Bending down slowly, the man placed his right knee on the reed-covered bank and lowered a rusty metal handle containing a small mesh net into the pond. He scooped the unsuspecting minnows into his net from the spring-fed water. His calloused fingers seemed oblivious to the cold water. I never knew the man's name. It hadn't seemed important.

Bucket filled, the man thanked Dad for the business and wished us good luck.

The smell of red clay and driftwood filled the air when I opened the car door. The lake was dark and deep, and I was certain a gazillion fish lurked below the choppy surface. I took the minnow bucket and the poles, and Dad placed the bag of food on the camouflage metal cooler, lifting it by its metal handles.

The late afternoon sun kept the air heavy and warm, though the tall pines hugging the lake provided ample shade. Not much talking occurred on the walk to the water as I stared at the beauty of the lake. I'm sure Dad was busy looking for snakes. Just the thought of snakes kept him on edge and always on the lookout. He had been known to cut short fishing expeditions and hunting trips if a snake was spotted in close proximity. Close proximity was a three-mile radius from his feet.

"This looks like a good spot," he said, setting down the bag of crackers, sardines, and unidentifiable pork by-products.

I placed the bucket by the bag, and Dad handed me my pole.

"Thanks." I realized how much I had missed times like those. We had spent time together through the years, but it had usually been with others around. I regretted we hadn't spend more one-on-one time. I should have asked him more about his life, his childhood, his thoughts, and his dreams, the first go around. How close to reality had his dreams turned out?

I wondered what Dad's thoughts had been the first time he held me. How had it felt to hold my tiny fingers when he'd helped me learn to walk? Had it meant as much as when Bobby was a baby? After all, Bobby was the first born, so it had been something so brand new for Dad to experience.

"Watch how long it takes me to catch one," Dad said, casting his minnow far away from shore.

"We'll see about that. My guess is that you'll spend most of the evening sliding my fish on the stringer. I plan on feeding the neighborhood when we get back. I'll be like Jesus feeding the multitude, only I won't have to perform a miracle to do it."

Dad shook his head and added a little slack to his line. Within a matter of minutes, his pole started to bend. "I got one," he said, stabilizing his footing on the lumpy rocks beneath his feet. Water splashed as the silhouette of a big rock bass rose to the top. The pole bent like a banana as he smoothly reeled in the fish. The bass tried to dive into deep water, but Dad refused to let him. He pulled the fish from the water and slid his fingers inside the bass' gill, causing it to stiffen like it was mounted on the den wall.

"He's huge!" I said, pulling the stringer from the tackle box.

Dad carefully pulled the hook out of the fish's mouth, and I handed him the stringer. After he had run the long stringer cord through the fish's gill, he handed it to me.

"Put the stringer deep in the ground so the fish can't pull it out and get away."

I did just that and placed it close enough to the water so the fish was completely submerged in the lake. Dad placed another minnow on his hook and cast again.

"Now it's my turn," I said as I cast my bait. I flipped the bail and looked out at the red and white float that would alert me when a fish had taken the bait. "Hey, Dad, was it hard to leave Tennessee?"

"I never gave it much thought," he said, his eyes fixed on his float. "I started work the day after we moved to town. By the time I realized I wasn't in Tennessee anymore, we were knee-deep in baby bottles and diapers."

"Was it hard leavin' Grandma?"

Dad surveyed the water as though he was looking for the Loch Ness Monster.

"Yeah, it was. Since Dad was gone so much, and I was the youngest, most of my family was already grown up and gone. So, when I got to be a teenager, I was pretty much the only help my mom had. I didn't like being so far from her, especially if she needed me."

"Must have been hard on her, taking care of that big house and the farm."

"It was. She was a soft-spoken woman, but she was tough as nails. And she knew how to get our attention. Plus, she made it clear that Dad would whip us when he got home if need be. He had this stiff, leather strap that my backside got to know quite well. Contrary to what your mom thinks."

"Mom does love telling us that Grandma spoiled you. But I do the same about Mom spoiling Bobby. So, who were you closest to growing up?" Dad reeled in his bait, looking for signs of life from the minnow, and recast. His eyes began to tear just a bit.

"Justin. I thought he was the toughest, but kindest, person that ever lived. When he wore his uniform, he was Alexander the Great and George Patton all wrapped up into one. The best part was that he didn't treat me like the young, tag-along brother that I was."

Justin had been killed in World War II, after surviving the Bataan Death March and three years in a prisoner of war camp. The saddest part was that he'd been killed by friendly fire one month before the war ended. British war ships had bombed the mine where he had been forced to work, as they had been unaware POW's were kept there.

"How'd your family find out he died?"

"I came home from school one day. Mom was crying and holding a telegram from the Army. He was the third one in the family to die young. My brother Carter died when he was three, before I was born. And then Rafe died when he was fifteen, from meningitis."

"I can't even imagine what your family went through. How did Grandma handle losing three of her children? Was it harder on her when Carter died, him being an infant, or when Rafe and Justin died?"

"I've asked myself that question many times. You know that an infant has had his entire life taken from him, and that alone is reason to be heartbroken. But you don't get the chance to learn who he is, or fully appreciate his personality, his being. So maybe you don't grow so close or become quite so fond of him. With regards to an older child, he's at least lived a fairly good stretch. But just the comfort of being around him, learning who he is, must make it that much harder to be without. Either way, mamas aren't supposed to outlive their kids."

I was seeing a side to Dad of which I wasn't familiar. "I never thought about it that way."

"Enough about that. Hey, how about grab me a beer from the cooler?"

"I got something better." I grabbed a soft drink and held it up for him to see.

"I guess a Pepsi will do," he said as he added slack to his line.

How about that? I presented the option, and he took it, though I admit I was caught off guard by his response. So much so, that I dropped the bottle opener into the lake. I quickly dipped my hand in, snatching it before it sunk to the clay bottom.

"Sure wish these were screw off caps," I commented.

"What? How can you screw off a metal cap from a glass bottle?"

I'd messed up again. You'd think I would have figured out how to keep my mouth shut with regards to things that pertained to the future. Instead, I pointed to the water. "Catfish! Must be the size of my leg."

Dad turned and looked at the calm water. "I don't see anything."

"He must have headed for the bottom." The diversion away from the screw off caps worked. "Oh, here's your Pepsi."

Dad took the bottle, tilted his head, and took a drink. "I forgot how good this stuff tastes."

"Not bad, huh? Hey, let me know when you want something to eat. I brought all your favorites."

"I'm good right now."

"Tell me again why we eat this garbage when we fish."

"I don't really know. Tradition, I guess."

"Tradition is good, but I wouldn't mind a piece of chicken every once in a while, would you?"

"No, I wouldn't. In fact, I could go for some right now."

"Next time."

The fishing adventure flew by. Dad, as usual, caught most of the fish. I spent the evening unsuccessfully casting my bait at the spot where Dad snagged an increasing load of bass. In between, I got to place his catches on the fish stringer.

"I think my rod's defective," I announced. "Either that, or the fish are chatting with my bait instead of eating it."

"Maybe it's a good thing it's defective," Dad said with a smile. "It's freed you up to string my catches."

"You're a comedian."

The long shadows of the tall pines stretched fast across the water as nightfall loomed. We decided to call it a day, and we loaded the fish into the cooler. The Vienna sausage and sardine cans were bagged and thrown away. Smelling of rock bass and processed pork, we walked to the car as a cool breeze blew off the dark water. Crickets serenaded. In that moment, I felt a closeness to Dad that I had never felt before or since.

Chapter Fourteen

If the world is a stage, as the saying goes, who writes the script? God? If so, is the script ever-changing based on His desires? Do we write our own? Has the play already been written, with a carefully planned set of actors to complete each act on the stage of our lives? Is the stage interchangeable, where we participate in the plays of others while starring in our own?

I don't think our scripts have been written, and that they change dependent upon the paths we choose, the choices we make, and with the people that come into our lives. Each script is unique to our heart and soul, though we share a kindred spirit in knowing we all walk a path, and all have to act out our own script. Maybe it's free will that God grants us so the responsibilities of the script fall on our lap after he places it there. Growing up, my family, friends, teachers, coaches, and neighbors had been the actors on my stage. And the stage had been the school, the baseball field, and our backyards. Belmont had been such a unique place to grow up. We'd been in on a secret that I think outsiders never could understand.

As much as we look forward to growing up, to experiencing life on our own, there's something a bit sad about leaving the nest. Not initially, I believe, but as time marches on, the feeling sometimes creeps into the recesses of our brains. I look back fondly at the years growing up, knowing that Mom and Dad had been there to take care of me, protect me. They'd provided that blanket of love and, by doing so, allowed me to be a kid. Adulthood can be a long, hard journey, and there is something to be said for allowing children to experience their youth, remain in their innocence, because when we grow up, it's hard to keep that innocence in our hearts.

And so, waking up that morning, still in the past, I drew once more on the warmth of childhood. I drew on the solitude of protection, when things were new and innocent. I noticed the sun was well up in the eastern sky. I had not realized Rick's bed was empty, and suddenly I felt like I was the last one on earth to get up. I stopped in front of the living room window, smiling at the peaceful neighborhood that I had taken for granted as a child.

The shrill of the rotary phone screamed across the house as if it were an emergency broadcast signal alerting us that a natural disaster was imminent.

"Chase, the phone's for you," Mom said from the dining room.

"Hello." The word came from my mouth groggily since it was the first word I'd spoken since the night before.

"You just now getting out of bed?" Robbie asked. Robbie rose daily with the chickens.

"Yep."

"Why?"

"I'm pacing myself."

"Listen, Van Winkle, we're going skating tonight. You in?"

"Let me ask." I placed the phone against my hip. "Mom?"

"What is it, Chase?" she answered from the back porch.

"Being the sweet, lovely, mother that you are…"

"What do you want?"

"Can I go skating with Robbie tonight?"

"Hmmmmm," she said, after a brief pause. She had always used the brief pause for effect. "Why should I let you go?"

"Robbie's got a couple of Asian hookers lined up. We thought they might like to skate before they have their way with us."

Mom leaned her head around the doorway and cut a stare split between anger and puzzlement.

Uh-oh. The adult humor comment had been aimed at the wrong audience.

"Maybe a little time confined to your room is what you need."

"Ha, just kidding! I was only trying to loosen you up a little bit. You know, add a little humor to your day."

"That's not the kind of humor I need."

"I'm sorry. Can I still go?"

After a long pause, "I guess."

Pulling the receiver back to my chin, I said, "I'm in. What time?"

"We'll pick you up at 6:30."

"Don't pick me up. I'll walk to your house."

"Huh?"

"Yep. I prefer to walk. See the neighborhood."

"Suit yourself. See you tonight."

The skating rink had been the first exposure I'd had spending time with the fairer sex in a setting involving music and soft lighting. It was puppy love palace, and just the mere prospect of holding a girl's hand had brought a rush. Plus, it was as close to dating as a twelve-year-old could get. I hadn't cared much for skating. In fact, I'd sucked at it. But, if that's where the girls were, it had been worth the sacrifice.

The heartbeat of the rink had been the music. I'm talking cheesy, bubblegum songs from the likes of Bobby

Sherman and Tony Orlando that had blasted through giant black speakers. I would never 'fess up to liking it, but I wouldn't deny it either. Regardless, the music had brought the blue oval floor to life while wild light patterns bounced off the giant party ball hovering above the center of the rink. Though I'd envisioned magic and romance occurring at the rink, it had never seemed to turn out that way. Not for me, anyway. It was probably a good thing, though, because if a girl had tried to hold my hand or kiss me, I'd have ended up drooling all over myself.

"Morning, Mary," Bobby said, walking from the bedroom, dressed for another day of work. "Did I hear you ask Mom if you could skate tonight? Won't that be just *precious*?"

"I'll tell you what precious is--that fruity, polyester tie of yours. Did Bozo have a yard sale?"

"This is called high fashion."

"And you call yourself a man."

"Pipe down, munchkin. Just remember to be home by eight. Don't want to miss your curfew."

"Isn't it time to carry little old ladies' groceries to their cars?"

"Whatever," Bobby said, lifting a doughnut from a glass-covered cake stand. "I'm going to hang out with the big boys and girls now."

"If your car starts."

It was time for breakfast, which had become like *Groundhog Day*, with me filling in for Bill Murray. A different morning, same scene—Ricky in his underwear, devouring cereal at the kitchen table. I thank God Rick had implemented an underwear rotation system.

"How about a poached egg and some prune juice?" I asked, hoping for some kind, any kind, of reaction from Rick as he inhaled his Lucky Charms.

Ricky shoveled through another bowl. Mom walked in from the back porch carrying a load of washed clothes that had dried on the clothesline. I loved that fresh smell of clean cotton.

"Mom, sit and eat with us," I said.

Eating breakfast at the table was a rarity, as she'd always been busy cleaning up behind four males. I fetched two bowls from the cabinet, two spoons from the drawer, and the cereal box. "Sit, and I'll fix yours."

"I really should put these clothes away," she said.

"Those clothes aren't going anywhere, but I can't say the same about the cereal. Rick'll eat it all if we don't take our share."

No response from Ricky. Mom smiled, shaking her head in certain wonder at her baby boy.

"Slow down, Ricky," she said. "It's not good to eat so fast." Her advice surely fell on deaf ears.

"It's kind of entertaining, watching him pack it in," I said.

"You know, you're right," she said as I placed a bowl in front of her. Her presence truly brightened the breakfast table. "Hey, this stuff's not bad."

"Crunchy balls of sugar and preservatives. The essentials of life."

The morning breeze slipped softly through the back porch screen-door, and the sun sparked the pines and oaks to a coating of gold, especially the underside of the pine needles. I wished I could have frozen the moment.

"Hey, Mom, it's kinda cool that you're eating with us," Ricky said, breaking years of silence at the breakfast table.

"I guess I should do it more often."

"Mom, you gotta make the most of every day," I said. I certainly had learned that was true, though it took stealing my youth before I truly understood that.

"Such wisdom from the mouth of a child. You sound like an old man reflecting back on life."

"Well, the day'll come when we won't be sitting here eating together on such an amazingly beautiful morning. I can tell you that much."

"Ever since you took that blow to your head, you seem preoccupied with aging. You act as if life has passed you by."

"That blow has opened my eyes, I'll tell you that. It's helped me realize how precious times like this really are. And we better soak in as much of it as we can because we can't keep it. Time is going to go on, and people will come and go in our lives, and all that will be left with are the experiences, the stories, and the memories."

Mom studied me for a moment, a puzzled look in her eyes. Slowly, she said, "Chase, honey, it's okay."

"No, it's not."

I took her hand. I wanted to tell her the truth. Was now the time? Would she rush me off to the doctor to get my head examined? I pictured them locking me away in a straight jacket, taking brain samples with long, sharp instruments. Just that thought was enough to deter me from telling her about the crazy time warp I was in. Still, I struggled, knowing that when the time came for me to go back to the 'future,' I wouldn't be able to see her again, at least not on Earth. When she brushed her hand through my hair, I fought back the tears.

"There's no need to cry. I'm right here, honey." She pulled me to her chest, circling me with those protective arms.

I stretched my arms around her neck. I couldn't help but picture her in that casket, and how gut-wrenching that sight had been. "But one day you won't be, and I'm gonna miss you so much. You'll only be a memory."

Ricky seemed to get caught up in the moment, and he stood and circled around the other side of the table, lifting Mom's arm. He placed his head just under her chin. She squeezed us both. "But I'm with you now, and that's all that matters."

What she said was correct, I suppose, but it was hard not to think about the future, when she would no longer be there to sooth the hard edges of life. I squeezed her hand once more, hoping it would in some way convey the love in my heart for her.

"What do you say we spend the day at Spring Lake?" she asked.

The pity party quickly faded.

Spring Lake was located east of town, and it sure beat running through the sprinkler in the back yard. The lake was basically an overgrown pond that offered up the basics: a swimming area, picnic tables, and canoeing. It had also contained the world's dumbest fish…

It was Labor Day weekend and our last trip to Spring Lake for the summer. It would have been nine months since we'd been able to swim in a body of water other than the bathtub. On that day, we stood in the morning shadows on a wooden walkway leading to a tiny dock. I remember how cool it had felt in the shade, a sign that fall was knocking on the door. The rickety boards of the dock were gray, almost colorless. Six-year old Rick had been anxious to break in a new Zebco rod-and-reel Mom had purchased with sixty-two books of Greenbax stamps. You baby boomers must surely have cashed in your stamps at the Greenbax store, the remnants of glue still on your tongue.

It had been Rick's first venture into catching something for the purpose of eating it. He'd caught his share of frogs and lizards, but none of them were captured with the intended destination of Mom's frying pan. Rick had known it would be his initiation into manhood — to become a hunter, to provide food for his family. That the food would barely cover a saltine cracker had been irrelevant.

I had struggled to push a fuzzy-legged cricket onto my fishhook, and Rick waited impatiently. His fascination with the unwilling cricket had caused him to unknowingly lower his pole, and his hook had dipped into the shallow water. Within seconds, his pole bent and, with a surprised look, I recall how he'd lifted the pole skyward. On the end of his baitless hook wiggled a bream the size of his hand. He'd then nodded, commenting, "This fishing stuff's pretty easy."

I finished my bowl of cereal. Ricky finished his fifth. The bowls were chunked in the sink, and we were off to the bedroom for swimsuits. Life was good.

I opened the top drawer of the oak chest of drawers. Choosing which suit to wear was simple, as I only had one. Living on a tight budget, as did most of the families in that day, required a streamlined wardrobe. A pair of swim trunks had only two requirements: cover private parts and dry quickly. Since trunks dried in minutes on a hot Carolina clothesline, the cover up was the only one that really mattered.

We slipped on our trunks, grabbed some towels, and Mom threw together peanut butter sandwiches, an industrial size bag of chips, and a Tupperware container filled with her homemade onion dip. The food would rank high on the taste scale for the outing, unlike the fishing trip. There would be no meat byproducts eaten on that day.

Though Spring Lake had offered up all the swimming amenities a young boy needed, it'd also provided the opportunity to check out the older, teenage lovelies. The lake had been a favorite hangout for high school girls in search of a tan and attention from the guys. It was the pre-global warming days, when ozone layers were without holes, and girls would lather themselves in baby oil like chicken legs at a barbeque. Sunscreen had been something to keep the flies off the back porch. These girls had been out of our league, but it didn't hurt to look.

The family wagon pulled onto the dusty dirt road that twisted between scrub oaks like a cottonmouth crossing a stream. The oaks were surrounded by sand, sugary to the eye but like flour to the touch. Music from the hi-fi speakers echoed up to the entrance as America sang 'Daisy Jane.' Our windows were down to help the natural air conditioner function properly. Good music, good weather, cool water, and cute girls. The car barely came to a halt and we were out the door, trying to be the first one in the water.

We made sure we wore shoes because the parking lot was lined with sand spurs. Those little meteor shaped barbs were sharper than a porcupine's quill, and to remove them required a large pair of pliers, ear plugs, and smelling salts.

"Boys, come help with the towels," I heard Mom say. Her request was for naught, as it was nothing but elbows and kneecaps as we sprinted toward the water. My excitement rendered me unable to help her. Ricky slipped slightly when I tugged on the back of his swim shorts, allowing me a slight, unfair advantage to the water. We shook off our shoes as we approached the water's edge. Running full speed into the water, our knees rose and fell like the pistons in Bobby's hot-rod, and we dove in like trained porpoises.

The tiny lake's bottom was always cold, but it was very warm at the surface. It smelled faintly of the maple and birch trees that populated most of the banks surrounding the water. Turtles sunned on the stumps that lined the back of the lake.

While we dove after each other in the water, Mom found a picnic table underneath a shade tree. She arranged the food in an easily accessible fashion. I remembered that the cooler was in the car filled with drinks. Not wanting to be a total slacker, I decided to retrieve the cooler. I slipped my shoes back on so as not to challenge the sandspurs without rubber protection. I was about to ask Mom for the keys but remembered we were in a time where doors need not be locked.

I lifted the ugly, camouflage cooler by its steel handles and slid it over the back gate of the wagon. It was as heavy as I remembered. The container was Dad's, and was usually stocked full of beer for road trips. In my childhood days, it hadn't been illegal to drink beer while driving. So, Dad had kept it in the back seat, keeping us busy by passing him cold ones to the front. Beer had been the only thing stocked. No soft drinks, no juice, and no water. One day, on a long ride to the beach, I'd pleaded for Dad to stop and get us a drink, but he didn't see the need. To shut me up, he'd offered me a sip of his beer. Taking him up on the offer, the liquid had never made it past my throat and I'd sprayed the inside of the windshield.

I lugged the cooler to the picnic table. "It always feels like we're carrying a body in this thing," I said, hoisting it onto one of the picnic benches.

"It's a heavy one all right," Mom agreed as she cut an apple. "Keep it in the shade so the drinks'll stay cold."

"Mom, this thing is so insulated it wouldn't matter if it sat on the sun, much less underneath it. These drinks will be like popsicles for days." I slipped my arms around her shoulders at the table. I couldn't resist the opportunity. "Aren't you gonna swim?"

"Maybe in a bit. I'm going to watch you boys and read a magazine."

"C'mon. You can read anytime. Swim with us."

"All right, all right," she said reluctantly. "You sure are getting bossy these days."

"I'm practicing for the future."

She hadn't swum much when we were young but, man, could she float. She was a human raft. She had tried to teach me, but perhaps I'd lacked the body fat necessary to stay buoyant. I swam like a fish but floated like a frozen dog.

Mom shed her green terrycloth swim robe and walked slowly into the water.

"Doesn't it feel great?" I asked.

"It does," she responded. "But I had forgotten how cold the bottom is."

Ricky flipped off the dock, a cross between a can opener and a cannonball. He didn't receive many style points, but did pick up a couple for effort. From the stereo speakers, 70's Top Forty tunes played, interrupted only by the sounds of happy chaps in the water. I watched Mom snatching a few moments of relaxation. Her natural beauty made her look like a movie star to me. She looked so healthy, death far away. Like it should be. She noticed me smiling, and smiled back.

"You're giving me that look," she said. "You want something, don't you? Chips? Cookies? A drink?"

"No, ma'am. How 'bout I get you something?"

"You boys have fun and I'll get the food ready."

"C'mon, Ricky," I said after he surfaced for air from the water. "Let's eat and then rent a canoe. I'll let you sit in front and we'll paddle wherever you want."

"Beat you to the picnic table," he said, splashing me.

We sprinted out of the water.

"There's no way you can beat me," I yelled as I exited the water ahead of Ricky. But, when I turned and saw the determined look in his eyes as he ran, I couldn't help but think it would be best if he won. When I 'accidentally' tripped over a pine tree root and Ricky flew by, raising his hands, I could tell he was feeling good about himself.

"Yes!" Ricky yelled. "I'm the fastest boy alive. I am *the* Kid!"

"What? The root tripped me."

"You're crazy. I beat you fair and square. And you better start getting to use it."

Mom and I exchanged smiles.

"You were lucky and you know it," I said in mock seriousness.

We sat at the picnic table which was positioned perfectly to shade the sun. The summer heat was bearing down, but I wasn't bothered at all. I wondered if it was because the heat felt good on my wet body, or whether it was because I was a kid again. For some reason, the heat and, conversely, the cold, didn't seem to bother me as a child. Thicker-skinned I supposed, as I could go all day outdoors in the summer, pleading with nightfall to stay away. And, on many blustery winter days, I would hit baseballs in my back yard until numbness crept in my fingers.

We ate quickly and walked to the canoe stand that was on the far side of the long dock. Renting a canoe consisted of basically saying that we would bring it back. I wondered if the guy renting the canoes thought we actually had the ability to carry a canoe home. Maybe he thought we had a truck, pedal driven, strategically hidden near the lake, where we would load the boat and make a getaway.

We each took a paddle, Rick playing air guitar with his while 'canoe guy' untied a red metal one tied to a river birch. The guy looked to be a college student making easy pocket change. His shoulder-length hair was wavy and sandy-blond. His bangs swept thick below his eyebrows. His tanned skin lay bare to the sun, covered only by his frayed, cut off jeans. Gently, he nudged us away from the bank. Ricky sat up front as promised, pondering which part of the lake to explore.

"You little dudes have fun," 'canoe guy' said before sliding into a metal lounge chair.

"Thanks a lot, captain," Rick said with a salute. "Want us to bring you back a turtle?"

"Only if it's a snapper."

We turned the canoe clockwise.

"Which way?" I asked.

"Let's go to the lagoon and look for snakes. If we don't see any, we'll scare turtles off the stumps." Again with the snakes.

The canoe rental was located at the edge of an elbow-shaped turn in the lake, which gave us the option of paddling back near the swimming area, or away from the crowd and into a quiet area which we called 'the lagoon.' We had chosen the name because it sounded eerie and isolated, even though we were no more than two hundred yards from the swimming area.

We ventured into the 'mysterious' water, bold and unafraid. Always careful not to tip the canoe, we'd never given thought that the lagoon was probably no deeper than three feet. We were aware it was stump filled, which no doubt contained dangerous creatures, lurking about, waiting to swallow little boys whole. Yet we paddled on.

The afternoon flew by as we covered every square foot of coastline of the oversized pond. When the day was finished, we took our tired, sun drenched bodies back to the car. Before Mom had driven back on the main road, we were out like fat kids in dodge ball.

Chapter Fifteen

I had showered the lake water off my skinny body. I'd not realized until going back in time how bony I was. A hipless wonder.

After I had dressed, sporting a pair of jeans and a Cincinnati Reds baseball jersey, I saw Mom counting money at the dining room table. She had a stack of ones and at least three dollars worth of coins.

"Counting out grocery money?" I asked.

"No, I'm counting out bus fare. I think it's time to take your friend living behind Frank's Market to the bus station. Let's get him to Charleston."

When we drove up to the broken down car, Clete stood behind it, an elm stick his walking cane. He appeared to be leaning on the stick, standing wobbly as he watched a cat chase a mouse into the weeds behind the store. A poor man's form of entertainment, I suppose. He slowly turned to look at us when Mom cut the engine.

"Hello, Mr. Clete," I said, waving my hand after I'd gotten out of the car.

"Hello there, young fella." He tipped his cap toward Mom. "Who's this angel you brung with you?"

"This is my mother."

"It is very nice to meet you," she said.

"Pleasure, ma'am," he said before returning his cap to his head.

"Mr. Clete," Mom began, "when Chase told me about you living in a car, it about broke my heart."

He shook his head and looked to the ground for a moment. "It ain't so bad. I got Mr. Frank looking out for me, bringin' me food every now and then."

"Well, this is no way for a person to live. Chase and I would like to get you to Charleston so you can be with your daughter."

"Ma'am, that's a mighty fine offer. But I don't want to be a burden."

"You are not a burden. Not at all. Would you let us drive you to the bus station? We're going to buy your ticket."

He looked at me, and I noticed his watery, tired eyes. "I thought you was just carryin' on when you said you would help me."

"No, sir. I meant it. But Mom is the one making it happen."

He extended his frail hand to Mom. "I don't know how I can thank you. I'll try my best to pay you back."

"No, sir. This is a gift. From our family to you."

Clete sat in the back seat, smelling strongly of sweat. As we drove, I turned and watched him looking out the window as though he were a child. His walking stick lay across his lap, and his hands were clasped in front of him as though he was in prayer. I wondered how long it had been since he had gone anywhere that wasn't by foot. He caught me looking at him, and he smiled, his eyes sparkling and alive.

"Mr. Clete," Mom said as she drove, "I'm going to give you cab fare when we get to the bus station so you can get to your daughter's house once you get to the station in Charleston." In between Mom and me on the front seat was a paper bag. "Chase, how about give Mr. Clete his lunch."

I took hold of the bag and handed it to Clete.

"You should have about an hour before you board the bus," Mom said. "That will give you plenty of time to eat. There are two sandwiches, some chips and dip, and a piece of cake. I put some change in the bag so you can buy a soda."

Clete opened the bag, and he looked at the food as though it was made of gold. "Yes'm. I'll surely do that. Thank you. Thank you, ma'am."

"Wait till you try that onion dip," I said. "It'll change your life. It's Mom's secret recipe."

When we pulled up into the station, I hurried out of the car and ran around the other side to open Clete's door. I helped him slide out carefully. He clutched his bag as tightly as his bony fingers would allow. He stood at the door, looking at us as though we had given him the moon and the stars. When I hugged him, I think it caught him off guard. He kept his arms to his side, the cane in one hand, his food in the other.

Mom walked inside to buy the ticket while I stayed with the old man.

"Mr. Clete, I wish you and your daughter the best. I have a feeling she'll be the happiest girl in the world, getting her father back. Speaking from experience, I know what it's like to get a second chance to see someone you love."

Mr. Clete nodded, and it was apparent he didn't know how to react to what we had done. Where a few dollars and a trip downtown seemed insignificant to us, I believe Clete felt it was a great sacrifice.

Mom handed him the ticket. "Do you want help getting inside?"

"No, ma'am. I'm gonna take my time and enjoy the stroll. Gonna eat this food as soon as I set down."

Mom placed her hand on my shoulder as we bid Clete goodbye. He walked slowly to the door, and we just watched him shakily open the glass door, nod at us, and walk inside.

I was certain Clete's stage was different from mine, and that his script, while taking on new chapters, would be a play I couldn't pretend to understand. I couldn't imagine living out of a car, and I'll never understand the burdens that some carry that just don't seem right.

After dinner, I left the kitchen to find something to wear to the skating rink. The pickings were slim. Sandwiched in between the psychedelic sixties and the polyester, disco seventies, clothing was more about expression than good taste. I laughed aloud when I ran my fingers along the options hanging in my closet. It wasn't as if I'd taken the fashion industry with me back in time. But then, if I had been wearing something from the modern era, I'm sure I would have suffered ridicule. Anyways, I settled for a pair of light blue slacks and a swirly blue-and-white pseudo-silk shirt. I would have to dazzle the girls with rayon.

I walked out the front door in style. Robbie lived a block away, and it was an easy walk. I found myself humming the tune to 'Stayin' Alive.' If I'd had enough hair, I could have primped it like John Travolta. As it was, I barely even needed a comb.

The sun hung low in the cloudless sky, and the tall pines, maples, and oaks provided a cooling shade on Brennan. Shadows stretched across the bumpy road, painting the street in dark stretches of charcoal gray like tentacles of some archaic beast. Patches of orange still found their way onto the road as the sun managed to slip through gaps in the trees. Though the shadows were building, heat still radiated off the street, providing warmth under my black high-top shoes.

Activity was light on Brennen, as the dinner hour still found most people indoors. I wrapped the peacefulness of the evening around me like a warm blanket. Passing in front of Mr. Lewis' house, I heard Walter Cronkite giving the latest updates on Vietnam on the CBS Evening News. Mr. Lewis' hearing had deteriorated through the years, requiring him to keep the volume knob on his television on high.

Next up was Asa Jackson's house. Asa's blue pick-up truck was parked by the street in front of the house. His Great Dane, Bubba, sat in the driveway. Bubba was the biggest dog I had ever seen. Certainly his ancestral background could be traced to the equine family. Though Bubba had been intimidating, he was a friendly dog. Unfortunately, he had a little Mississippi leg hound in him and tried to impart his amorous intentions on anybody too slow to get out of his reach. The key to surviving his advances was to, at all costs, not get knocked to the ground. If and when it reached that point, Bubba would lock into overdrive like a jackrabbit on Viagra.

Bubba's eyes sparkled when he spotted me, and in two bounds he was at the edge of the driveway. "Whoa, Bubba," I said as I ran for the truck. To Bubba, no might mean no, but whoa must have translated to yes as he roared into a full trot. I realized he had cut me off at the pass, and so I faked a step to my left. He lifted his front paws high in the air like Silver being ridden by the Lone Ranger. As he raised his gangly legs, I cut right and sidestepped the beast. As Bubba turned for another mount attempt, I leapt head first into the bed of the truck. He placed his bear-sized paws on the tailgate and barked with frustration for me to exit the truck.

Sorry, Bubba, not today.

I stood at the front of the bed against the cab in the event Bubba made a leap for me. He continued to bark and circled the truck. Relief from avoiding his advances evaporated as I realized I was now a prisoner. Robbie's house was five homes away, so outrunning the lovesick beast was out of the question. I looked through the picture window of Asa's den and noticed him nodding in his recliner. Bubba seemed content to wait, and he sat beside the passenger door.

After a few minutes the standoff showed no signs of ending. I saw Robbie walk out his front door, and I waved my arms and yelled. "Robbie! Bubba's got me penned in!"

"Looks like you two want to be alone!"

"Maybe from your vantage point," I yelled with my hands cupped around my mouth like a megaphone, "but I think I'll sit this dance out. Can your mom drive up here and get me?"

Robbie nodded and smiled. Soon he and his mom walked to the car and backed out of the driveway. As they drove up to the truck, I slid to the edge of the driver's side. Seeing the back passenger window down on Robbie's wagon, I said, "Pull up and I'll jump in." I slid into the back window while Bubba watched his date slip away.

"That was close," I said. "Hello, Mrs. Foster."

"Hi, Chase. Nice of you to jump in."

The ride to the rink was a short one and we were dropped off at the front door, which no doubt impressed the ladies. Instead of arriving James Dean style on motorcycles wearing leather jackets, we got curbside drop-off in a family wagon dressed in permanent press.

We pulled out our slim-budget wad of cash from our pockets. I guessed that I would pay the entry fee only and save my money by standing rink-side since I couldn't skate for bat droppings, but Robbie wouldn't let me. On the ball field, basketball court, the back yard, I was fleet of foot, as balanced as could be. It frustrated me to see others skating as if they were on air while I skated as if being electrocuted.

As we entered the rink, the music wrested memories from a place I hadn't realized still existed. Familiar faces were everywhere, and I was busy trying to associate the names that went along with them.

"Come on, Chase," Robbie said as we tied the laces of our skates. "Let's check out the action." Action was a relative term.

Robbie was on the rink in no time, his eyes examining the playing field. I walked to the rail like a newborn calf. Trying to look cool while leaning against the rail, I scoped the oval floor. While I stood there, keeping a firm grip on the rail so as not to split my lip, a soft hand gently rubbed mine. I just knew it would be Vicki. Wrong. Wanda Farley, a spindly girl with stringy black hair, horn-rim glasses, and teeth that looked like baked beans, stood next to me. Her hair always looked as though it was washed once a week. And, by the gooey shine at the part on top of her head, it was obvious that that day wasn't the appointed shampoo day.

"I knew you'd come around," Wanda screamed, her voice rising over the music. "Let's skate."

"What? What are you talkin' about?"

"Robbie just told me how you feel about me, so let's not waste time. Let's get this party started."

I looked over Wanda's shoulder, only to see Robbie extending a raspberry. "Wait a second," I said. "Let's not rush into this. Can't we just stand here and talk?"

I saw the disappointment in her eyes. She seemed excited, and I was deflating it. *What would it hurt?* It wasn't as if I was being forced to marry her. "Come on," I said, taking hold of her hand. She grinned.

Stepping onto the floor, I braced for the first fall. Wanda was rock steady. In fact, she was very good. She held tightly on to me to prevent me from falling and making a fool of myself. We circled in front of Robbie and a couple of the other guys. They were surprised, I'm sure, to see that I was fine with the situation. Wanda looked thrilled, as it was most likely her first couple skate with anyone other than her brother. The lights from the party ball bounced off her large glasses and the greasy buildup in her hair.

"This is so cool," she said, smiling at me. "I can't believe I'm skating with you."

"I can't quite believe it myself. You know, you're a good skater."

"I'd say the same about you, but I don't think you're that stupid."

I laughed, causing me to lose my balance, and I fell hard to the floor.

"Chase! Are you okay?"

My backside pulsated with pain. "What were you saying about stupid?"

She shook her head. "I meant intelligence stupid, not looking stupid."

"Thanks for the clarification."

She sat beside me on the floor and motioned the other skaters around me. I was touched by her kindness, and it made me feel guilty for wanting to run for the door when she had asked me to skate earlier. And so I leaned towards her pasty face and kissed her gently on the cheek. Her smile grew large, her eyes glassy, as if in disbelief.

"I never realized you were such a sweetie," I said.

Wanda was speechless. She helped me to my feet and we skated to the rail where she helped me to a table. "Chase," she said quietly, "I didn't want to come here tonight. It's not much fun to be passed over for the popular girls. I try not to let it bother me, but it does. Not getting to skate with boys, that is. So, thank you. By the way, the kiss wasn't bad."

"One day, the guys will line up to be with you. Wait and see." Tears formed in the corners of her eyes. "C'mon now, no crying."

She nodded her head and wiped her tears. "Go on. Go hang out with your buddies. I'll never forget this night."

"Neither will I." I skated carefully toward Robbie.

"So, have you made the wedding plans yet?" Robbie asked as he flashed a big smile.

"We couldn't resist," added Jimmy, one of Robbie's teammates.

"I'm glad you did. She's somethin'."

"Are you kiddin'?" asked Robbie. "She's a goofball."

"She's not the prettiest girl in the place, but she's sweet as sugar. You watch. She'll be quite a catch one day."

"Whatever," Robbie said.

When Vicki walked in, I was busy defending Wanda. When she smiled at me, I almost fell into the railing. I'm sure she thought it was a smooth move. I had to get out of those skates. It was making me look bad.

"Well, what are you waitin' for?" Robbie asked. "Go talk to her."

I removed the irritating skates and walked to the table where Vicki had stopped to visit some friends.

"Hey," she said sweetly.

"Hey. I was hoping you'd come."

"You looked a little shaky over there. Is that why you took off your skates?"

"I just didn't want to look too tall for you. You are a short one, remember?"

"I'm sure that's the reason."

"Do you want to skate? If you plan on skating with me, I strongly suggest head gear and knee pads. I'd also like you to sign a waiver first."

"Wait a sec. Just how bad are you?"

"Think Tasmanian Devil on wheels."

"I think I'll just sit here and suck down a few sugar packets."

I took her by the hand and helped her to her feet. My knees buckled and I felt light headed. I remember hitting the floor hard, but not much else. I could hear faint voices, but I couldn't open my eyes. Familiar voices, I could detect the angst in their tones.

"Dad? Dad? Can you hear me?" It was Lauren's voice.

"Wake up, Dad!" Brett shouted. "Lauren, there's the ambulance. Run to the parking lot and flag them down."

I tried to open my eyes, and I think I could sense a bright light. The sun, perhaps. Hard as I tried, I couldn't open them. I heard a siren in the distance.

"Chase!" Vicki said, rubbing my face. I felt her hand lightly touch my chest, as if she were making sure I was breathing. I heard her talking with someone...an adult. Slowly, I was able to open my eyes. The manager and Vicki were kneeling beside me. It was at that moment I began to sense my trip to the past was temporary.

"Chase," Vicki said. "Are you okay?" There was relief in her voice. Her warm hands felt good against my face. When she rubbed my temples, I looked into her pretty eyes. There was such compassion in them. I rolled over on my side, trying to get the cobwebs out of my head. "You scared me."

"Son, do you need me to call your parents?" the manager asked.

I sat and looked around for a second. "No, sir. I'm okay now."

"You sure?"

"Yes, sir."

The manager walked to the counter, but I could see he was keeping an eye on me.

I rubbed my eyes. "Something's wrong. Something's wrong with me."

"What is it? Is your head hurting? Blurry vision?"

"No, in the future. It sounds bad."

"I'm confused."

"I heard Lauren and Brett. They were trying to wake me."

"Who?"

"My children."

"Oh," she said, putting her hands to her mouth. "Oh, my."

"I heard a siren. I heard Brett tell Lauren to flag down an ambulance. I must still be on the ball field, and I must be in pretty bad shape. They were trying to wake me. I was about to come to, I think. Something tells me I don't have much time left before I have to go back."

Vicki helped me to my feet.

"What are you going to do?"

"I don't know. I think of my mother lying in that casket, and it makes me sick to my stomach. But I miss my family. I hate to think of what they're going through, wondering if I'm dying on that dusty ball field." I rubbed my fingers through my hair. Vicki then took my hand.

"Skate with me."

She rented a pair of skates and we took to the floor, hand in hand. We skated through three songs and she held my hand so delicately. She wore a melancholy look. When we stepped off the rink, she began to cry. She wore her heart on her sleeve, and I was humbled by her sincerity of affection. I hugged her while The Temptations serenaded.

"You are such a pretty girl," I said.

She blushed. "Are you sure you have to go back home? You know, to the future. Can't you stay here with me?"

"I don't think I've got any say so about that."

Soon it was time to go, and we walked outside to find our ride. I told Robbie to give me a minute, and I took Vicki by the hand. We walked around the side of the building, and the streetlight illuminated her eyes. Clenching both of her delicate hands in mine, I gently kissed her.

"I've got to go."

"Will I see you again?"

"If you don't, just know I'll never forget you." A tear rolled slowly down her cheek. She forced a smile and ran her hair behind her ear. She lowered her head and I turned away. I ran to the car, wanting to turn around.

The ride home was slow and agonizing. Talk was confined to the front seat.

Chapter Sixteen

It was a restless night. I flipped and flopped in my bed like a goldfish tossed on the sidewalk. The frantic pleas of Brett and Lauren played through my mind. I imagined the worries they were going through. I wondered about my condition. Was I in a coma? Was I in the hospital? Was I still lying on the infield of the baseball field? Was my journey back in time one that equated to the length of a normal dream, or was it a dream matched minute for minute with the time I'd spent on my trip back in time? I wondered how much time I had left before it was time to return. What if I never went back? That thought made me break out in a sweat. Was I destined to repeat my life? Was it intended I carve out an entirely different future?

I couldn't sleep and went to the kitchen. Maybe a full belly would help me sleep. I opened the pantry door, but nothing looked appealing. I looked on the counter and spotted a chocolate cake sporting thick, creamy icing. It cried for a tall glass of milk to keep it company. I pulled the silver handle on the refrigerator door and placed my skinny fingers around the cold carton of homogenized. No skim milk. No one-percent, two-percent, or any other percent, only good, old-fashioned homogenized. No worry about clogged arteries.

As a kid, I had been fascinated that the milkman delivered milk to our doorstep each week. Every Monday, a metal case containing four one-quart bottles had been delivered like clockwork. One morning, when I was four or five years old, the milkman had offered to take me on his route. With Mom's permission, I became the youngest milkman to serve the neighborhood. Though I got to sit behind the wheel of the truck, I had been a little disappointed that I hadn't gotten an official milkman's hat. That way, I could have completed the look. Well, not entirely: I'd needed those vintage white shirt and pants.

I cut a super-sized portion of cake and sat at the kitchen table. Since my waist was a size twelve, I was going to suck down as much as I wanted without any regrets. The only sounds I heard from the darkness outside was an occasional cricket, and the only noise inside were the faint sounds of snoring coming from Mom and Dad's bedroom. I couldn't distinguish who was doing the snoring, or whether it was a tag-team operation. Either way, it was a soothing setting, and I had never felt quite so at ease in the middle of the night. There were no thoughts of bad guys or thieves, no thoughts of bills or business meetings. I felt absolutely no desire to leave the kitchen table. As far as I was concerned, that night could have gone on and on.

After the cake was finished I stared out the kitchen window into the deserted night. A dog barked. The trees and the shadows were perfectly still. The Midway tower flashed a red, silent beacon. The whole world was asleep except for me.

I walked into the living room and found a picture album. At first, I was puzzled as to why the album was so small until I realized that many of the photo memories hadn't occurred yet. I turned on the stereo in the room, turning the volume down so as not to wake the family. Roberta Flack sang 'The First Time Ever I Saw Your Face.' Her voice carried through the speaker in angelic fashion. I noticed some unfamiliar pictures. They must have been lost or misplaced down through the years. I spotted one in particular, where Mom was hugging me while I sat on her lap. Our smiles jumped off the picture. I appeared to be about seven or eight. I touched the picture, emotion mixed with joy and sadness—joy from the memories, sadness that the memories would become just that if, and when, I awakened from this crazy trip to the past. I wondered what Mom looked like in Heaven. Was she young again? Surely she had the biggest set of wings in the clouds.

The squeaking front door awakened me as Dad walked to the box for the morning paper. Realizing I had finally succumbed to sleep while looking at pictures, I rose slowly from the couch, rubbing my sore neck. Clearing cobwebs from my sleepy brain, I realized my early rising presented a great opportunity.

I pulled a Dixie cup from its holder in the bathroom, filling it up about one-third of the way with cold water from the sink. I sneaked into Bobby's room as he lay perfectly on his side, dead to the world. You know where this is going, right? Revenge is a dish best served cold, and I wanted it as cold as possible. I held the Dixie cup above Bobby's right ear, and slowly poured the water into his eardrum. Bobby rolled forward, falling out of the bed.

"What the..." he yelled. He leapt to his feet, furiously bobbing his head up and down to expunge the water from his ear.

"How's it feel, dipwad?"

I shut Bob's door and took off to the kitchen. 'Vengeance is mine,' sayeth the Lord, but I have to admit it felt pretty dang satisfying. The way I saw it, I had just earned myself a nice breakfast.

"What's all that ruckus about?" Dad asked as I entered the kitchen.

"Nothing. Just making sure Bob is warm and cozy."

Dad didn't appear to give my comment much thought, as his eyes returned to the newspaper.

"Hey, Dad, how about I whip up some breakfast?"

"That's all right. Your mother will be up in a bit." Dad had been quite the handyman, and could build, fix, or design most anything for the house. But when he was in the kitchen, he'd been a lost pup without Mom. I wondered if he even knew where the plates and silverware were kept.

"Let's give her the morning off. How 'bout French toast?"

"French toast? Where'd you learn to make French toast?"

"Overseas, when I was stationed in the war."

We laughed.

The sun peeked through the backyard trees, illuminating the smoke from Dad's morning cigarette. I removed four slices of bread from the light green, tin breadbox. I found eggs and milk in the fridge and removed a green mixing bowl from the cabinet. I noticed Dad watching me remove two small plates, butter, and the syrup, apparently impressed not only with the swiftness and ease I prepared breakfast, but that I knew where to find everything. Perhaps now was the time for me to give Dad kitchen orientation. Within minutes, I had a hot stack of lightly fried toast sitting on the kitchen table.

"This looks good," Dad said. He cut into the toast soaked in butter and syrup, and took a bite. "Maybe you should skip your plans to play baseball and go to culinary school instead."

"I don't want to wear the goofy hat."

"A ball cap does look better."

"Hey, Dad, can I ask you a question?"

Dad seemed to sense my hesitation. "What is it?"

I picked at my French toast, keeping my eyes on my plate. I took a deep breath. "Why do you think you've been drinking so much?"

"What? What are you talkin' about?" I could tell I had caught him completely off guard, and that was the way I intended it.

"It's just that I've noticed you seem to be struggling with it these days. Are you unhappy? Unhappy with Mom? Unhappy with us?"

"Son, that's not something you need to concern yourself with."

"Yes, it is. Let me help. Let us all help. All you have to do is let us."

Dad flipped a piece of French toast on his plate, looking unsure of what to say.

"Wish I had helped you more the first time," I muttered.

"The first time?"

It was time to come clean. It was my only option. I had to help him. "Yes, the first time. There's something I have to tell you." I took a deep breath and looked about the room for a moment. "What I want to tell you is that I am not a twelve year old boy…"

"Mornin', Son," Dad said to Rick as he entered the kitchen. Rick didn't respond. Why should he? His stomach was empty, and talking would only complicate matters of filling it.

"We're out of milk," I said.

Ricky snapped the refrigerator door open. "Shut up," he mumbled after realizing a half-quart sat on the top shelf.

"Hey, he spoke before breakfast," I said, looking at Dad. I knew our talk would have to wait, but it didn't mean I had to stop doing what I could. "Ricky, you want French toast instead of cereal?" Ricky's unchanging expression strongly implied 'no.' "You can't eat the same thing over and over your whole life. Change it up a little." Rick poured his cereal as if he were alone. As changeable as a dead chameleon.

"You know Doc will be here today," Dad said. "Sometime around noon I'd say."

That was great news. I had never been around someone as entertaining as my uncle, and it was really hard to understand unless you'd met him. Doc had such an aura of warmth and happiness about him, always having a joke to tell, a story to share. I guess now would a good time to tell you a little about him.

Doc had moved to town when I graduated from college. Retired, bored and lonely in snowy Ohio, he had begun a new chapter in life in our town at the age of seventy-two. A bachelor for forty years, he had lost all ties to the northern town on Lake Eerie, as his closest friends had passed away. He'd lived to be ninety and had been very independent and well able to take care of himself. That was, until the last three years of his life. Alzheimer's had come fast and furious, and he'd became a shell of his former self. And, even when he did start to fade, he had somehow held on to his sense of humor.

One of my favorite 'Doc' moments had come not long after Mom and Dad had placed him in a retirement home, when Alzheimer's was in its early stages. The facility had been a top-notch, fairly exclusive place in a very nice part of the city. When I had gone to visit him one day, I'd found him sitting in the lobby waiting for the dining hall to open. The lobby had been full of people, and most of the tenants were women. The ladies were dressed nicely, as if they were going out for an elegant evening of dinner and a Broadway show. Doc, on the other hand, wore clothes more suited for riding down country roads looking for deer. He had been very particular about his appearance, always combing his hair, but he'd dressed for comfort, not for style.

On that particular day, when I walked into the lobby, I'd spotted Doc sitting on a very ornate couch. He was sitting in between two very sweet-looking ladies.

"Hey, Uncle Doc," I said. "How you doin' today?"

"I'm doin' everybody I can," had been his reply, and he'd lifted his right arm, fist clenched, his left hand smacking the right arm in the bend at the elbow, forcing it upward in some phallic gesture. Both ladies had walked off in disgust. Doc had flashed his devilish smile. Without hesitating, he'd said, "Sit down and take a load off. I'd buy you a drink, but I haven't found a bar in this sorry joint."

Another memory that has stuck with me occurred on a winter day not long after Doc had moved to town. A nice snowfall had fallen overnight. Snow was rare in our part of the country, yet I'd driven to Doc's house to check on him. This made little sense, since Doc had lived sixty years in a part of the country where snow was as common as rain. If anything, Doc should have checked on me.

The combination of wind and snow that day had made the situation ripe for freezing pipes. I had helped

Doc check the pipes under his house. Together, we'd tried to remove a garden hose that was still attached to an outdoor faucet. The hose was rock solid. With our hands on the hose, Doc had commented on how he wished that a certain part of his anatomy was as hard as the frozen hose. I'd laughed so hard I dropped the hose, falling on my hands and knees in the white powder. Doc had looked at me as if I were the crazy one. He was being as serious as he could be. Remember, this occurred in the pre-Viagra days.

Doc's brown Chrysler wagon pulled in the driveway.

"He's here!" Ricky yelled from the front steps. "Uncle Doc's here."

We walked out the front door and down the four steps to the driveway. Doc opened his car door and removed his hat, displaying his full head of white hair. Tall, broad shouldered, he bit down on a lit, slender cigar in the corner of his mouth as he reached for Ricky.

"Hello there, sluggie!" Doc shouted. Rick jumped into his arms and Doc studied him. "I think you've doubled in size since I last saw you. Are you drivin' yet?"

Ricky laughed as Doc placed his dark gray fedora on Rick's head. Setting Rick down, he pulled a bag out of his front seat. "Grab hold of this mother," he said, handing me a giant salami loaf.

"Wow, that thing's huge," I said, grabbing the massive log of cured meat.

"That's what she said on our wedding night," Doc said with a twinkle in his eyes. Mom shook her head while Doc smacked me on the back.

He looked healthy and strong. Though silver-haired and sixty-something, he looked like someone on the short end of fifty. I could see a look of mischief in his eyes.

Mom slid up to get a hug. "Glad you made it safe and sound," she said, patting Doc on his shoulder. "Ray had to work, but'll be home by five-thirty. Did you have any trouble finding the place?"

"Nope, not at all. It's a straight shot down seventy-seven. I'd be lying if I said it's not great to see you guys." He tipped the bill of his hat, which was swallowing Rick's tiny head, with his middle and forefinger, causing the bill to drop over Ricky's eyes. "When you guys going to come up to my place? You want to know something really interesting?"

"What?" Ricky asked while raising the bill of the cap.

"That it's the exact same amount of miles from here to my house as it is from my house to here. Which means, you guys need to get your fannies up to my place soon."

"Can I help you with your luggage?" I asked.

"No, thanks. I'm staying at the motel out on the main highway."

Doc had enjoyed setting up his traveling bar in his motel rooms, turning them into instant party rooms. All had been welcome, and it hadn't mattered if it was a family member or the guy at the front desk. Drinks were always on 'good ole' Doc. He drank every day, but rarely got drunk. He'd been a social drinker. A very, very, social drinker. Years later, when he'd moved down south, I would visit him when I could. No matter what time of day or night I stopped by, Doc had wanted to 'buy' me a drink. I would try to oblige so as not to hurt his feelings, but I'd quickly realized I would be going home drunk if Doc poured the drinks. So I began pouring my own, which amounted to a teaspoonful of alcohol, and a lot of soda. Once, Doc had noticed how small an amount I was pouring into my glass, and he'd offered me an eye dropper.

One morning, I had stopped by on the way to work to borrow one of Doc's tools. I had just gotten out of my car, not realizing that Doc was outside doing yard work. As I knocked on his door I heard, "How 'bout an eye opener?" I turned around to find him, rake in hand, smiling.

"An eye opener?" I asked. "It's seven-thirty in the mornin'. Besides, I have to go to work."

"Ah, work's an overrated experience. You know, I been lookin' for a job that pays fifty thousand a year, with two paid vacations, each six months long."

"Where do you think you'll find such a job?"

"I'll be a suck egg mule if I know. Come on inside."

Doc had walked straight to the kitchen, opened the cabinet, and filled a shot glass with bourbon. He'd slung it down in one quick chug. "Wish I could find a cow that gives milk like that." He'd been the life of the party, morning, noon, and night.

We escorted Doc, the salami, and a honey-baked ham inside. We sat at the kitchen table.

"Doc, let me fix you something to eat," Mom said. I knew Doc wouldn't allow that to happen. He was the king of dining out, and somehow made sure he got to pay the check.

"Why don't you let me take you guys out for dinner?" Doc offered. "If you cook, the kitchen will be a mess and you'll have to clean a lot of dishes, and all for the sake of something that will be eaten in about five minutes. Makes no sense to me. So, that's that. Where you boys wanna go?"

Ricky was geared up like a sailor on port leave following a six-month tour. Because of a tight budget, and because Mom was a stay-at-home mom, eating out was considered frivolous and unnecessary. So, if an opportunity arose to dine out, we weren't about to pass up the chance.

"Can we, Mom, can we?" Ricky asked, pulling on Mom's apron. He gave her a puppy dog look, and I knew she couldn't say no.

"I guess," she said hesitantly. "Doc, you sure I can't just fix you somethin'?"

"The kids want to go out, so let's give 'em what they want." Doc looked at us. "Right, boys?"

"Yes," Rick shouted while running for the bedroom for his shoes.

Doc drove us down the street and out of the tiny neighborhood.

"Doc, take a right up here at the stop sign and it will lead us to a restaurant that has everything from biscuits to burgers," Mom said.

"I believe I could tear up a bucket load of biscuits," Doc said. "How about you guys?"

Ricky smiled at me, slowly nodding his head.

The restaurant was called Rose's, and it was actually a lunch counter in a small department store. It belonged to the Sestokas, the only Greek family in the neighborhood. Rose was the owner's wife, a short, stocky lady with jet-black hair pulled tightly in a bun. Miss Rose sat at the register most of the time, greeting guests as they entered the restaurant. Otherwise, she'd wander about the restaurant chatting with the customers in their booths.

For being a department store restaurant, it had a unique look and feel. It had a black-and-white checkerboard floor. The j-shaped counter was made of Formica, and the stools were silver with red seats. The seats rotated, and with a strong push, I could spin three evolutions before coming to rest. That isn't exactly important news to any of you, but it impresses me.

The warm smell of cornbread and brown beans filled the air. A long row of booths sat opposite the counter, with high wooden backs and a hat rack. Doc threw his hat on the first one and said, "You ankle biters sit your fannies down and order anything you want."

We slid in on one side, Mom and Doc on the other. The booth tables were also Formica, with rounded corners, colored a nondescript beige. Within seconds, the waitress appeared with four large, plastic menus. When Rick and I opened ours, we lost sight of Doc and Mom.

"I want a grilled cheese sandwich and some fries," Ricky declared.

"Don't order just one sandwich," Doc said. "You know it's bad luck orderin' an odd number. What about you, Chasie?"

My taste buds had changed through the years. "I wonder if they have salmon."

The others looked at me like I was an alien come to visit.

"Salmon?" Mom asked. "You've never eaten salmon. Why would you get that?"

"What is salmon?" Ricky asked. "Some kind of Chinese food?"

"I don't care if it's Chinese or chicken knees," Doc said. "If you wanna eat it, get it."

I looked at the waitress, and she shook her head. *So much for salmon.*

"Guess I'll just get the roast beef and mashed potatoes."

"Now you're talkin'," said Doc. "Ellen, get whatever you want."

"The roast beef sounds good too," she said.

"Listen," Doc said to the waitress. "I want four of your biggest biscuits, and I want 'em smothered in sausage gravy. I also want two eggs, fried, but don't cook 'em long. I want 'em real snotty." Doc even made ordering entertaining. With his flip-up sunglasses pointing to the ceiling, his marble-blue eyes gleamed as he talked about the first time he'd tried to eat a scrambled egg.

It was amazing to see Mom and Doc sitting across the table side-by-side, healthy, happy, alive. I wondered if they had a clue as to the number of people they had touched during their time on earth.

Sweet tea, not water, was soon at the table. One had to specifically ask for water or it wouldn't be served at all.

"When's Bobby gonna be home? I need to take him and Rod out to dinner too."

"Now Doc, you're not taking us out for every meal," Mom said. "I'm going to fix supper tonight."

Doc shook his head. "I can't understand the need to dirty up your kitchen."

The waitress carried a large, round tray filled with plates. Oval, off-white plates overflowed with roast beef and potatoes. Smaller plates held biscuits and rectangular slabs of butter. Ricky took the cheese sandwich from his thick ivory plate, biting the corners before working his way from top to bottom. Uncle Doc threw three butter slabs on each biscuit. He put butter on almost everything. It was amazing that had he lived ninety years, eating the foods he ate. Genetics had to play a large part. Bacon, eggs, sausage gravy, and butter by the pound were daily staples for the man. While we ate, Doc told us about a blizzard he'd endured in January. Mom offset that with talk with the heat and humidity of the south.

"If you finish that sandwich, I'll give you a quarter," Doc said to Ricky.

Ricky knew the quarter was guaranteed, whether he finished the sandwich or not. Doc gave us quarters at every meal, always challenging us to eating contests. The quarters were based on effort more than actual consumption.

"I'll give you a quarter if you finish off that roast beef," he said to me. It would be a quarter that I wished I could take with me when my time was up.

The meal was over. Only morsels remained, and our full, happy bellies were content and ready to go home. The afternoon sun warmed my shoulders when we walked outside the chilly restaurant.

Soon we were home. Doc dropped us off at the driveway and drove to the motel to check in and take his afternoon nap.

Chapter Seventeen

Doc returned not long after Bobby and Dad arrived from work. When he entered the den, I noticed his unusual hat. A baseball-style cap with a mesh back, it had an outline of Alaska on it, with the words 'Alaska Forecast' at the top of the bill. There were three cities on the map, and the forecast for each. An expletive was used to describe each city's forecast. For Fairbanks, let's just say the forecast equated to something you might need Kaopectate to treat. For Juneau, the forecast was very Kaopectate-worthy, and for Anchorage, it was going to be really Kaopectate-worthy. Bobby and I laughed hysterically. Mom turned red, and Dad shook his head in disbelief. Fortunately, Ricky couldn't see high enough to read the forecast.

"Waddaya say there, Ray, old boy?" Doc shook Dad's hand vigorously. "Bobby, you've grown a foot." Bobby smiled.

Doc removed his hat, held it in his left hand, and looked for a seat. I slid down on the couch to make room. We listened as Dad and Doc brought each other up to speed. Though there was fifteen years difference in their ages, the brothers were very close.

As I knew it would, the talk turned to deer hunting. Deer season in Ohio had permitted only one deer to be slayed per season, and Doc always got his one. Conversely, the deer season in South Carolina had been four months long, and was like a skeet shoot. No limit, antlers optional. Size was good, but not a requirement. If it was bigger than Bambi, pop it full of lead had been the state motto. Just knowing that Dad could bag as many deer as he wanted, for a quarter of the year, had made Doc envious.

"Bagged my buck on the second day of the season," Doc said. "Good mother Moses, he was huge. Twelve points. Two hundred and fifty pounds if he was ten. The snow that mornin' was up to a tall Indian's under drawers." Mom shook her head, but it would do no good. "He came sneakin' up the ridge, down through the high line, and I dropped him in one shot."

I was never sure what a high line was, but every deer Doc shot had come through one. He'd owned a hunting cabin in the Alleghany Forest, and fed most every animal that might roam the woods. Between the salt lick for the deer, the corn bin for the raccoons, and the tree stump of bacon for the bears, Doc had looked out for every animal on the green earth except one—cats. He'd hated them with a passion. He had kept a pistol in his glove compartment so he could snuff out roadside felines he came across.

Remembering that thought, I felt the need to bring up the subject. "You keepin' the cat population under control?"

"Gosh, yeah," Doc answered. "Saw one outside camp last week on the side of the road. I peppered him with a couple of rounds. Cats. All they do is kill the young of other animals. The only good cat is a dead one." We laughed loudly.

"Doc," Mom said. "You should be ashamed of yourself."

"I'm not kiddin'. I'd rather kiss a dead moose's butt than let some cat wander around killin' other animals."

Doc tried to convince Mom and Dad to let him take us out for dinner, but Mom stood her ground. "I've got supper simmering on the stove," she said. "It'll be ready in just a little while, so you relax."

Doc looked disappointed, but he would have a full evening to spend with his brother and our family. The television was on, but no one paid attention. Besides, the show going on in the den was better than anything that could be found on television. Dad and Doc volleyed between stories, tossing tall tales on baited hooks that none of us could resist.

Because of their age difference, neither Doc nor Dad had much on each other as far as gossipy tales. Instead, their stories were of odd characters that had lived along the valleys and hillsides of their mountain home. Doc told of Ted Canton, an old timer who had smashed Doc's bare feet with a tobacco stick while Doc rode in the back seat of a car one summer afternoon, his feet positioned out the window to cool his tired feet.

It had been all Daisy, Doc's girlfriend, and the one behind the wheel, could do to keep Doc from grabbing the wheel and turning the car around to even the score with Ted. Dad talked about Tater Thompson, who'd got his family jewels zapped while peeing on an electric fence while coon hunting.

To give us a breather from the heavy laughter, Dad walked to the kitchen. I followed behind him. When he opened the refrigerator, I reached around him and retrieved two sodas from the refrigerator door.

"Let's try one of these tonight," I said, unsure of the response. I smiled, but I think he saw the hope in my eyes.

"Sounds like a good idea." Dad took the bottle and rubbed my head.

We returned to the den, and I felt that a perfect evening lay ahead. And I was right.

I sat beside Doc on the couch, and he caught a glimpse of a shapely young thing on the television. "Would you look at the bazookas on that gal," Doc said. After a scolding from Mom, Doc shook his head and smiled. "Looks like she's carrying midgets in her sweater." I was hoping I'd carry back memories of the evening to the future when this journey was complete, which I did. If not, how could I be telling them to you now?

Ricky and I were sent to bed before the others. I wanted to let Dad know that, being a fully grown man, I should be able to stay up as late as the others. But I knew I couldn't spill the beans just for the sake of staying up late.

"Night, night, little boys," Bobby said to us.

"Shove it," Ricky whispered as he walked by Bob's chair. "I'll get you tomorrow."

"I'll probably turn in around midnight," Bobby said, aggravating Ricky even more. Ricky kicked Bobby's shin.

"That's enough," Mom said.

"Come on, Ricky," I said. "We get to spend time with Uncle Doc tomorrow while Bobby's bagging groceries."

"Oh, yeah," Rick said, perking up. "Don't forget to stack the eggs on top of the bag."

We retreated to the bathroom to brush our teeth. The water from the faucet sprayed our toothbrushes, as there was no filter to slow the flow of the water. Rick's mouth was quickly full of toothpaste, and he looked like a rabid dog.

Soon we were in bed, lights off, with the light from the streetlight splitting the curtain. Talk was small, and Ricky faded off in a matter of minutes. I reflected on the day, thanking God for the opportunity. I tried to listen as best I could to the conversation emanating from the den.

I, too, soon drifted away, and it didn't seem long before I was in a foggy dream. In the dream, I opened my eyes, knowing that I was lying in the bed of my childhood room. But I wasn't looking at the bedroom ceiling, or the surroundings of the bedroom. Instead, I saw blurred visions standing beside me, and I heard Lauren crying. Blake was trying to console her, and I tried to speak but couldn't. I was trying to tell them to look at me, to see that my eyes were open, but they wouldn't. Finally they did, but they looked at me as if I were still sleeping. Were my eyes not open? I wanted to tell them that I was fine, and that I would be coming out my sleep state soon. It was as if my mind knew the score, but my body had not caught up yet.

I heard other voices, and then I lost the ability to see. One unfamiliar voice was talking about the importance of prayer. I felt Blake's hand holding mine. I felt Lauren's fingers lightly rubbing my hair. I tried to move my mouth, to blink, to move, but couldn't. I felt claustrophobic, like I'd been tossed in a casket while still alive.

"Chase, wake up. Wake up, son." I opened my eyes and looked foggily into Mom's. "It's okay Chase. It's okay."

I looked about the dark room, the light from the bathroom forming a silhouette around Mom. "Sorry I woke you, Mom." I rubbed my eyes. "Man, what a crazy dream."

"Would you like a glass of water?"

"Yes, ma'am."

I sat on the edge of the bed, trying to figure out what was going on. Mom handed me a cup of water and ran her fingers through my hair. Her hand felt warm and soothing. Within minutes I was asleep again.

When I awoke, I tried to make sense of what had happened the night before. I couldn't understand it fully, but the best I could figure, I was in the hospital. I sensed my time was very short, my days in the past nearing the end. I showered, soaking up the hot steam while I tried to make sense of it all. I knew I had best hold on to each moment, as I felt I could be taken away any second.

I looked at Dad's razor and picked it up before remembering that I only had peach fuzz. A definite benefit of being a kid again. Although, when I showered, I noticed shortcomings in certain areas of my body that I'd forgotten was all part of being a young boy.

It was Saturday, the best day of the week. With Uncle Doc in town, the chances of a good day looked promising. I walked to the kitchen where Mom fixed biscuits and sausage gravy, and the aroma drifted through the house. Dad filled light blue glasses with orange juice. His happy disposition brightened the overcast morning.

"Chase, how 'bout you take out the trash," Mom asked, anxious to rid the kitchen of unsightly eggshells and sausage grease. I was the designated trash boy, as Bobby had refused since he wasn't 'on the clock.' A mist fell from the sky as I walked out the back door. It was an unusually cool morning for early summer, and the crisp, humidity-free breeze was a welcome change. The air had a feel of fall, which suited me just fine. I'm sure it felt good to Doc, who had never been big on Carolina summers. I closed my eyes, breathed in the cool air, and the soft, moist mist gently caressed my face. The clouds were low, but solid like a sheet of gray cotton. Looking across the back yard, I felt content absorbing the serenity of the misty silence. I heard Mom calling that breakfast was ready, but I stood just a while longer in the light rain.

The kitchen table bustled with activity as we passed the plates, bowls, and cartons of cholesterol around the table. Doc's eyes were all aglow as he placed three fluffy yeast biscuits on his plate, covering them with so much sausage gravy the biscuits disappeared.

"Okay, who wants to take the first bet?" Doc asked, reaching in his pocket for quarters.

"I will, I will," Ricky said, stepping out of character by not only eating something besides cereal for breakfast, but speaking at the breakfast table.

"Attaboy," Doc said. "But I should warn you I'm really hungry this morning. You might want to reconsider."

"It doesn't matter," Rick replied. "I'm hungry too."

"You're on then."

"What about you boys?" Doc asked.

Bobby and I took the bet as well. Ricky got off to a fast start, eating two biscuits in no time at all. He slowed a bit as he ate his third, and belched twice to allow enough room for a fourth. Bobby and I ate two, and Doc three.

"Well, I know this little guy ate more than me," Doc said, tossing two quarters beside Ricky's plate. "And I couldn't keep a good count of you boys, so I better pay up just in the event I miscounted." He flipped two quarters to Bobby and me.

"Thanks," we said in unison.

We glazed over the other breakfast items, so Mom and Dad concentrated on eating those.

"What are we doin' today?" Bobby asked. "I got the day off."

"I thought we'd ride to the beach," Mom said. "It's only a couple of hours away, and Doc hasn't seen the ocean since...how long has it been?"

"My honeymoon. Miami, September of '39. What a disaster that trip was. Drivin' through one-horse towns, sleepin' in the kind of motels that woulda made Norman Bates wet his pants. Just a miserable time."

"Well, then," Mom said between our laughter, "this trip will be a breeze compared to that. What do you say?"

"I'd be a monkey's uncle if I said no," Doc replied.

"Good call, Mom," I said.

"It won't take but a few minutes to pack some towels and fix a basket of food for lunch," Mom said. "Get your swim gear."

"Hey, you guys want me to drive?" Doc asked.

"No!" Mom and Dad shouted simultaneously. Doc never had to worry about being offered a position as a driving instructor. He'd spent as much time in the opposing traffic's lane as his own. Whether it had been because he always had alcohol in his system, or if age had gotten the best of his driving skills, I wasn't sure.

"I'll drive, Doc," Dad said.

We gathered our beachwear, which, by the way, was the same as our lakewear, which was the same as our pool wear. As a matter of fact, it was the same as our run through the sprinkler wear.

The seating selection unfolded as we hopped in the wagon. Mom and Dad sat up front, Doc and Bobby in the back, and Rick and I were relegated to the 'no man's land' seats by the rear-wagon tailgate. Of course, 'seats' was a misnomer in this case as there were none, just a carved out space for the likes of spare tires and tool boxes. It was a foxhole on wheels.

The streets of the sleepy town slowly faded into two-lane country blacktop and, within an hour, the wagon carried us through the doorway of the Lowcountry, one of my favorite areas in all the world. It was a flat-bottomed region where moss-covered live oaks watched silently over black water streams. It was home to cypress trees, a thousand years old, surrounded by the bony cypress knees that crept up from the shadowy swamp. I had heard, and read, countless tales of ghosts and 'haints' which supposedly roamed the area. I had spent a lot of time in the Lowcountry as a child, and I'd often spotted figures moving about in the shadows and tree lines.

As the old highway cut through fields of corn and soybean in east to west fashion, Rick and I viewed it in reverse as we faced the back window of the wagon. It was if we were getting to verify that the world didn't change after we passed it by. I also kept close watch for flying hubcaps, as I was sure that I had long since been designated the hubcap retriever...

I had often been forced to recover wayward hubcaps that fell off the family auto. During my early days, I'd retrieved hubcaps from neighbor's yards, city street corners, and parking lots. One of the more eventful times had occurred when a hubcap flew off while Mom was cutting through a manufacturing district in town. It had seemed like we were running late at the time, for what reason I can't recall. We always seemed to run late thanks to Rick, Bobby, or me, especially if we were headed out to do boring things like running errands or visiting Mom's friends.

On that day, the right rear cap had popped off and rolled into the parking lot of an auto body repair shop. It was on a Sunday and the shop was closed. I hadn't given much thought to retrieving the metal disc until I heard an angry bark from a Doberman Pincher, who surely was sworn to protect the repair shop property. *Wasn't the dog supposed to be inside the gate?*

Holding the hubcap behind me with my hand for protection, I'd almost come out of my Chuck Taylor's as I made a beeline for the car. The dog, nipping at the bottom of the hubcap, must have decided my calf might have provided tastier fare and was getting ready to latch on just as I leapt through the open window of my door. It was probably the only time I might have been glad that we didn't have air conditioning, if I had known back then it even existed.

Mom, stunned to see me face down in the back seat while a Doberman tried to climb through the window, had mashed the gas pedal, barely leading us to safety. Ricky, who was in the front seat playing with a Kung Fu Grip G.I. Joe, had simply asked, "What took you so long?"

The clouds yielded to bursts of sunshine, and blue sky became more and more dominant as the trip unfolded. Doc looked for deer and turkey, providing us with commentary about the prospects that some were nearby. He had a hunter's eye, three hundred and sixty five days a year.

"Hey, there's a stupid cat," he shouted. "Pull over and I'll give him a lead-filled enema." He reached into a small travel bag and removed a twenty-two caliber pistol.

"Doc!" Dad shouted. "Put that gun away. You don't need to be carryin' a gun in the car. And you can't go around killin' every cat you see."

"Well, at least pull over and let me pet it," he said with a sly grin. "I've got a little present for him." The car continued down the road as Doc watched the feline leap off into the underbrush, obviously itching to shoot it.

The air from the windows barely cooled the back of the wagon, making the ride feel like a trip in a closet. At that particular moment, I would have traded a kidney for air conditioning. Rick pulled two dice out of a brown lunch bag. Along with them, he removed a pencil and a note pad.

"Wanna play a game of football?"

"How do you come up with these games?" I asked. "How's it work?"

"What you do is roll the two dice," Rick said excitedly, "and the outcome of each die means somethin' different. If the first die ends up with one, two, three, or four, it's a running play. Five or six means it's a pass. The second die tells how many yards you gained, and whether the pass is complete, incomplete, or intercepted."

"Sounds fun to me. I'll be Green Bay."

I knew Green Bay was his favorite team and absolutely no one but Rick was allowed to choose the famed Packers.

"You can't be the Packers, dummy. Pick another team."

"Why can't I be Green Bay?" I was baiting him just for the fun of it.

"Because I invented the game. You invent one and you can be anybody you want."

"Okay, okay. Let's just play the game. Roll them bones."

"What are you talkin' about?"

"Never mind. Let's play."

I picked up the dice and rolled them on the pseudo-carpet in the back of the wagon. While we tallied up yardage and touchdowns, Doc continued on in his search for shootable wildlife. I'm surprised he didn't keep a scope on his dashboard to enhance his chances of running over deer in the offseason.

Dad spotted Jackson's General Store, and he pulled into the dirt parking lot. The old store had been built in the '20's, and we stopped there every summer. It had everything from cured hams to ice cream. Unfortunately, it had been leveled not long after I graduated college, another link to the past wiped away.

The store was a large, white wooden building with a red roof. Inside, it contained a small lunch counter with a jukebox and a shuffleboard game. Indoor shuffleboard was Doc's favorite pastime. Well, after hunting, drinking, and killing cats.

"Come on, sluggie," Doc said. "Let's play a quick game."

We looked around to see which 'sluggie' Doc was referring to, as he called us all by that name. He looked at Bobby. "What do you say?"

"Sure, I'll play," Bobby answered.

The shuffleboard was a wooden table, two feet wide and twelve feet long. It wasn't quite as tall as a pool table, and the playing surface was as slippery as ice. Participants would take turns sliding wooden discs the size of drink coasters toward the opposite end of the table, hoping to land them in sections allotting points. The goal was to knock the opponent's discs off the table while keeping their own discs on.

Rick and I took to a bowling game similar in design to the shuffleboard. It was ten feet in length with a wooden bowling ball and pins that hung from an electronic board. The idea was to roll the baseball-size ball down the 'lane' so it would trip metal clips that would force the pins above it to snap like a folding lounge chair. The scoreboard that tallied points looked like it had been snatched from a pinball machine.

While we played, Dad pumped gas. Mom shopped for suntan lotion and boiled peanuts.

The cherry floor felt dusty under my tennis shoes. 'Everything I Own' was playing on the *Rock-Ola* jukebox. After the fill-up, Dad joined Mom at an indoor picnic table and they ate the boiled peanuts out of the brown paper container. I noticed Dad and Mom sitting on the same side of the table, laughing. Mom plopped a peanut inside Dad's mouth, his hand guiding hers to his lips. I nudged Ricky to watch our parents, but his only interest was rolling a strike.

The salty smell of country ham curing in the rafters of the general store filled the air. A few locals stopped by to chat and purchase bait and soft drinks. An elderly man working behind the counter spoke to all who entered his store.

"You boys need to finish up soon," Mom said. "We've still got a ways to go to get to the beach. You want an ice cream cone dipped in chocolate before we go?" The blend of cold soft serve and hot chocolate was hard to beat. We needed no coaxing and moved to the counter quickly, causing a teenage girl to rise from a wooden stool.

"What can I get for you?" she pleasantly asked.

"We need three cones dipped in chocolate, please," Mom answered.

"No, that's not right," I interjected. "We need six."

"No, just three," she said.

"No way. If we get ice cream, you get ice cream." Looking at the girl I said, "Six, please."

My brothers and I sat on the picnic table while the adults found wooden rockers facing the back side of a wood stove. The sound of hardened chocolate crunching between teeth carried across the room. Ricky had chocolate on his nose, but either didn't have the time to wipe it off or didn't care. The elderly owner walked from behind the counter and pulled up a rocker beside Doc.

"Where you people from?"

"From the state capital," Dad answered. "We're headin' to the beach for the day. Your store is a required stop every time we come to the beach."

"Well, we appreciate the business," the storeowner said. "I've had this store for thirty-seven years. I took it over when my daddy died. He built it, and at one time this was the only store on this old stretch of highway. I hear talk about a super highway being planned north of us. If that happens it will take the traffic away from this road. It'd probably do this little store in."

"I haven't heard about a new highway," Dad said.

"Sure you have," I said. "He's talkin' about I-20. You know, the one that runs from Augusta to the coast."

I realized, too late of course, that I'd supplied news of the future again.

"What are you talkin' about?" Dad asked. "There's no interstate that goes to the beach." The family looked peculiarly at me, and I bit on my lower lip as I found myself once again searching for an answer to keep my secret intact.

"Wait a minute," I said. "I'm thinking of I-26 that goes to Charleston. I don't know why I get highway name and numbers mixed up. I'm an idiot."

"That's why we call you Magellan," Bobby said, not passing up the opportunity for a jab.

"Well, I just hope the highway stays filled with folks like yourselves," the storeowner said. "Ya'll have a safe trip and a great day." And, with that, he walked behind the counter and sat on his stool, waiting for the next car full of hungry, thirsty travelers seeking respite from the road.

We returned to the family wagon. The grand total for the stop, including gas, totaled four and a half dollars.

Chapter Eighteen

Dad turned off the highway and onto Ocean Drive. Though the road was built for two-way traffic, the accumulation of silt-like sand along the edges tightened the street into a one-lane avenue. The contrast of the faded blacktop and the windblown sand could almost be mistaken for a snow-laced road if it were a winter's day. Small wooden cottages, some white, most grayish-blue, occupied the roadsides in sparse, random order. The Ocean View, a single wing motor lodge, flashed 'Vacancy' in dimly-lit neon outside the door of a tiny lobby. I looked to the eastern horizon where the midday sky blended with the aqua-colored waters of the Atlantic. Only the sun's reflection on the ocean distinguished the two.

"By golly, there it is," Doc said matter-of-factly.

"I can't see diddly," Rick added. "All I see is Bobby's fat head."

I was caught off guard by the simplicity of the beach that would later swell and become a vacation destination for millions. Missing were the condos and high rises that smothered the beachfront. Instead, dunes of reeds and wax myrtles offered a view north and south as far as the eyes could see.

The beach again held the look of a family beach where the only necessities were towels and sandals. Speaking of sandals, they were more important than sunscreen, life jackets, and lifeguards. This was because sandals were the main line of defense in protecting delicate feet from beach sand that reached furnace-like temperatures. More importantly, the sandals were necessary for protection from the dreaded beach sand spur, which was even deadlier than its lamer cousins around Silver Lake. Beach sand spurs were harvested from a nuclear experiment gone horribly wrong. Stings from jelly fish and stingrays paled in comparison to the skin-piercing hell the beach spur unleashed.

As for the sand, it was a bed of hot coals, but only in the dunes leading up to the beach which were fifty to seventy-five yards from the ocean. After that, the sand felt good, especially around the water's edge. The beach was long, flat, and wide. Throughout my life I had walked along the ocean on both coasts and the Gulf of Mexico, in the Bahamas and Europe, and there's no place more perfect than the Carolina beaches.

Dad found a spot along a designated public access parking area, and I was the first to exit, climbing out the rear window. The aroma of the salt air rode a soft breeze blowing off the water. Mom asked for assistance carrying the lounge chairs, towels, and the cooler, but we had already bolted for the water. Safely past the dunes, we discarded our t-shirts and sandals in the sand.

Within seconds we were diving over the first set of waves rolling into shore. Mom, Dad, and Doc positioned the lounge chairs on the sand facing the water, thirty yards from where the tide rolled in. Doc was decked in plaid shorts, a Hawaiian style shirt, white tube socks, and black canvas shoes. He had no intention of entering the foamy waters of the Atlantic. Parking his backside in the first available lounge chair, he folded down his pop-up sunglasses and gave me a quick salute. It was at this point Doc seemed to realize that the beach was filled with an over-abundance of bikini-clad young ladies. Anchored in the chair, he seemed intent performing an inventory check of each and every one.

I spotted Mom and Dad holding hands, combing the beach for shells. I can't express how that sight warmed my heart. Mom occasionally glanced at us, surely keeping a head count. She had complete trust in our swimming abilities, but that didn't mean we were not kept in the watchful eye of our parents.

Kids in my day were taught how to swim at an early age. I had been taught before I'd been shown how to ride a bike. Whether it had been done so for safety reasons, or because swimming was a necessity to escape the hot Carolina summers, I had no clue.

I'm just glad I knew how. I had spent so much time in pools, lakes, and the oceans by the time I walked through the school doors in the fall, my fingers would be wrinkled like a prune. Maybe that's why I struggled to keep hold of my pencil.

While Bobby and I dove for large rocks on the ocean floor, Ricky chased a large group of minnows toward the shore.

"Let's see who can ride a wave the furthest," Bobby said. I had never been one to pass up on competition, especially with my brother.

"Good idea. You go first, but get out of the way when I sail by. I plan on ending up on Uncle Doc's lap."

"Yeah, sure you do."

The water was choppy, as the afternoon winds had increased. The swells, good for body surfing, were spaced twenty yards apart, allowing the waves to build to a nice apex. The success of riding a wave depended on the body surfer's ability to position himself at the base of the wave as it reached its peak. When timed right, the water level in front of the wave would drop suddenly, creating an undertow at the base. At that instant, the body surfer could push towards the shore, allowing the wave to carry him like a surfboard. The swells were cresting at about four to five feet, normal for that stretch known as the Grand Strand.

Bobby soon picked one out, and I knew, by the pull of the swell's undertow, it would carry him a long way. I dove under the wave, reappeared on the back side, and watched Bob ride it like an unmanned raft. It took him a good thirty, thirty-five yards before it fizzled out. Bob shook the salt water out of his eyes and hair, turning around to marvel at the distance he had ridden.

"You're gonna have to ride in on a boat to top that," he boasted.

I drummed up some adrenaline and scoured the horizon for the mother of all waves, needing a turbo charged ride. Several waves passed, some that looked good, but not quite the one I was waiting for.

"Sometime today would be nice," Bobby yelled. I paid him no mind.

A hundred yards back, I spotted a huge swell that was gaining size and momentum. If the crest didn't peak too soon, it would be perfect. Two more waves moved in ahead of it, and I could sense by the budding undertow my patience was paying off. The water depth dropped from my chest to my kneecaps in a matter of seconds, and the wave began to peak. It was twelve feet if it was one.

I stiffened my body, pushed towards the shore, arms extended forward, and caught the wave perfectly. I felt extreme pressure below me at first, and then felt my body lift up, just below the crest of the big wave. Eyes closed, I wondered if that was what it felt like to be shot from a cannon. The deep breath taken prior to taking on the monster wall of water came in handy as I skimmed the water like a wayward missile. The ride was fast, and I began to feel the sand of the surf rub my chest and stomach. Quickly I pulled myself up from my knees, and turned to admire the distance I'd ridden.

I raised my fists. "Yes!" I looked at where Bobby stood so as to estimate the winning margin of distance I'd gone. As I mentally calculated the distance traveled, I felt something rubbing against my feet. It was my swim trunks. The force of the undertow had removed them along the way. Bobby laughed so hard he fell in the water. Ricky stopped chasing fish long enough to point and yell. Uncle Doc flipped his sunglasses upward, apparently to make sure he saw what he thought he saw.

"Go get 'em, sluggie," Doc yelled, slapping his right knee.

I snatched my shorts and ran into deeper water, diving into a wave. Struggling to slip my shorts on while being pounded by waves was no easy task.

"Don't worry about the fish," Bobby shouted. "There's not enough bait for 'em to nibble."

"I can't help if the water's cold."

Fortunately, Mom and Dad had ventured far enough down the beach that they didn't have to witness the incident. Unfortunately, that wasn't the case with several of the young ladies on the beach. After I emerged from the water with shorts securely tied, two teenage girls waved at me and laughed. Of course, I blushed. If winning the wave riding competition required me to expose my nether regions, it was worth it. Besides, I wouldn't ever see any of these girls again. It was a good thing, because my reputation would not have been a flattering one.

We resumed swimming, diving, and rolling through the waves. The ocean floor was as smooth as glass, and the saltwater felt great on our sun-splashed shoulders.

Some of my most memorable moments had occurred on the beach. When I was sixteen, I had shared a kiss with Stacy Bennigan one night on a blanket by a sand dune. Stacy was two years older than me, and kissing an older girl, a college coed, had made me feel like I was a man. The beach had been where I'd told Blake I loved her, though at the time I had gotten a lukewarm response at best.

We had been lying on beach towels, getting some sun after swimming in the ocean, and I'd written 'I love you' in the sand beside her towel while she had her eyes closed. When she opened them, I'd guided her eyes with mine to the sand. She had looked at what I'd written and then rolled over on her back and took a nap. How's that for impact? I guess I should mention that she'd told me she loved me a few days later.

Mom and Dad returned and waded into the water. Dad was wearing a light purple pair of swim trunks and a matching shirt. He left the unbuttoned shirt on, surely to prevent the sun from burning his pale shoulders. Being the only trunks he owned, he observed the one pair trunk limit just like we did. Dad motioned for Doc to come in the water, but Doc shook off his brother's offer. He looked to be thoroughly enjoying the female scenery. I decided to take a shot at getting Doc's feet wet, and walked on shore.

"Come on, Uncle Doc," I requested. "The water feels great."

"Forget it," Doc replied, waving his hand in the air as though he were swatting a fly. "I hate the feeling of sand crammed between my toes. Besides, I'd rather have a drink."

"You mean you've traveled all this way, haven't seen the ocean in fifty years, and you don't want to at least touch the water? You can't find this at Lake Erie. Come on, at least wade in up to your knees. "

"Tell you what. Give me a few more minutes in this chair, and I'll come get my toes wet. Right now, I need to make sure these ladies don't misbehave."

"Okay, then. I'm going back in the water. Take it easy."

"At my age, I'll take it any way I can get it."

What a crazy man.

The midday sun stood bold above, and the heat was building. The soft ocean breeze chased away thoughts I had about the furnace that was sparking to life around me. The beach was becoming more active as people hovered near the ocean's edge. Some families set up tents to escape the sun, or perhaps keep food and drinks cool. I heard a few snores coming from under the tents. Children were everywhere, and they looked content with the simplicity of the water, the sand, and each other. Their laughter was muted only by the crashing of the waves against the surf.

I dove into the water and quietly swam to where Dad waded in chest-deep water. Doing my best to imitate a claw, I pinched his Achilles tendon. He leapt out of the water. "What in the world?" He pulled his knees to his chest, and I could see him treading water above me as if some horrid creature lurked beneath. I heard him yell, "I just got bit by a crab." When I emerged from the water, he splashed me. "Very funny. I'll get you for that one."

After the laughter subsided, Mom looked towards the shore. "You boys want to walk up to the pier?"

"Does Ricky pick his nose?" asked Bobby, his warped way of confirming his vote of 'yes.' Dad and I

267

found the question amusing. Mom and Ricky, of course, did not.

The pier was a large draw, mainly because it allowed one to walk above the ocean. On calm days, especially when the sun was bright, stingrays, jellyfish, and dolphins were easy to spot. I had fished countless times on the pier, day and night, watching the pole bend with each passing wave.

Rarely had I ever reeled in anything besides an empty hook. I couldn't decide whether the fish were just better at eating the bait while it clung to the hook, or whether the roll of the tide made it impossible to know the difference between a tug by a fish or a passing wave. Regardless, I drew a fine line between fishing and just standing on the pier looking stupid. I guess I had kept coming back for more because fishing always brought the possibilities of catching some large ocean creature.

The pier had been a hub of activity twenty-four hours a day during summer months. Fishing for kingfish was popular at night. The pier's lunch counter had been a place to find a greasy meal, day or night. When I was a teen, I'd awaken at sunrise and walk to the pier for breakfast. After I had kids, I would pull an unlucky, and unwilling, child out of bed at dawn to accompany me to the pier. The food was decent at best, but the view of the sun coming up over the horizon of the ocean had been absolutely beautiful.

"Let me get Doc," Dad said. "He'll want to walk on the pier. He'll probably want to sit under the air conditioner in the restaurant too."

We walked the two hundred yards to the pier. Ricky ran ahead of us, looking again for small fish wandering up the shore. White clouds built slowly, like massive bundles of cotton candy. The clouds did their best to hide the sun and provide a temporary break from the heat. Walking up the sand-caked steps, we entered the restaurant at the base of the pier and were immediately greeted by the cool air of the overworked window unit.

"Now this is the place to be," Doc said, removing his hat and flipping up his shades. "I sweated enough out there to fill up a pool. After I run to the little boy's room and shake hands with the guy who stood up for me on my honeymoon, I'll buy you guys something cold to drink."

The restaurant was filled with fisherman, as well as beachgoers seeking food or just a place to cool down. The brown, paneled walls were adorned with all things, great and small, pertaining to fish. Various types of fish were mounted on the wall, from swordfish to catfish, from shark to barracuda. I looked at a picture guide that labeled the fish found in the Atlantic. Mom and Dad looked at a small shelf of souvenirs filled with ceramic sharks, shark teeth, and glass dolphins. Rick and Bob chose drinks from the tall glass cooler by the bait counter. Doc emerged from the bathroom. I looked at him and noticed a slightly devious grin.

"Everything okay?" I asked.

"You bet your ass it is," Doc replied, patting me on the shoulder. "Now get yourself something to drink. I'm buying."

Root beer was the drink of choice for the boys. The refrigerator was as tall as Bobby, with multiple shelves, soda and beer on the top and bait on the bottom. Mom and Dad selected lemonade.

"If they don't serve whisky, I'll take the lemonade," Doc said in a somber tone.

"Let's walk on the pier and see if they're catching anything," I said. I turned to a diminutive man behind the lunch counter, dressed in army fatigue pants and a tee-shirt with 'I'm with Stupid' written above a giant hand, index finger pointing sideways. "What have they been catchin'?"

"Mostly spots and flounder today," the little man replied, a crooked smile revealing a mouth about six to eight teeth short of capacity. "One guy caught a barracuda this morning. Teeth on that sucker must have been two inches long."

"Maybe one of those will tickle your foot when we go back in the water," I said to Dad.

"I think I've gone in the water for the last time," Dad responded.

Dad paid the twenty-five cent per head entry fee for us, and we walked onto the pier. Fishermen lined the pier on both sides. Many sat on wooden benches facing the water, their fishing poles resting in front of them on the rail. Activity was at a minimum. The fishermen looked a bit bored, and the afternoon sun seemed to be zapping what optimism remained in their hopes of landing the big one. The smell of bloodworms and fish heads loomed heavy in the air, combated only by the smell of Coppertone. Sunburnt shoulders and noses were everywhere on the mammoth wooden structure.

I peered through the wooden boards below my feet, watching the waves roll underneath. We walked to the end where the pier opened up on both sides like the head of a hammerhead shark. I stared out on the horizon of the mysterious blue sea, where I used to think I could see Europe on the ocean's horizon.

"Hey Dad, think there's any whales out there?" Ricky asked.

"Sure," said Bobby. "Look, there's Ahab on a dinghy, smacking Moby with an oar."

"How'd you like me to jam an oar up your—" Rick said before Dad interrupted with, "That's enough."

I took hold of Mom's hand. "It sure is peaceful isn't it?"

"Yes, sweetie, it sure is. It makes you appreciate what God has created. Can you imagine what Heaven must be like?"

I bit my lip a moment before I spoke, knowing she would be experiencing just that when my trip to the past was done. "I just hope you're waiting for me when I get there."

"With open arms, son. With open arms." I leaned my head onto her shoulder. "Hopefully, that will be many years from now."

"Man, would you look at that!" Doc shouted, looking over the rail into the water.

A shark glided across the top of the water, sleek and smooth. I had only seen one shark in the ocean before, and that was as an adult in the mouth of an inlet. To make things interesting, I had been crossing the inlet in waist-deep water at the time.

Several fishermen tossed their bait towards the shark, hoping for the opportunity to battle the beast. It appeared to be around six feet long. The shark seemed disinterested in their offerings and skirted around the outer edges of the wooden poles of the pier.

The shrill sound of a lifeguard's whistle cut the air, serving notice for the swimmers to evacuate the water. His whistle set off a chain reaction as lifeguard stations down the beach signaled the swimmers to get out of the water. Although the shark was probably a sand shark, and posed no threat to the swimmers, the lifeguards took no chances. Though there were probably other sharks in the water more dangerous, it created some excitement for the lifeguards, who, except when talking to girls, seem bored and under-worked. The shark disappeared from view and the beachgoers resumed normal activities.

We moved about the pier, observing the fishermen. Doc struck up a conversation with a middle-aged woman, discussing her choice of bait. From the look in his eyes, he was hoping to offer her some bait of his own. The afternoon sun beat off the time-worn wood, increasing the temperature on the pier to stifling proportions. The ocean breeze's ability to provide relief was stifled on the hot, wooden surface. Mom had seen enough and wanted to entice her boys off the pier.

"You boys ready to eat?" she asked. Like trained mice, we quickly exited the pier, ready to devour lunch.

The beach had filled with beachcombers and sun worshipers. Though the ocean's edge was alive with activity, there was a sense of peace and order.

"Man, it's strange to be on the beach without hip hop music thundering everywhere," I said. The family looked at me as if I was Elvis arriving for surfing lessons.

"Hip who?" Bobby asked. "What kind of music?"

My mind moved quickly. "It's a new style of music on the west coast. I think the Beach Boys are playing it."

"Well, I've never heard of it," says Bobby. "I think you're full of malarky."

"Wait and see. You'll hear more of it than you'll care to one day."

We soon arrived at the lounge chairs and the wooden picnic basket. Dad poured sweet tea from a Tupperware pitcher into some plastic cups while Mom spread out a cream-colored blanket. She pulled several sandwiches from the basket and a huge bag of chips.

Bobby opened the bag and looked inside. "Great. Six chips and a bag of air."

"You can have the air," I said, "and I'll take the chips."

Uncle Doc snagged a ham sandwich. "Ellen, you got any butter?" he asked.

"You put butter on ham sandwiches?" Ricky asked.

"You better know it. A sandwich ain't a sandwich without butter. What do you think you're eatin'?"

"I'm eatin' a peanut butter and jelly sandwich," Rick said proudly.

"Well, there you go. Butter in your sandwich too."

Few words were spoken as we ate our homemade lunch on the blanket covering the soft sand.

"I'm done," Ricky said after swallowing the last of his sandwich. "I'm gonna go back in the water."

"Oh, no," Mom said. "You can't go in the water for thirty minutes. You have to let your food digest."

I had often wondered where the food-digest-timetable-translator originated. Every mother had seemed to know the table by heart, presumably after attending some secret class whereby they had been taught the length of time children must stay out of the water after consuming food. The amount of time had differed, depending on the food. Peanut butter and jelly had equated to a thirty-minute waiting period. Lunch meats had required forty-five minutes. Tuna salad, twenty minutes. Without a doubt, it had been a sophisticated system developed through years and years of motherly study.

"Aw, Mom," Ricky protested. "You don't really believe that do you?"

"Don't argue, Rick. It's a proven fact that it's dangerous to swim right after eating. You'll develop cramps if you do."

"And since you will be swimmin' in a whole three feet of water," Bobby added, "you won't be able to walk out of the ocean back onto shore."

"Very funny," Mom said. "You can whine all you want, but you're not going into the water for thirty minutes."

I was in no hurry to return to the water. The ocean would always be there, but my family wouldn't. Mom glanced at the ocean and I again noticed just how beautiful she was. I wondered what a sister might have looked like. Surely she wouldn't have been as pretty as Mom. Pretty or not, she would have been overprotected, that's for sure. With three brothers and a father who possessed three shotguns and mounds of ammunition, we would have made sure the boys treated her as though she were a leper.

As we continued our ocean-side picnic, Dad gently touched Mom's hand. Doc stared again at the young ladies walking the beach. Ricky tried to entice a fiddler crab to come out of his hole in the sand, and Bobby and I watched a chubby boy try to fly a kite without decapitating the other beachcombers. The kite constantly nosedived like a bat chasing mosquitoes at dusk. The kid was so focused on keeping the red, white, and blue kite airborne that he stepped across a blanket full of teenage girls.

"Watch it, tubby," one of the girls shouted.

The boy, hanging on for dear life, didn't seem to notice, or care, what was going on around him. He only seemed interested in controlling the bipolar kite.

"Hey," Bobby said. "Kite boy's hangin' a quarter moon over there. He needs to yank those shorts up a foot or two. I'm losin' my appetite."

"Bobby!" Mom said. "Be nice. He can't help it."

"I bet he could if he did a few deep knee bends," I said.

"You boys stop it," she said in a losing cause. We were there to have fun after all, even if it was at the expense of others.

Doc stopped his babe-staring and finally noticed the struggling kite flier. "What's a matter with that fella? Looks like he escaped from the zoo." The boy's kite show lasted long enough to satisfy the food digestion wait time.

"Okay," Mom said. "You boys can go back in the water for a little while longer, and then we've got to head back home."

We enjoyed one last swim. Mom and Dad packed up the blanket, the picnic basket, and the towels. I spent my time in the water watching Bobby and Ricky as they made the most of their time before it was time to head home. I breathed in the salt air and glanced down the beach one last time. What a shame the beach couldn't have remained as quaint as it looked right then. No high rises, no jet skis, no twin-engine planes flying down the beach with advertisements hanging from its tail.

The ride home was a quick one, mainly because of the nap that I took. The sun and water had taken its toll on us, and we took advantage of time on the road to catch up on some much-needed rest. It was a perfect day, and I'm sure I slept with a smile on my face.

Chapter Nineteen

The weekend came to a close, and Doc prepared for his trip home. I never liked seeing my relatives leave, and this time was incredibly hard, for I knew it was the last time I'd ever see my uncle. I hugged him, and I did a poor job of hiding my sadness. When I let go of him, he looked at me and smiled with his eyes, something hard to explain, but it was true.

"Well, sluggie, I guess this is it," he said, extending his hand. This time it truly was, and I had trouble letting go of his hand.

"Uncle Doc, I just want you to know I love you, and you have meant a lot to me."

Doc looked as though he tried to keep the situation light. "Well, dadgummit, we gotta stay in touch. I'll get back down as soon as I can. You get your fanny up to Ohio soon and we'll stir up a little trouble."

I wanted to tell him that wasn't possible, but I dared not. I pulled away and walked to the house to hide the tears. Once inside, I became emotional.

Mom walked in a few minutes later, and placed her arms around me. "It's okay, Chase. You'll see him again someday soon."

"No, I won't."

"What makes you think you won't?"

"I can't explain now, but I know I won't. Soon I won't be seeing you either." I grabbed her, hugging her with all my might, and the tears poured like a fountain. I had held up quite well, given the whole, 'she'll be dead when you wake up,' scenario. But I knew my time was short, and the only part of her I'd be able to hold would be memories.

"Chase, don't say that."

"It's true. Soon I'll be gone. I wish I could explain it, but I can't. Life for you will be normal, and I'll still be in your life. But you won't be in mine."

"Nonsense. How can that be?"

"Just trust me. It's just the way it is and there's nothing I can do about it. It might happen while I'm sleeping, or maybe while I'm right beside you. I don't know. My spirit, my soul, is going to leave."

Mom looked confused, probably attributing my wild thoughts to the fact that Doc was leaving. She held me without speaking.

Dad, Bobby, and Rick walked back in to the house.

"I sure am gonna miss Uncle Doc," Bobby said. "He's one of the greatest guys I've ever met."

"Yes, he is," Mom said.

Even Dad's eyes told of sadness, as if he wondered himself if he would see his brother again.

Dad had spent the whole weekend without a drink.

The family settled in for a quiet Sunday evening of popcorn and television. We watched Ed Sullivan on the black-and-white. A late evening storm rolled in, and the distant sound of thunder made the television a bit cloudy. The warm evening began to turn cooler, and the air conditioner unit got a much-needed rest.

"You boys want to stay up late?" Dad asked. "I think we can extend bedtime a while tonight."

Ricky, in a look of disbelief, raised his eyebrows as if it were a trick. "Can we really stay up late?"

"Sure," Dad replied. "It's summer time, and you boys don't have to get up in the morning. Ellen, can you make some more popcorn? I don't think one bowl is going to be enough."

"I'll turn the stove on," Mom said. It was pre-microwave days.

Dad let Ricky choose the television show following Ed Sullivan. They were shows Ricky had only seen while hiding under the dining room table after he had snuck out of his room after bedtime. He and I had become quite proficient at crawling behind and around furniture to get late night glimpses of the television.

We had to work our way through the bedroom hallway, across the living room, and then slip into the dining room. It was under the dining room table where we had watched everything from the Cartwrights to Marshall Dillon.

It was a time when television was changing from safe, conservative subjects to topics like racism, the Vietnam War, and sex. There had still been plenty of wholesome shows available, but there were some that pushed the envelope on sensitive subjects. The subject of sex had seemed to catch my attention, I'm sure because I was steadily becoming more interested in girls. I figured I could use all the help I could get.

I had no idea that the shows I considered racy would be considered prudish by today's standards. There had been no need for child safety features in my day. Besides, how much could a boy see when there were only three channels?

We sucked down popcorn and sodas, disregarding the fact that we would be making bathroom runs throughout the night. Mom finally ignored the dishes in the kitchen sink to hang out with the men in her life. After Archie Bunker finished a tirade on the infiltration of 'Commies' into the American public, Ricky fell asleep on the carpet, his head resting on a sneaker. His first shot at staying up late had fizzled. Mom traded the shoe for a pillow and covered him with a blanket from the back of the couch. The faint smell of the evening rain, a hint of wet copper, penetrated the den windows, and the gentle patter on the front porch awning assured that Ricky would do his Rip Van Winkle impersonation the rest of the evening.

Television had never seemed so much fun as it did that night. Even the commercials were worth watching. As an adult, I avoided commercials like The Plague. I've worn out many remotes changing channels, putting the family through misery in the process. But, on that evening, my nostalgic bones were just anxious for anything from my childhood. My eyes began to get heavy, and I fought it with all my might, not wanting the evening to end. And, for a brief moment, I dozed off on the floor beside Ricky.

Briefly, thanks to Bobby. As I began to enter a deep sleep, a loud bang shook everyone in the room except Ricky, who remained in a vegetable-like state. I rose quickly and looked to see who'd been shot.

"What in the world?" Dad yelled.

Bobby was laughing hysterically, slapping his leg with his right hand, and pointing at Dad with his left. I squinted to look closely at Dad's lower lip and chin, which looked grotesque. The butt of his cigarette was still clenched tightly in between his lips, but it rested on his chin like shredded wheat. Dad stared at the match he'd used to light the cigarette.

"These matches are defective," Dad said, unaware he was a victim of Bobby's practical joke.

"It wasn't the match," Bobby said in between laughs. "It was the load I placed in your cigarette."

Dad shook his head, trying to hide a smile. "If I was you, I wouldn't close my eyes tonight. Otherwise you might wake up in the back yard, or maybe the middle of the street. You might wake up hanging upside down on the streetlight."

We all laughed, Mom included. Bobby had always been the joker of the family, and Ricky and I had to endure our share of humiliation. But most of the jokes had honed in on Dad, and it seemed only logical. Dad had seemed the easiest in the family to pick on, for some reason. Maybe it had been because the cussing and fussing was more profound coming from Dad. For Rick or me, we typically would throw something at Bobby and be done with it. Not Dad. He would rant and rave for days, and it had just made it that much funnier.

~//~

Sometimes things happened to Dad that weren't practical jokes by design. They just turned out that way.

I was about nine, best I can remember. I had been hammering carpet tacks into a broken bat, and I remember Bobby walking to the crawlspace that led under the house. Dad had slithered into the crawl space, trying to track a leak from the bathroom floor. It had been a hot, muggy day, typical for a summer day in South Carolina. Bobby had yelled to Dad that he had a very important phone call. I can still recall Dad's voice echoing out through the vents underneath the house, "How do you know it's important?"

Bobby had replied, "Because the man said so. He sounded like it was urgent."

Mom had gone to the grocery store a little earlier, and maybe Dad thought something bad had happened to her. I remember hearing him cussing as he'd crawled over and under the vents, brick columns, and other items such as the lawn mower and wheel barrow.

"What the...!" he yelled from underneath, "I'm stuck."

I ran to the doorway of the crawl space and looked over Bobby's shoulder. Dad had gotten lodged between two air ducts and a nail had caught the collar on the back of his shirt. The harder he'd pulled, the madder he'd got. For the sake of decency, I'll not relay the profanity that came from his mouth.

Finally, he had broken free and, when he'd climbed out from underneath the house, his clothes and his face were covered in a dark layer of dirt. His hair was ruffled and he'd been so ticked off. After dusting himself off, he had walked in the back door to the kitchen and picked up the receiver. After the caller had identified himself as one selling burial plots, Dad had not only hung up the phone, he'd yanked the phone line out of the wall.

"Unbelievable!" I can still hear Dad shout from the kitchen. He had walked outside and stared at Bobby. "How about screen the calls next time, for the love of Pete? Burial plots." He'd then started towards the crawl space. "You're the one who'll be needing the burial plot if this ever happens again."

~//~

The evening flew by, but eventually it was time for bed.

"Don't forget you have a game tomorrow," Mom said to me. "I've got your uniform cleaned and ready on the dryer. Sweet dreams."

"Thanks, Mom. You, too. Night, Dad. Have a good day at work tomorrow."

"Okay, son. See you at your game."

I had never looked so forward to playing a game.

"Night, Bobby," I said as I walked through the doorway of the den. "Yell if you get scared. I'll bring your teddy bear and blanket."

"Riiight," said Bobby. "Don't sleepwalk naked."

The emotions of the day had zapped my energy. I'd never see Uncle Doc again. Soon, the same would apply to Mom. My boyhood would soon return to the corners of my mind, no longer able to carry me to the ball field and never again to take me down the streets of my youth. Those thoughts were hard on my heart. But Dad had a grip on his drinking, and perhaps I had helped the future enough that he would forever have won the battle with the bottle.

Wrapped up in the warmth of the love shared by our family that day, I drifted off to sleep. I'm not sure how long I'd been asleep but I woke up to the sound of music and, at first, I thought I was dreaming. I opened my eyes to stare, unfocused, at the dark bedroom wall that stood linear, like a black canvas. The music couldn't have been coming from the television. The house looked dark, so everyone must have been in bed. I turned my head slightly so I could hear more clearly, and I rose slowly on my elbows. Curious as to the origin of the sweet sound, I tiptoed towards the hallway, the cool wooden floor lightly creaking under my bare feet. I stepped into the hallway as 'Unchained Melody' by the Righteous Brothers played softly on the living room stereo.

The room, lit only by beams of the streetlight drifting through a half-opened curtain, revealed the silhouette of two people slow-dancing. Gently swaying to the soft beat of the music, they glided about the floor. I smiled, watching Mom and Dad hold each other in the darkness. I was careful to remain in the hallway so as not to disturb them, and I stood motionless. I had never, ever, seen them dance.

With Mom's head resting gently on Dad's shoulder, her brown hair just under his chin, I watched my parents rekindle their love. They had shared the highs and lows of marriage, of life, like everyone else, but they knew they were meant to share them together. I had heard the stories from aunts and uncles. I'd seen pictures of them together when they were barely out of their teens, and I gathered that they had broken quite a few hearts when they'd got married. Maybe the stories were just that, but I know I'm no different than anyone else in truly believing that my parents were beautiful, the heartthrobs of the county and the envy of all. And I know I will never think otherwise.

And so, in my mind, their dance carried them back in time, back to when they first fell in love. I imagined them sitting along the bank of Spears Creek in the spring, fields of purple and yellow mountain iris their backdrop, a sun-drenched valley, and being serenaded by the creek that was as old as time itself.

The steady flow of tears beat down my cheeks, and I'm man enough to admit it. I leaned against the wall and saw Mom's tiny fingers covered gently inside Dad's hand, resting at his chest. The memories and images created in my journey back in time were plentiful, but the silhouette of them dancing will be forever etched in my memory.

Chapter Twenty

The next afternoon, the fruits of my labor were in full bloom. Well, I'm taking credit for more than I should here, but it's my story, so that's the way it goes.

Rick and I were throwing the baseball in the backyard when Dad pulled into the driveway. Mom was pulling clothes from the line, and I could hear the breeze flapping the sheets like they were keeping time to some symphony nature had composed. At first, Mom looked worried when she saw Dad walk around the side of the yard to the patio. I was a little apprehensive too, and so I held the ball in my glove and watched him. It was three-thirty, a good two hours before he normally came home from work.

"Where's Bobby?" Dad asked. He opened the porch door and took hold of a bat from the rack and reappeared on the patio. He looked like a man who couldn't wait for answers.

"What's wrong?" Mom questioned.

"Not a thing. I was sitting at my desk, and I got to thinking. Thinking about how awesome this family is. About how nothing should ever be more important than you—more important than us. And so I walked into the boss's office and told him I needed the afternoon off."

He looked at the bat and gave it a swing. "What do you say we all go to the ball field?" He smiled at Mom, and she looked puzzled. "Let's see if these young punks can hang with their old man."

We walked toward Dad, and my first thought was to check and make sure he was sober. "What do you say, boys? Want a little lesson on how to play the game of baseball? Ellen, don't think you're going to be a spectator, because you're playing too."

"Me? You must be crazy. I'll watch from the dugout."

"No way. Go dust off your sneakers, if you remember where they are." He laughed. "Is Bobby working?"

"He went in early so he gets off at 4:00."

Rick took his bat excitedly from the rack and placed the handle of it through the strap of his glove. He was armed and ready. I removed two balls and placed them in my glove with the one I had been throwing with Rick. Mom and Dad changed while we waited on the front steps.

"What's gotten into Dad?" Rick asked.

"I've got a hunch. But whatever it is, I sure do like it."

"Me too. He's been fun to be around lately. Have you noticed?"

"I sure have."

Mom left a note on the door for Bob with instructions to change and meet us at the field.

The field sat empty, as it was an hour before parents would arrive to line and drag it, and an hour and a half before players would arrive. My team wasn't scheduled to play until the next day, so I was free to play a family doubleheader if time allowed. It was the first time we'd seen our parents on the ball field. I had brought two spare gloves, and I handed one to Mom, the other to Dad. Dad took a ball that I had tossed behind home plate and lined Mom up in front of him, twenty feet down the third base line. She laughed when her throw fell short of Dad by several feet. By the time it made it to his glove, the ball had almost come to a stop.

"This is going to be ugly," she said.

"You're doing fine, Mom," I said. I walked beside her and watched her catch the ball Dad had thrown, a soft, crescent moon toss that she trapped between her glove and her stomach. "It will hurt a lot less if you use more glove and less body when you catch it."

I took the ball from her glove and placed it in her right hand. I pushed downward on the webbing of the glove to open it. "Keep it open as wide as you can so you'll have as much room to catch it as possible."

I stood behind her and took her hand with the ball, her hand so soft and gentle. A hand that had soothed away my aches and pains for a lifetime. A hand that had made my worries disappear. I loosened her wrist.

"Make it like a wet noodle." I moved to her right. I'd given a hundred baseball lessons in my day, but none could compare with helping her. "Point the ball towards me," I said. "Curve your wrist so that your arm and the ball look like a snake ready to strike. Now, point your shoulder at Dad and when you're ready, step towards him and throw as hard as you can."

Mom, in sleeveless white blouse and denim shorts, was the daintiest player I had ever seen on the diamond. She shook her head as if to warn the family not to expect any accuracy, and she stepped and threw the ball to Dad. The ball was not thrown hard, but it went directly to its target. She smiled and pressed the glove against her chest.

"I did it." She smiled. Such a beautiful smile. Her eyes sparkled. A scene also etched in my memory forever.

"Nice throw," Dad said. "Okay, it's coming back to you." He tossed a soft one and she straightened her arm in front of her, blinking briefly as the ball dropped into her mitt.

"There's nothing to this game," she said, laughing. She and Dad continued to throw while Rick and I paired up. Within a few minutes Bobby's car roared into the parking lot. Soon he was on the field, puzzled to see his family gathered on the field with gloves.

"What's going on?" he asked, hands on his hips.

"We're getting ready to play a game," Dad replied. "It's time for your mom and me to teach you boys a lesson in humility."

"Well, let's get it on then," said Bob.

He threw with Rick while I ran to the equipment shed and removed three flat, rubber bases which teams used on the playground of the school when the ball field was occupied. I watched Mom laugh, and I saw Dad smile that smile at her that I'm sure made her fall in love with him. I thought of how Dad's shoulders had become worn with age, and how healthy he looked now on that field, his tank-top undershirt revealing shoulders from a generation ago.

Clouds of white, moving under the blue sky like a ghostly armada, sent patchy shadows across the infield, intermittent refuge from the summer sun. Bobby went to first base and Rick took the mound. I went to shortstop. Dad handed Mom a bat, and she eagerly stepped in the batter's box. She bent her knees slightly, and moved her backside back and forth like a pendulum. Her elbows outward, pointing in opposite directions, she squeezed the bat tightly.

"I've been wanting to do this since I was a little girl," she said. She looked to the mound. "Okay, Ricky, don't hit your mother. It wouldn't be nice to clonk the woman who brought you into this world."

Rick smiled and held up the ball for her to see. "Okay, Mom, I'm going to blow this by you. I just wanted you to see what the ball looks like now because, once I pitch it, it will be nothing more than a blur."

"We'll see about that," Dad said from the on deck circle, swinging the bat that he used to hit us pop flies in the backyard.

Rick used his Juan Marichal windup, and he raised his left leg high and stiff as he twisted his upper body, his arm flailing the ball as it twisted around his body. Mom swung and missed.

"Having a little trouble?" Rick asked.

Dad picked up the ball and threw it to Rick. He whispered into Mom's ear, and she smiled. She resumed her stance, again shaking her tail with confidence. Again the same result.

"Strike two," Rick said.

Mom smiled again. "Bring that steam ball one more time."

"Steam ball?" I yelled from shortstop.

"Steam ball. Fastball. Whatever you call it. Just bring it."

Rick delivered another pitch, and Mom hit a hard ground ball to second. Bobby gave chase and it headed for the outfield. I ran to the edge of the infield where it met the grass of right center field.

"Go, go, go," Dad yelled as Mom took off down the first base line. She stepped on the flat rubber base at first and almost tripped. She moved on down to second as Bobby grabbed the ball against the outfield fence. He threw it to me, and Rick ran to home for the relay. Mom made her way to third, laughing every step of the way, her arms stiff like they were in casts up to her armpits. She turned for home, Dad waving her on as I threw the ball to Rick. He caught it, standing in front of home plate, smiling because he knew she had no chance to score. As he began to apply the tag, Dad lifted Rick up by his pants and spun him so that he faced the pitcher's mound. By the time he had swung full circle, Mom had stepped on home plate. Bob and I smiled while Rick protested. Mom jumped into Dad's arms.

"A home run your first at bat," Dad said. Rick had his hands on his hips and he walked to the mound, mad but able to give a slight smile. "Hard to top that," Dad called out.

"I think Mom and Dad have their own set of rules," Rick said.

Dad stepped into the batter's box, and it didn't take long for him to show off. He sent Rick's first pitch into the trees behind center field, and when he jogged the bases I yelled at Rick, "Can you serve up a bigger meatball?"

"Pipe down."

Mom hugged Dad when he stepped on home plate.

It was a baseball game to end all baseball games. Dad pitched while Mom played first. Ground balls hit to Dad he'd swallow up like air, tossing softly to Mom for the out. Dad in his glasses with flip up-shades, Mom in her dainty white sneakers. Us in shorts and tee-shirts, getting dirtier by the pitch. It was the game of my life, a game where no score was kept, where every out recorded was done in laughter, where every run scored was celebrated. It meant more than any World Series game ever could, watched by no one else, but in a way I imagined it watched by the entire world. It was a game made for heaven, a celestial gathering of one angel and four ordinary men.

Chapter Twenty-One

I've had people tell me that life is a journey. Webster defines journey as an 'act of traveling from one place to another.' Does that mean life is a metaphor for one's evolution in finding true meaning? Or does it imply transference to some place far away? Not physically, necessarily, but a state of being, a state of purpose? To me, it implies life's beginning and end are polar opposites.

But I'm not so sure that's how it works. At least, not for me. With any trip, whether it's crossing the country or walking a nature trail, there is intent of reaching some destination, to find something at the end of it or, perhaps, to find something along the way. Perhaps it's to help us grow, to uncover some mystery of life. Some mystery within ourselves? What if it's not to uncover a mystery, but an awakening that the essence of life, or the essence of being, is found not in some far-away place, but in the subtle things surrounding us in everyday life?

Early morning sunbeams streamed through the curtain in my bedroom, offering a laser-light-show on the white wooden closet doors. I rubbed my eyes, yawned, and stretched my body in the warm bed. I felt odd. It's hard to describe, but it was like I had jetlag. Like I had been traveling for days on a plane and had just stepped off, not sure of where I was, what day it was, or whether it was night or day.

I made my way to the kitchen, thinking breakfast would shake me from the funk I was in. Mom reminded me, when I entered the kitchen, that my game began at 5:30. That meant that warm ups began at 4:45. Bobby had a rare day off from the grocery store and, as always, needed rest, which translated to a heavy dose of couch and television time. Ricky was busy at work on a new masterpiece with his Lego blocks.

I removed the last cinnamon roll from the Tupperware bowl and took a tall glass of milk to the front steps. Wearing a pair of gray cotton shorts and a white tee-shirt, barefoot, I sat, covered by shade on the top step. I breathed deeply, filling my lungs with the morning air, listening to the sounds of a distant lawnmower, of two children riding their tricycles in the driveway down the street, their mother watching closely as she folded clothes.

I caught the song of a blue jay in the tall pine above the house, and the gentle flapping of sheets on Mrs. Mackie's clothesline. The faint melody from wind chimes on a nearby porch rode the soft breeze. Familiar sounds, and I realized how much I had missed them.

When I was a boy, I'd heard those sounds every day, but I hadn't given them much thought. I certainly hadn't appreciated them. Perhaps the innocence of youth had led me to think life would always be filled with those sounds. And maybe they have been, but it doesn't sound the same as it did then. I think that life dulls the senses when it comes recognizing the little nuances of chimes or a warm breeze. But, on that day, I made sure to soak it all in like I would never experience it ever again.

A convoy of red ants climbed the steps below my bare feet, moving at a fast pace, single file. They had found crumbs from my cinnamon roll to their liking, and began carrying their feast to the anthill. The concrete steps, cool against my legs, slowly warmed as the sun chased the shade from the front porch. I disregarded the heat building on the back of my sun-splashed neck. For over an hour I sat in silence, soaking in the tranquility of the slow pace of the neighborhood.

"Chase," Mom called through the front door, "come eat."

I took another long look at the peaceful street in front of my house before I walked inside. Rick took a break from his construction work and joined Bobby and me at the kitchen table. Again, I asked Mom to stop her chores long enough to eat with us.

Roast beef and gravy poured over toast sat on the table.

"How come we're eatin' supper stuff for lunch?" Ricky asked.

"'Cause we'll be eating hotdogs at the game tonight," Mom explained. "I want something decent in your bellies at lunch."

We wanted to ensure that something decent reached our bellies too, and we ate everything on our plates.

The afternoon slipped away as game time approached. I removed my freshly washed uniform from atop the dryer, and the light aroma of starch skirted across the back porch. After pulling off my tee-shirt and slipping out of my shorts, I put on the gray pants, a blue stripe running along the seam of each leg.

I slipped my arms into the jersey, a stripe on each sleeve as well as along both sides of the button holes, left it unbuttoned and slid the thick blue belt through five wide loops of the pants. I hopped on the washer and pulled the thick, white socks to my kneecaps.

It may have been just putting on a uniform, but to me it was like putting on armor before a battle. After slipping on the blue stirrups, which were pulled up just above the kneecaps, I buttoned my shirt. Across the chest spelled Phillip's Garden Center, with a blue '5' on the back. My cleats and glove sat in the wire clothesbasket, and I carried them to the bedroom, then removed my cap from the bedpost.

I heard Mandy barking, and I walked outside to see if she was okay. She looked very unsettled, running back and forth along the fence. I opened the gate and let her out, figuring she had pent up energy she needed to release. Instead of taking off across the yard, she leapt into my arms and knocked me down. It was as though she hadn't seen me in years. I made it to my knees, hugged her, and scratched under her floppy ears. She whimpered as though she were hurting.

"What's a matter, girl?" I continued to pet her as I checked her paws and legs. I didn't notice anything that would make her whimper like she was. It was such a rare thing for her to be panicky.

She kept placing her face against mine, and slobber soon covered my chin. I knew I needed to get to the ball field, so I tried to lead her into the kennel. She slid along my legs as though she was trying to get as close to me as possible. I knelt and looked into her eyes and she looked afraid, or sad. I'd never seen such a look from her.

"It's okay, Mandy." I stroked her head. "It's okay."

I nudged her through the gate as though I was following behind her, but I quickly shut the gate. She looked at me and began to bark, again running back and forth along the fence.

"Easy, now. Easy." My commands did nothing to soothe her. I backpedaled, talking to her as I walked.

When I was near the back porch door, I heard the fence rattle. She had climbed it, falling sharply on her side. Unfazed, she ran toward me in full gait and, when I knelt, she again knocked me on my back.

It was all I could do to get her back in the kennel, and I had to fasten her leash from the corner of the fence. I knelt in front of her, talking to her. Trying to soothe her. It was though she sensed I was leaving for good. I promise she had actual tears in her eyes, and soon I did too. I hugged her and she whimpered.

"I love you, girl. You are the best dog in the world."

She barked at me again as I walked to the house, and I couldn't bring myself to turn around and see her again in such agony.

I had to leave for the field. Just a ten-minute walk, it had seemed much longer when I was a boy. Isn't it amazing how time and space seem tighter and slower when we are kids? Maybe it's because our world is centered on fewer things, thereby reducing our world to a few, specific places and events.

"Bye, Mom," I said, hugging her at the den door.

"I'll see you there," she said with a smile. "Be careful. Watch for cars."

"Yes, ma'am."

On the porch steps, I sat and put on my dusty, black cleats. As my feet stepped off the downward sloping driveway and onto the road, I felt an odd desire to turn and look at the house. When I did, I spotted a silhouette of an elderly woman at the curtain's edge of the picture window in the living room. Her smile, her hair of silver, her petite stature, were all so familiar. I looked closer and whispered, "Mom?" I stood motionless, squinting my eyes under the bright sun. The woman slid away from the window. Puzzled, I glanced down at the driveway, removing my cap, and rubbed the bill against my forehead. Again I looked at the picture window, but only the curtain was in view, with no movement at all. I figured the bright sun was casting shadows through the living room window. Turning back to the road, I erased the vision of the woman from my mind, and my cleats were soon on the gravelly pavement.

The heat of the day had kept most of the neighbors indoors. A black-and-brown German shepherd barked as it ran along its imprisoning fence, providing the only sounds for the first two blocks. Getting closer to the field, I saw cars roll by as parents began dropping off the boys at the ball field who lived too far to walk.

A block from the field, I noticed Perry Williamson's lawn entrenched in foot-tall grass, and the flowerbed overrun with weeds. I was thinking how nice the yard had looked just a few days earlier when I rode by in Toby's Impala. I stopped in the road, confused. A tiny lady, dressed in a green-and-white dress, with long silver hair tucked under a wide-brim straw hat, sat on her knees, slowly tugging at the weeds.

I walked up the driveway.

"Hey Gramma Williamson," I said as she continued battling the weeds. "What's the deal with your lawn? I bet it's grown a foot in less than two weeks." Either unable to hear, or unwilling to stop, she was oblivious to me. "Um, excuse me," I said, "has Perry left for the ball field? I thought we could walk together."

The woman, stopping to scratch an itch on her chin, stood as though to ease the stress on her knees and back, but still had not responded to my questions.

"Grandma Williamson?" I called out loud and clear.

"Well, hello there young man," the elderly woman said.

I stepped closer, and I'm sure I couldn't hide the look of disbelief on my face. "Mrs. Williamson?"

The woman was Perry's mother.

"Yes?" she replied, removing her gloves and straw hat.

What was I supposed to say after that? I tried to act normal, but that was next to impossible. "Um, uh, I was hoping Perry was here. We have a game today."

"A game? I'm not sure what you mean. Perry lives in Reno. I got to visit with him and my precious grandchildren just last month. But he hasn't been here to visit in over three years."

I was speechless, and my heart began to race. I felt nauseous and lightheaded. I wanted to sit. "How do you know Perry?" she asked.

A slamming car door turned my eyes towards the road. A man, small in stature, closed the car door to his late model Buick. "Can I help you?"

"I was just talkin' with Mrs. Williamson," I told the man.

"Who?"

Holding my glove under my arm, I pointed, turning towards the house. There was no one there but the man and me. "Um, I was just talking to..." and I looked around the yard. "Did you see where Mrs. Williamson went?"

"Son, there's nobody here by that name. I think you got the wrong house."

I regarded the man as one seeing a ghost. *Wrong house*, I wondered. This man's crazy. But when I looked again at the house, seeing nothing but the weeds and tall grass, I knew I was the crazy one. "I'm sorry. I guess I do have the wrong house."

I jogged to the road.

"Son, are you alright?"

I kept my eyes on the pavement and ran for the ball field. I ran through the parking lot and down the grassy path, and, when I saw my team in the dugout, I breathed a sigh of relief.

The fathers were preparing the field for play, and the mothers were getting the concession stand ready. I smelled hotdogs cooking as I ran onto the field and into the dugout.

I wondered why we hadn't started warming up, and then Coach Cooper, visibly upset, asked us to sit on the bench. "I'm afraid I have some bad news," he started. I knew immediately what the bad news was. "This past weekend, Joe went on a camping trip, and, well, uh," said the coach, struggling to keep his composure, "he had an accident."

"What happened?" Rusty asked, surely unprepared for the forthcoming answer.

"Well," Coach Cooper continued, "he fell into the river and was carried over a waterfall. He didn't survive."

The team was silent. Players looked at each other. A few began to cry. I noticed Perry at the far end of the bench, and I'm sure he noticed me giving him a strange look. Reno?

"Now, boys," the coach said, "sometimes things in life happen that we don't have answers for." The players sat motionless. "I wanted to postpone the game out of respect to Joe's family, but his mother said Joe would have wanted us to play. That he wouldn't want sad faces, but happy ones playing this game we love. Because of her wishes, the game will go on. It would be great for us to win for Joe's family and sign the game ball and present it to them. We can all present it to them, together." Tears trickled down Coach Cooper's cheeks, and Coach Long placed his hand on Coach Cooper's shoulders.

Although I'd known for almost thirty years the outcome of Joe's trip to Flat Rock, it still was a punch to the gut. Slowly, I rose from the bench, and said, "Live each day as if it's your last fellas, 'cause one day, it's gonna be."

Word soon spread, and the mothers in the concession stand came down to the dugout to console their sons as well as the others on the team. Slowly, the team walked down the left field line to warm up. I noticed Benny crying. Walking over to him, and using my sleeve, I reached down to wipe the diminutive boy's eyes.

"It's okay, Benny. It's okay to cry."

Benny pulled the bill of his cap down to cover his face and cried so hard his body began to shake. We all surrounded him, patting him on his shoulders. It touched me to see the players come to the aide of their teammate.

"Well, guys," I said, rubbing tears away with the top of my cap, "I say we give it all we got for Joe. Let's play the best we've ever played today. Waddaya say?"

The boys nodded their heads, and even Benny nodded slightly.

When we warmed up, not a word was spoken. As the bleachers filled, the news about Joe spread. The league president said a prayer on home plate just prior to the first pitch.

The game started with an air of somberness as the players fought to keep their minds on baseball. It seemed so insignificant at the moment. But, after the first inning was complete, a little pep, a little energy, returned to the players on both teams. Pitching dominated the game early on, with no hits generated by either team through the first three innings. That changed in the fourth.

Rusty and Cary Gilliam lined back-to-back singles to start the inning. I was next to bat, and I hoped to break the scoreless tie. Standing in the on-deck circle, I grabbed a handful of sand with my right hand, holding the bat with my left. I let the bat rest against my shoulder and rubbed the sand between my palms and fingers, letting it spill slowly like an hourglass. The tiny grains absorbed my sweat. When I turned and looked at the bleachers, I noticed Mom and Dad sitting side-by-side on the second row. Mom smiled at Dad, and he placed his arm around her back. Bobby sat two rows back, resting his elbows on the row behind him. It was a beautiful sight.

"Get a hit," Bobby yelled. "It's the least you can do since I came to watch you play."

Ricky stood behind the fence and handed me a piece of gum through an opening in the chain link fence. I slipped it in my back pocket. "Hit one over," Ricky said.

"I'll try. Hey, thanks for coming to my game."

"No problem. You're the best player on the field."

"Aw, you're crazy." I couldn't help but smile. "Do you really think so?"

Ricky nodded.

"Thanks, little man. You're pretty awesome too. Think you can show me how to build a stadium out of Legos some day?"

"I can try."

"Let's go, batter!" the umpire yelled.

"Gotta go hit now," I said, winking at Ricky.

I walked to the batter's box, and I wanted nothing more than to make my family proud. Isn't that what we all strive for? I took my practice swings, my eyes focused on the pitcher, a lanky lefty name Stan Jenkins. Stan was a hard thrower who had control problems. He was known as one of the wildest, and scariest, pitchers in the league. The first pitch to me was low and outside, so I stepped a little closer to the plate for the second offering.

"Knock it out of the park!" screamed Ricky as I again took my practice swings.

Stan reared back and threw with all his might. The ball came fast, tailing to the inside of the batter's box. I tried to back away from the pitch, but the ball caught my left cheekbone so solidly that the crowd let out a collective groan. My body fell hard onto the dusty sand. Lying on my side, I fought for consciousness.

Mom and Dad were soon by my side, and I heard Coach Cooper call to the concession stand for someone to bring ice. There were footsteps all around me, like people positioning themselves to help.

I felt Mom slip to her knees as she called my name. She pulled my limp body into her arms. "Wake up, baby," I heard her say. Her voice faded as she pleaded for me to open my eyes. My head was cloudy, and I had trouble distinguishing voices. I heard Mom call out, and I could feel the worry in her arms. I heard other voices, all familiar ones, but I could not distinguish their source.

Finally, I heard a tender voice saying, "Dad, can you hear me?" I tried to open my eyes but I couldn't. "Dad, respond if you can hear me. Blink, move your toes, do something." It was Lauren's voice, barely audible, and she sounded as nervous as Mom. I tried to open my eyes again but could not. And again I heard Lauren call out.

It was then I knew my trip to the past had come to an end. I could feel myself slipping toward the voices of my wife and children. It felt good to hear them, and I had missed them. But the realization that my time with Mom was done was hard to take. To know I would never see her smile, or feel her arms around me, crushed me. To know that Dad would no longer have the strength to hit a baseball, that Rick would never again be that scrawny little wildcat running up the street, that Bobby would never again sit at the kitchen table being served like a king, broke my heart a bit.

As I felt Blake's hand surrounding mine, I knew I couldn't go back just yet. Not without that final chance to say goodbye. And so I opened my eyes and looked into Mom's tender face. I touched her cheek and tears began streaming down my face. "Mama," I said with a tremble.

"I'm right here, baby," she said, placing her left hand under my neck for support.

"I just want you to know that I love you more than I can ever tell you."

"I love you too. Hang on, sweetie."

"Don't ever forget that, okay?"

"Chase, son, try not to speak." She rubbed her fingers delicately under my rapidly swelling cheek.

"You taught me how to love. You showed me how to love our family, my family."

Mom began to cry as she removed my cap.

"Honey, you're talking crazy. Just lay here and let's get some ice to your head. Hold on, sweet boy. Help is on the way."

"Remember yesterday when I said I'd be leaving soon..."

"Sssshhhh," she said, lightly pressing her forefinger against my lips.

"Remember?" I asked again.

"I remember," she said, surely to appease me.

"It's that time."

"What?"

"I have to go."

"No, baby, I've got you. You're not going anywhere." She ran her fingers through my hair, gently kissing my forehead.

"Mama?" I whispered, struggling to keep my eyes open.

"I'm here sweetie. I'm right here."

"Will you wait for me in Heaven?"

"Oh, baby," she said, and she began to cry as she pulled me close to her chest. "Please don't talk like that."

"Just tell me you will. It's the only way I can make it."

"I will," she cried. "I will."

Looking over Mom's shoulder, I saw Dad hand a bag of ice to her, and she placed it softly against my cheek. Dad knelt beside Mom, staring intently at me. Bobby and Ricky stood over Mom's shoulders. I smiled at them all. We were together, just like we should be. We were a family, and I couldn't have asked for a better one. We loved each other with all we had, the way it was meant to be.

"I gotta go, Mama. Bobby, Ricky, Dad. I love you guys." I felt Mom's arms tighten around me, holding me in a way only a mom can do, and I felt myself slipping away. I faintly heard her cry out, but I could not fight any longer.

"Chase!" she cried. "Chase!"

Those were the final words I would hear my mother speak.

I soon began to hear familiar voices, and I was able to open my eyes. I felt Blake's hand squeezing mine. When I was able to focus, I was looking into Lauren's hazel eyes.

"Dad! Mom, he's awake."

I looked about the room and saw relief ignite in the eyes of my family. I tried to rise up on my elbows.

"Easy," Blake said. "Easy." She rubbed my forearm gently as she stood, looking into my eyes as though to make sure I was coherent. When I smiled, Brett headed for the door.

"I'll get the nurse," I heard him say.

"Dad, are you all right?" Lauren asked. "How do you feel?"

I looked around the room and, for a moment, I had trouble speaking. A nurse walked in and checked my eyes with a small flashlight and checked my vital signs.

I took a deep breath. "I'm okay," I said slowly. "I'm okay."

Lauren and Blake reached over and hugged me, and then Sarah did the same.

"It's bad enough I had to miss Grandma's funeral," Sarah said, "and you made it look like I was going to miss yours too." She squeezed my hand.

"It sounds like I've missed a lot of excitement," I said. "What happened?"

"You got knocked out by the baseball when Brett was hitting you grounders," Lauren said. "We had to call an ambulance since we couldn't wake you up. We were scared to death."

"How long have I been in the hospital?"

"Almost two weeks," Blake replied. "The doctors didn't know if you were going to come out of it. We've been here trying to get you to respond, to wake up. There was a moment two days ago when it looked like you were going to open your eyes. How do you feel?"

"My head feels like a freshly cracked pecan. Other than that, I'm okay."

"Your dad, Bobby, and Ricky are down the hall," Blake said. "Ricky has stayed in town since you got hurt. We've all been worried sick."

"Can you get them?"

Within a couple of minutes, Brett returned to the room with his uncles and grandfather. They certainly looked relieved.

"Dad," I said anxiously, "are you okay?"

"That's what I was getting ready to ask you. You had us worried."

Though I was happy to see Dad and my brothers, my heart felt an emptiness without Mom there.

"What was it like being asleep for so long?" Brett asked. "Did you feel anything? Did you have dreams? Were you just dead to the world?"

"You wouldn't believe it if I told you. I went on a wild ride."

"What do you mean?" Blake laughed. "What kind of *ride*?"

"It was a journey back in time, and it was incredible. Amazing. That bump I received was the best thing that could have happened to me after Mom's funeral. It was exactly the medicine I needed."

"I think the nurse has been slippin' silly serum in Dad's IV," Lauren said with a smile. "Maybe she can give us some too. We'll all take a trip together. I've always wanted to go to Hawaii."

The room filled with laughter, the family's worry gone.

As time passes, the memories of youth still burn in my mind, though the edges have faded. Like a portrait from a hundred years ago, the outer circle of that canvas of memories is now a blurry coat of gray. And so I settle in the warmth of the paled details, knowing that, although I might not recall the past as clearly as I once did, the memories are remarkable nonetheless.

And so I've come to realize that the road to my youth can be re-traveled. Whenever a light, summer breeze brushes against my face, whenever the sun chases shadows from the dew-drenched lawn in the early morning. And when I capture those moments, I again smell the sweet honeysuckle behind the baseball field, I again feel the soft cotton uniform against my skin. I again hear the sounds of the ballpark, and the happy chatter of children playing behind the bleachers. I again feel the summer sun warm my shoulders as it did when I was a wide-eyed young boy. I again feel the simple pleasures of games played with my brothers, and relish the joy of knowing Dad won his battle with alcohol. But, most of all, I again feel the indescribable completeness found in the arms of my young, healthy mother.

As the years pass, I've realized my journey didn't take me far away. It simply took me full circle. I am at the place I first began, though I've found the answer to so many things: who I am, the dreams I've chased, and why. And, in the end, I've returned to the starting point but transformed in the way my heart knows is most important: that what I chased was what I had when I was a child--the love of family, the safety of a father's arms, the gentle touch of a mother's caress.

I often seek comfort in the recollections of my youth.

Author Acknowledgments

A Passage Back was a vessel that carried me back to childhood days. Even though it was a journey of the mind, a metaphysical event, it took me back nonetheless. And in that journey, a reawakening took place whereby a house, a backyard, a baseball field, and a tiny neighborhood rose from the recesses of time, becoming vibrantly alive in my heart and mind.

Crucial to that awakening were the people who impacted my childhood, who exemplified what love, kindness, compassion, and laughter was all about. And to those I would like to acknowledge and give thanks.

To the people of Belvedere—the old adage, "it takes a village to raise a child" is so true. I couldn't have asked for a better place to grow up, and the kindness, love, and yes, even discipline, bestowed upon me has made an everlasting impact, where the mere thought of childhood days brings tender feelings of warmth.

To my boyhood friends, teammates, and classmates—together we learned what our parents, coaches, and teachers taught in the value of true friendship and selflessness.

To my brothers, Bill and Russ—thanks for confirming that brotherly love is nurtured through many pathways. For us, it was through sport, through competition, and even in the well-crafted art of sarcasm that Dad passed down to us.

To Dad—I wish you were still here with us and miss you every day. When we were growing up, our backyard was a lifeline to sports, games, and learning the importance of playing together without diminishing the desire to be successful on an individual level; to be the best we could be. When I think back on what you constructed for us to play on, play with, simply to make a kid's life fun, it fills my heart with gratitude. It was a wonderful way to show your love for us.

And finally, to Mom—because of you I am now a writer, primarily for two reasons: you being diagnosed with breast cancer years ago made me want to write something to you, for you, to tell you how much you mean to me, and it opened up a part of me artistically that I didn't know existed. Secondly, because of the way you love me, care for me, and set an example loving others, I aspire to not only do the same, but to apply that same caring approach in creating characters that readers will love. Words can't fully describe how much I love you. Thank you for loving me, loving us, with all your heart, soul, and being.

About the Author

Chuck Walsh is a co-author of *Faces of Freedom* (featured on Sean Hannity's book list), a book that recognizes the noble lives of U.S. soldiers who died while fighting in Iraq or Afghanistan. His debut novel, *A Month of Tomorrows*, is based on the life of his uncle, WWII hero, Rubin Stout. His book about travel, *A Passage Back*, is scheduled for release in 2015. Chuck lives with his wife in South Carolina.

Please visit Chuck's website, www.chuckwalshwriter.com, and follow him on Twitter at @ChuckWalsh

Dear Reader,

If you enjoyed reading A Passage Back, I would appreciate it if you would help others enjoy this book, too. Here are some of the ways you can help spread the word:

Lend it. This book is lending enabled so please share it with a friend.

Recommend it. Help other readers find this book by recommending it to friends, readers' groups, book clubs, and discussion forums.

Share it. Let other readers know you've read the book by positing a note to your social media account and/or your Goodreads account.

Review it. Please tell others why you liked this book by reviewing it on your favorite ebook site like Amazon or Barnes and Noble and/or Goodreads.

Everything you do to help others learn about my book is greatly appreciated!

The author kindly acknowledges the following trademarks:

Rawlings – Rawlings Sporting Goods Company, Inc. CORPORATION DELAWARE 510 Maryville University Drive, #110 St. Louis MISSOURI 63141

Easton – EASTON BASEBALL / SOFTBALL INC. CORPORATION DELAWARE 7855 Haskell Avenue, Suite 200 Van Nuys CALIFORNIA 91406

Count Chocula - General Mills IP Holdings II, LLC LIMITED LIABILITY COMPANY DELAWARE Number One General Mills Boulevard Minneapolis MINNESOTA 55426

Cap'n Crunch – The Quaker Oats Company CORPORATION NEW JERSEY 555 West Monroe Street Chicago ILLINOIS 60661

A&W – A&W CONCENTRATE COMPANY CORPORATION DELAWARE 5301 Legacy Drive Plano TEXAS 75024

Plymouth – Revel Holdings, LLC LIMITED LIABILITY COMPANY OKLAHOMA 200 East 171st Street South Glenppool OKLAHOMA 74033

Tabasco sauce – McIlhenny Company CORPORATION MAINE Hwy. 329 Avery Island LOUISIANA 70513

Magnavox – MAGNAVOX COMPANY, THE CORPORATION DELAWARE 2131 BUETER ROAD FORT WAYNE INDIANA 46803

Lego – Kirkbi AG CORPORATION SWITZERLAND Neuhofstrasse 21 CH-6340 Baar SWITZERLAND

Tupperware – Dart Industries Inc. d.b.a. Tupperware Home Parties CORPORATION DELAWARE 14901 S. Orange Blossom trail Orlando FLORIDA 32837

Chia Pet – JOSEPH ENTERPRISES, INC. CORPORATION CALIFORNIA 425 California Street, Suite 300 San Francisco CALIFORNIA 94104

Kellogg's Frosted Flakes – KELLOGG COMPANY CORPORATION DELAWARE P.O. BOX 3599 ONE KELLOGG SQUARE BATTLE CREEK MICHIGAN 490163599

Fruit of the Loom – Fruit of the Loom, Inc. CORPORATION NEW YORK Legal Department 1 Fruit of the Loom Drive Bowling Green KENTUCKY 42103

Superman - DC COMICS composed of Warner Communications, Inc. a Delaware corporation and Time Warner Entertainment Company, L.P., a partnership organized under the laws of the State of Delaware, composed of American Television and Communications corporation, Time Warner Operations Inc., Warner Communications Inc. and Warner Cable Communications Inc., all Delaware corporations and Capital Cablevision Systems, Inc. and People's Cable Corporation, both New York corporations and Memphis CATV, Inc., a Tennesssee corporation PARTNERSHIP NEW YORK 1700 Broadway New York NEW YORK 10019

Popeye – Hearst Holdings, Inc. CORPORATION DELAWARE 300 West 57th Street New York NEW YORK 10019

Curious George – Houghton Mifflin Company CORPORATION MASSACHUSETTS 222 Berkeley Street Boston MASSACHUSETTS 02216

GQ – MEN'S WEAR SERVICE CORPORATION, THE CORPORATION DELAWARE 612 NORTH MICHIGAN AVENUE CHICAGO ILLINOIS

Fisher-Price – MATTEL, INC. CORPORATION DELAWARE M1-1518 333 CONTINENTAL BOULEVARD EL SEGUNDO CALIFORNIA 90245

Buick – GENERAL MOTORS CORPORATION CORPORATION DELAWARE 3044 West Grand Boulevard Detroit MICHIGAN 48202

Keds – SR HOLDINGS, LLC LIMITED LIABILITY COMPANY DELAWARE 191 Spring Street Lexington MASSACHUSETTS 02421

Nascar – National Association for Stock Car Auto Racing, Inc. CORPORATION FLORIDA Attn: Legal Department One Daytona Boulevard Daytona Beach FLORIDA 32114

Chrysler and Dodge – Chrysler Group LLC LIMITED LIABILITY COMPANY DELAWARE CIMS 485-13-32 1000 Chrysler Drive Auburn Hills MICHIGAN 48326

National Cash Register –

NCR CORPORATION CORPORATION MARYLAND 700 Building 3097 Satellite Boulevard Duluth GEORGIA 30096

Chuck Taylor – CONVERSE INC. CORPORATION DELAWARE 160 North Washington Street Boston MASSACHUSETTS 02114

Briggs & Stratton – Briggs & Stratton Corporation CORPORATION WISCONSIN attn: Lynda Hargreaves 12301 West Wirth Street Wauwatosa WISCONSIN 53222

Reader's Digest – The Reader's Digest Association, Inc. CORPORATION DELAWARE 44 South Broadway Legal Dept White Plains NEW YORK 10601

Chevrolet – General Motors LLC LIMITED LIABILITY COMPANY DELAWARE 300 Renaissance Center Detroit MICHIGAN 482653000

Wheel of Fortune – CALIFON PRODUCTIONS, INC. CORPORATION NEW YORK 10202 W. Washington Blvd. CULVER CITY CALIFORNIA 90232

Barnum & Bailey – Ringling Bros.-Barnum & Bailey Combined Shows, Inc. CORPORATION DELAWARE 8607 Westwood Center Drive Vienna VIRGINIA 22182

Wizard of Oz – Turner Entertainment Co. CORPORATION DELAWARE Bldg 156, Rm 5078 4000 Warner Blvd Burbank CALIFORNIA 91522

Meet the Press – NBC News GE Building 30 Rockefeller Center, Midtown Manhattan, Manhattan, New York City, New York, U.S.

Puff the Magic Dragon – Lipton, Lenny INDIVIDUAL UNITED STATES 25 Corte Lodato Greenbrae CALIFORNIA 94904

Royal Crown Cola – ROYAL CROWN COLA CO. CORPORATION DELAWARE 41 PERIMETER CENTER EAST, NE. ATLANTA GEORGIA 30346

Nehi and Tahitian Treat and Canada Dry - DR PEPPER/SEVEN UP, INC. CORPORATION DELAWARE 5301 LEGACY DRIVE PLANO TEXAS 75024

Nutty Buddy – DEAN INTELLECTUAL PROPERTY SERVICES II, INC. CORPORATION DELAWARE 2711

Bazooka Joe – TOPPS COMPANY, INC., THE CORPORATION ASSIGNEE OF DELAWARE ONE WHITEHALL STREET NEW YORK NEW

Kaopectate – CHATTEM, INC. CORPORATION TENNESSEE 1715 WEST 38TH STREET CHATTANOOGA TENNESSEE 37409

Zebco – W.C. Bradley/Zebco Holdings, Inc. CORPORATION GEORGIA 6101 East Apache TULSA OKLAHOMA 74115

Neosporin – JOHNSON & JOHNSON CORPORATION NEW JERSEY One Johnson & Johnson Plaza New Brunswick NEW JERSEY 089337001

National Geographic – National Geographic Society CORPORATION D.C. 1145 17th Street, N.W. Washington D.C. 20036

Twinkies – HOSTESS BRANDS, LLC LIMITED LIABILITY COMPANY DELAWARE 1 EAST ARMOUR BLVD. KANSAS CITY MISSOURI

Greenbax - Greenbax Enterprises, Inc. CORPORATION SOUTH CAROLINA Box 118407 Charleston SOUTH CAROLINA 29423

Plan Your Next Escape!
What's Your Reading Pleasure?

Whether it's brawny Highlanders, intriguing mysteries, young adult romance, illustrated children's books, or uplifting love stories, Vinspire Publishing has the adventure for you!

For a complete listing of books available, visit our website at www.vinspirepublishing.com.

Like us on Facebook at
www.facebook.com/VinspirePublishing

Follow us on Twitter at
www.twitter.com/vinspire2004

and join our newsletter for details of our upcoming releases, giveaways, and more!
http://t.co/46UoTbVaWr

We are your travel guide to your next adventure!

Made in the USA
Lexington, KY
08 July 2016